JUDGE ANDERSON
YEAR TWO

An Abaddon Books™ Publication
www.abaddonbooks.com
abaddon@rebellion.co.uk

This omnibus first published in 2019 by
Abaddon Books™,
Rebellion Publishing Limited,
Riverside House, Osney Mead, Oxford, OX2 0ES, UK.

10 9 8 7 6 5 4 3 2 1

Creative Director and CEO: Jason Kingsley
Chief Technical Officer: Chris Kingsley
Head of Books and Comics Publishing: Ben Smith
Editors: David Thomas Moore, Michael Rowley and Kate Coe
Marketing and PR: Remy Njambi
Design: Sam Gretton, Oz Osborne and Gemma Sheldrake
Cover Art: Christian Ward

Judge Anderson created by
John Wagner and Brian Bolland.

ISBN: 978-1-78108-618-6

Printed in Denmark

JUDGE ANDERSON
YEAR TWO

DANIE WARE // LAUREL SILLS
ZINA HUTTON

**ABADDON
BOOKS**

WWW.ABADDONBOOKS.COM

Introduction

I HADN'T REALLY encountered Judge Dredd before I arrived at Rebellion. I knew the comics existed, but they were for someone other than me; they were gritty and dark and involved strange swear-words and hulking, stone-faced men riding around on huge motorbikes. Even when I started reading the comics as research, I found Dredd off-putting; grim and humourless and bleak.

Then I encountered Judge Anderson.

I liked her when I first read her, all through her battles with Judge Death and travels across the galaxy; but I think it's the battle with Satan—in the 1995 storyline of the same name—that made me love her. It's the stubborn refusal to give up, or to give in; it's the tenacity and the sheer bull-headed belief that humanity is worth fighting for... even if they are drokking stupid at times. She even makes Dredd more human, and that's saying something.

So when David suggested that I take on *Judge Anderson: Year Two*, I jumped at it; a chance to work with three female authors writing new stories? Getting to read more of Anderson's background and past, seeing how she turns from rookie to Judge to the Cass that we first meet, battling Judge Death—and, if not winning, then at least containing him?

In Danie Ware's *Bigger Than Biggs*, Cass takes on the monster in the basement, and finds out just how far greed and ambition can take someone; Laurel Sills' *Devourer* resurrects a cult that's targeting Psi-Judges; and in Zina Hutton's *Flytrap*, a spider's setting a web for victims—and Cass is the fly.

I'm absolutely in for those stories, and I hope that you are too. Cassandra Anderson, Year Two—buckle up, we're in for a psychic ride.

Kate Coe
June 2019

BIGGER
THAN BIGGS

DANIE WARE

MEGA-CITY ONE
2101 A.D.

One

THE CITY WAS quiet.

Well, not 'quiet' exactly, the Big Meg didn't get quiet. It may be the dead hours of the morning, but eight hundred million cits were still one hell of a lot of life. Streams of vehicles ran in lines over the Expressways; the shimmer of neon was unending.

Parking her Lawmaster at the end of the overzoom, Judge Cassandra Anderson walked to the edge of the lookout platform and looked down, the drop dizzying past the toes of her boots.

Shouting came from the block behind her, a sharp detonation of violence that echoed in her head like cymbals...

But Anderson wasn't up here to run a bust.

No, she'd come up here to clear her thoughts—Doc's orders. Up here, the endless tinnitus hum of a thousand background fears could be tuned out. Up here, the noise faded to whispers, the faintest psychic echoes of the endless guilt, the reflexive lies. Everyone was hiding something—she'd learned that one pretty quick—and sometimes, the racket just got too much.

As the block's violence faded to slammed doors and resentment, Anderson looked out across the unfamiliar view.

She was away from Psi-Div, up here, on secondment to Chief Johnson up in Sector 19. Johnson had a job on; he was busting gangs like it was going out of fashion—just your usual rounds of kooks and perps and futsies, all destined for the cubes. And she'd earned her stripes already: taken a Block boss down with the exploding black sun of a psi-blast... but sometimes, hell, this stuff left echoes. So she'd talked to the sector's doc about them, needed a way to let go.

The doc had taught her a new thing, a mental purge like blue light, something that could rid her mind of toxins and overspills, and of the seething crap of the city's endless noise.

Anderson inhaled, then let her breath out again.

One-two-three-four...

Blue light. Everything's fine.

Everything's—

The roar of the overhead Manta shattered her concentration and she swore, her visualisation scattering like so much pebbled glass. The violence behind her had re-erupted and was now all fury and gunfire.

Quiet, for Grud's sake.

The Manta banked and soared away. It paused over another of the huge, shimmering citiblocks, and lowered itself gently to rest.

Anderson stepped back from the edge and turned for the Lawmaster. She should can this crap and get back to sector house; the chief'd told her to hit the sleep machines before they shipped out on a whole new search-and-seize tomorrow...

Another day, another perp to book.

SHE TOOK THE ride easy, heading over the Jim Bob Morrison Expressway towards the Department's Eagle logo, visible even from here. Its spread wings hung above the night-time streets, protector and predator both.

Out of pure habit, she called up the Lawmaster's data-screen, checked for crimes in progress, for the blips that were Street-Div, out there busting heads. There was a glut of activity round a couple of nearby blocks, but she'd already had the reports of the wars in the basements: the Dripping Skulls and the Monkey Gang had been at it with acid, edged weapons, and a certain no-holds-barred creativity. The blips were closing fast, though, and Anderson reckoned that playtime was over.

Leaving them to it, she leaned into the corner—and a movement in the mirror caught her eye.

There was a bike on her tail.

It was a good twenty yards back—too far for a scan—and it wasn't trying to race her, it was just sat there like some gruddamn stalker. And it was unusual; her screen showed a rotating scan of an old, Brit-Cit frame and a tek-built, custom engine...

Nice piece of kit.

She spoke another instruction, but the screen pulled no licence plate, no ident.

Creep'd stolen the bike, or she was a mutie's uncle—she should stop and pull him over. Hell, he was probably just some overeager kid, riding it 'cause he'd stolen it, and proving how tough he was by taking on a Judge...

Yeah, that's gonna end well.

Traffic tore past her. Mouthy cits leaned out of car windows, jeering and throwing garbage. She twitched the Lawmaster sideways and a synthi-plonk bottle sailed over her and shattered at the roadside. Unbidden, the screen tagged an ID.

Oh, drokk this for a game of squaddies...

She indicated, leaned sharply into a second corner. A squeal of car brakes and a shout of 'Bitch!' cursed the sudden movement, but the last-minute turn had shaken the bike—

No, it hadn't. Gruddamn thing was still there.

You're lucky I've not got time for this, kid.

She put her wailers on and dumped the Lawmaster into top

gear. Four thousand ccs of engine bellowed and the bike surged. Sirens blaring, she wove through the traffic, and the rockcrete became a blur, lights shooting by to either side. A munce-truck thundered past her with an irate scream of its horn. She'd leave that teen in the dust—

The headlight of the stalker stayed put.

It'd made no attempt to gain ground; it was just sat there, following her round every bend. Fully aware of the speed they were now doing, and of the open drop to either side, she took one hand off the bars to draw the Lawgiver.

Instantly, the data-screen flicked ammo-counts, crosshairs, possible targets. She dropped back, intending to ride parallel and make this creep pull up. They wore leathers, she saw, black and worn and completely unmarked. A tinted visor covered their face.

Fat lotta good that's gonna do you. I'm gonna bust your ass, after all...

But they were just too gruddamn quick. As she dropped back, siren still going, the figure on the bike gave her a brief salute, then hung a sharp left and shot off down the sliproad towards the Les Carter Tower.

The tail light merged with the background neon glare, and was gone.

Anderson had missed her chance for a scan; her screen had come up zilch.

But she'd gotten two things.

One was the figure's hair-braid, black and scarlet and very long. The other was the red-clenched-fist 'Knux' symbol on the back of the jacket.

Her data-screen flashed trajectories, possible routes, anticipated destinations, but Anderson wasn't chasing this kid through half the gruddamn night.

Not for a stolen bike and an attitude problem.

She shut the wailers down, re-holstered the Lawgiver. It had been a long day, and tomorrow was gonna be another one juuust like it...

Enough.

Another time, she thought. *C'mon, Cassie, time to hit the sack.*

THE PROBLEM WITH sleep-machines, Anderson had always figured, was that morning came waaay too soon.

Especially when you had to be up, out, and hitting the streets by oh-five-drokking-hundred.

The rising sun had lit the city's pollution to a gleaming, seething smog. The alleyway she stood in was littered with garbage, human and otherwise. Everything stank of piss and despair, and she'd sell her left kidney for another half-hour's shut-eye—hell, she'd not even journalled her dreams. Yet here she was, back to the wall, taking point for another day of the sector's search-and-cleanse.

A broken-down cleaning droid sat watching her, one of its eyes picked free and hanging loose on a cable.

Opposite the warehouse doorway, her assigned partner Judge Marshall was holding up three gloved fingers, so she waited. He was too long and gangly for his uniform, but she rather liked him—and he damned-well knew his stomm.

Silently, he counted them down.

Two... one...

On zero, his boot slammed into the sagging doors. They crashed apart, and hit the warehouse floor with a clatter and cloud of crud.

"Justice Department!" He moved into the building. "On the ground! Now!"

Anderson spun, pointing the Lawgiver, her retinal tac-display tracking the goons...

Nada.

What?

Zip. Zilch. Zero.

Light filtered down through the broken roof; the overhead gangways creaked half-loose, casting odd shadows over the floor.

The warehouse was deserted.

But... Anderson blinked, tried to focus. *I know they're here...*

"Drokk!" Marshall barked into his comm, "I got nothing. How you guys doing?"

Two reports came back to Anderson's ear—the other simultaneous entries had both come up empty.

Marshall swore. "C'mon, Cass," he said, aloud, his tone soft. "Where'd they go?"

"They're in here, all right," Anderson told him. "Maybe there's a basement, undertunnels."

"Bit early for that, don'tcha think?" He pulled a mock-grimace, then spoke back into the comm, "All right. Cass insists they're here—we clear the building."

"*Roger that.*"

Additional mutters followed, but not clearly. Chief Johnson had delegated this op to Marshall's command—and none of the other Street-Div goons were about to argue with him.

Carefully, Anderson moved into the building, her mind open, searching.

"You got these 'skills,' rookie." Chief Johnson's initial briefing had been both curt and humourless. "And I need my teams protected. I want you at the front. I wanna know what's waiting, and what it's packing. I wanna know where the gang-leaders are, what they've got, what they're scared of. And I wanna know how to take 'em down. I wanna hit my Department's targets, and I don't mean with a Lawgiver." He'd been pointing at the holo-map on the wall, its zoom function picking out the streets and buildings. "You're my robo-canary, blondie. And I want you to *sing*."

Johnson was young, an early promotion—her 'skip-and-dip' scan had found a mind like a filing cabinet, like a wall of framed certificates in perfect, linear order. He was a man of precision, he liked his rules, and he liked them unbroken. And yeah, out here in the backstreets, she was one hell of a lot happier listening to Marshall...

Even if he *had* been assigned to keep an eye on her.

"Cass." Marshall's voice brought her back to the warehouse. "We need a location. Stat."

"Roger." She nodded. "Let's see if I can pin 'em down."

Mutters still came over the comm—whatever Johnson's orders, the squad-level goons didn't trust her. And hell, why should they? It wasn't like her previous partners'd ended up dead or brain-friend or both—

"Cass," Marshall said again.

"Hang on."

She stopped, honed her focus fully, and let her mental scan creep out through the building.

C'mon, I know you're in here...

There, at the walls, residual taints that lingered like leftover graffiti—a flare of violence, a bark of gunfire, a man with thumbs in his eyesockets, kicking and screaming as they pressed in... The images were bloody, but they were just background noise, nothing unusual. They were not what she wanted.

She opened the scan wider.

C'mon, you bastards. Out you come.

The mote of sharp calm was Marshall, steady at her shoulder. She picked up the others—two at the rear, two at the loading bay by the overzoom. Unlike their officer, they were a grumble of agitation.

Gruddamn mutie...

Dunno why we even need her...

Yeah, she thought back at them. *You guys can kiss my ass.*

Then: older memories, people living here, crying children,

hunger and cold. Soft drizzle, gusting though the ceiling. Bitterness. Loss. People going missing, posters and fear and desperation and grief. And then, vicious and more recent: an outbreak of fighting, backwards and forwards, spiteful and swift. For a moment, she was flooded by an onslaught of pure outrage—a gang of teens, chrome-flashed leathers and teeth bared in shouting. Bloodied faces, weapons raised. The people who lived here had nothing, yet they still weren't safe from a rampage of greed that'd stormed about their warehouse walls. And they'd mustered their strength to hit back...

Was that anger theirs?

Or hers?

Her empathy was strong; sometimes, it was hard to untangle where one thing ended and the other began.

Her hand tightened on the Lawgiver.

"Cass?" Marshall's voice was calm, and not over the comm. "What is it?"

"This was someone's home," she told him, frowning. "There were families here, and not very long ago. They were attacked—"

"They lost." The touch of a gun-muzzle came up against her jaw. "And you Jays shouldn't've come here."

"Take it easy, kid," Marshall said evenly. "Don't do anything dumb." He kept his tone calm, but didn't lower the pistol.

"You shut the drokk up." The kid was seventeen and alone, but the gun muzzle was pressing hard under Anderson's jaw. "Drop 'em, both of you, or I decorate the wall."

Marshall carefully lowered his Lawgiver, talking easily and non-stop. "C'mon, you don't wanna do this. You gotcha whole life ahead of you. Think about where this'll end..." Only half-listening to the standard spiel, Anderson lowered her own pistol. She'd been too focused on her scan to feel the kid coming, but now, Marshall was offering her the perfect distraction...

And she could flick through this kid's thoughts like she was reading a screensheet. Too intent on his aggression, the kid didn't even notice.

Oh, yeah. Now I gotcha…

Surface thoughts: a predictable teenage tumble. Youth and confusion, sex and ego, the need to prove himself. Anger and nerves were curled round each other, inseparable. They were patterns of insecurity she'd seen many times before.

But they weren't what she wanted—she eased them all aside and went deeper. Into the limbic system and the amygdala, into the complex pulses of his emotions, the colours that beat through his mind. He had the very last trails of the drug 'White Heat' in his system, giving him adrenaline and confidence—but its offerings were fake, and fading, and beneath them, he was awash with fear. His gang has raided this hideout, taken it for their own. But the Judges weren't supposed to be here, weren't supposed to know. And she was real pretty, too, and he just didn't wanna hafta pull that trigger, man…

But he would, yeah, he *so* would…

Because…

Because they weren't s'posed to know, okay? Not about any of it, not about what was going on. And the Boss was gonna drokk him right the hell up—

Boss, eh? Anderson grabbed the thought like a gambling jackpot. Carefully, with a bandit's precision, she prised it open. *What boss? What's he gonna do?*

The kid's thoughts roiled; she pressed harder.

Look at me, trust me. She played on his reaction to her appearance. *It's not like I'm gonna hurt you…*

And he just didn't have experience to resist.

The kid's name was Rikki. He didn't like the Judges, didn't want them here. He was afraid of them. They'd put him in a box, alone. And they weren't supposed to *be here*…

Why?

The question was wordless; a concept planted like a mine, there to cause a reaction.

And then—*whoosh!*—the answer came in a flood.

Screaming, people being pulled from their homes. Kids, mostly, some older. Some wealthy, some poor, many just lost. And one image, stronger than all the rest—a blond lad, maybe sixteen, expensively dressed. He's in Rikki's hands and he's scared. He's twisting, struggling, his wrists are secured with gaffer-tape. He's in tears. He just wants to go home, please, just wants to go home...

Somewhere, she was aware of Marshall still talking, still making 'Ease down, you don't wanna do this' noises, but Rikki was starting to panic now, his thoughts blurring into fuzz. He clung to the BudJet pistol like a lifeline. The White Heat was leaving his system, leaking from his body like piss down his leg, and saturating everything in fear...

You shouldn't be here shouldn't be seeing this why are you here ohhhh Grud this is all gonna go wrong so wrong...

Puzzled, Anderson went still deeper. She shouldered her way through his white-noise-panic like a snowdrift.

And there: a confused jumble of overlapping memories...

The blond kid's from a lux block, somewhere close. Figures break down the hab door. The lad's dragged, shouting, from his family. There's a security guard, and a bewilderment of dark bodies and hot lights and engine noise. There are cold creds in dirty hands; there are more flashes of bright chrome, like gang-colours...

Then violence, vicious and bloody. The chrome-flashed gang are fighting. Someone staggers; heat sears skin. There are synthi-booze tins, scattered across a rockcrete floor; there's graffiti, bright and harsh and scrawled across crumbling walls—

And then, out of nowhere, the image of the Knux-biker hit her with the force of a full-on premonition.

The same figure, the same worn jacket. He's chest to the fuel tank of that Brit-Cit bike, and haring like a demon across the Expressway.

And the blond kid is on the back of the bike, cowering to stay out of the wind.

Anderson blinked.

What?

Somehow, the two things had crossed over; she'd been knocked off-course. She'd come clean out of Rikki's memories and was now seeing something else, something like a full-on precog...

Behind the biker, there are broken lights, spelling a name down the outside of a Block...

Eee-Zee Rest.

She didn't know what that meant—she wasn't familiar with the sector—but she could find it. She turned back to Rikki and drove the cold, hard spear of a psi-scan right into his brain-stem.

Show me. I need to understand.

But instead of an answer, something hit her back—something dark and slavering and savage and starving-hungry, something huge and clamouring and greedy. Something that filled Rikki's head like a tangle of metal cabling. Something like pain, like screaming, like absolute fear, like—

BAM.

Rikki's thoughts went suddenly, utterly blank, stopped by a single, sharp retort, by the sharp reek of cordite. She yanked her awareness out of his head before that sucking darkness could drag her down with it...

The silence in the warehouse was deafening.

"He panicked," Marshall said, shrugging. "Dunno what you hit, Cass, but he tried to blow your face off. You okay?"

Her limbs felt cold; the tumble of light through the broken roof seemed oddly unreal. "Yeah. Sure."

"What the hell did you find?"

She shook her head, struggling. It had all happened too fast, was too jumbled. Gang-violence and kidnapping, they were all in a day's work. But that final flash...

...*something huge and clamouring and greedy...*

She edged around it, trying to comprehend where it had come from. But even as she rummaged after it, it'd gone.

She found herself looking down at the body as it lay cooling on the floor.

What the hell was *that...?*

Shouts still came from further into the building, occasional coughs of Lawgiver fire. Voices over the comm reported retreating knots of resistance. Marshall put out the call for a catch-wagon—this might take time.

"Cass?" The tilt of Marshall's thoughts was troubled.

But Anderson was still looking at Rikki, at the exploded mess of brain and bone that'd been his face.

...*huge and clamouring and greedy...*

"Something's wrong," Marshall commented.

She snorted. "You a Psi-Judge now?"

A pool of gore was spreading out across the rockcrete, reaching the toes of her boots.

"I've met Psi-Div before," he told her, half-smiling. "That's why Johnson assigned you to me." The smile spread. "You don't scare me, mutie."

His tone was teasing, but she turned away, not wanting to know his thoughts. They needed to get the drokk out of here, and she *needed* to find out what the hell was going on.

One way or another, she was going after that biker.

Two

"I'M NOT INTERESTED in your hunches, blondie." Chief Johnson stood at his desk as if it were a barrier, defending himself and his sector from her mutoid abilities. "You're here to do a job. No futsie freakouts, no side trips. And you'll follow my orders 'til I send you back to Psi-Div."

"Sir—"

"I don't need to hear it, rook—"

"Sir, I had a full-on premonition, and it was pretty clear." She kept her tone steady. "Whoever that blond kid is, I need to get him back."

And besides, I wanna get that biker, and know what in every drokking hell we just found...

Johnson eyed her over the desk. He was small, and square, and angry, and had very little patience with Departmental creativity. She could feel his hostility, shoving at her like an Academy bully; feel the subtle and complex envies that bubbled under his thoughts. Johnson was ambitious, and he resented her edge.

He leaned his knuckles on the desktop, doing his best to loom. "I gotta schedule," he said, like a threat.

"I know you do, sir." Hell, Johnson probably had a schedule for taking a dump. "But reading my instincts is what you got me out here to do—"

"You get any *proof?*" The word was scathing, and her cautious scan showed his motivations well enough. He didn't give a drokk about her precog—he just wanted the clean-up done, the boxes ticked, and the report filed neatly between the Chief Judge's cheeks.

"I don't need proof, sir," Anderson told him, trying to keep her tone respectful. "I'm Psi-Div—"

"You're Psi-Div under my command, blondie," he told her. "And I'm not having you opening random cans of wrigglies in my sector."

She blinked. "Sir?"

"You listen to me." He lowered his voice, leaned forwards further. "I'm not touching Eee-Zee Rest with someone else's hands. It's a community support charity, been providing low-cred housing for the sector's poorer cits for years. We go stomping about anywhere *near* it and PR-Div will have a collective hernia. Whoever that blond kid is, you're gonna hafta let this one pass."

Anderson came right up to the desk, faced him across his blotter pad and his colour-organised pens. "Sir, it's just one kid." *Something huge and clamouring and greedy.* "And I can get him, if I get out there quick enough." She paused, letting her words sink in—there was a fair amount of psychology in being a Psi-Judge. "And it's all kudos—you gonna just let this pass?"

Johnson stopped, chewing at the inside of his mouth. He was watching her closely, and she could feel the machinery of his mind click and shifting. He was re-filing, re-evaluating, thinking about the implications, and about the consequences. At last, he said, "Look, Eee-Zee Rest's a cover, and we all know it. It's a gruddamn mess down here. There are multiple bike gangs— the Knux, the Boozters, the Runners, the Pink Chickens—and they trade in everything from drugs to illegal droid parts. Whole place is a filth-pit that I'd *love* to wipe out."

"Then why don't you, sir?"

He stood upright, huffing in annoyance. It felt like an admission. "Because the owner is one of the most powerful men in the sector. His name's Reginald Biggs, and I got nothing on him, blondie, not as much as a parking ticket. He owns the entire area outright, and his paperwork's white enough to wipe your butt. Biggs is cleaner than a futsie on a mind-ream."

Frustration flared, a conflict between his Judge's authority and his own adherence to rules and regs.

But Anderson stopped herself smiling—she had him now. She said, like a peace offering, "Then why don't you just let me handle this, sir? Let me save the boy." She spared a thought for the Big Zero Six kookhouse. "And maybe I could even... y'know... get close enough to take a look round?"

Johnson sucked his teeth. He was still watching her, and she could see her own recent record flashing through his memory. He said, "We don't do undercover, up here, Anderson. We're Judges, not thieves."

She noted the use of her name.

Yeah, but you just think: who'll get aaall the pats on the back if I do find something icky...

As if she'd planted the thought in his head, he stopped, rearranging his pens in proper colour order. The motion soothed him, cleared his thoughts. "All right," he said at last. "Get the kid. Get him—and that damned Knux-biker—back here. And then, we'll ask them a coupla questions." She opened her mouth, but he spoke straight over her. "But you take Marshall with you. And no funny business. And a full report on my desk!"

"Yes, sir."

"And Anderson?"

"Yes, sir?"

"*Everything.*"

"Yes, sir."

As she turned to leave the office, his thought was loud as a shout, *And you'd better not make me look bad, rookie, or I'll have that shiny-new badge of yours before you can say 'Titan.'*

"So," ANDERSON SAID into the comm. "Short version: we're going out to save the kid. And if we do uncover something nasty, he'll get a big-ass promotion. If we drokk it up—"

"*He'll pretend he never knew us,*" Marshall told her, then snorted. "*Plausible deniability, Cass, way of the world.*" He grinned. "*Don't take it personal.*"

They rode through the traffic, heading for the Chris Barrie, the Eee-Zee Rest block with the broken lights. It was one of four owned by the charity, and they stood at the corners of a private, fenced-off tangle of habs, roads and overzooms.

All of it owned by this 'Reginald Biggs.'

Anderson had called up Biggs's details on the Department's data-screens—and had found absolutely nothing. There wasn't even a mugshot, just a date of birth, a hab-listing and a record of the purchase of the land. As Johnson'd already told her, this guy had a record you could eat your dinner off...

Hell, he was a crim, all right—no cit in the Meg was that clean.

Impatient, she wove the Lawmaster through the traffic queues and the rising fumes, through the flashes of nervousness as the drivers spotted the Judges.

Oh, Grud, should've renewed my licence...

...I only touched her shoulder, I swear...

...just the change from the caff-machine. I'll pay it back...

"*There,*" Marshall said, pointing. "*That what you saw?*"

Across the far side of the Hattie Hayridge Expressway, a silent, grey tower rose hard into the sky. Down one side, it bore the familiar, broken lights of the Eee-Zee Rest name.

"Yeah."

She slowed, trying to make the image fit exactly to her memory of it, trying to remember the angle.

Come on, Cass, think.

She spoke the instructions aloud, "Trajectory mode. Angle: ten degrees from current. Twenty degrees. Advance forwards two hundred metres." The map flashed options, likely locations and routes. She zoomed in on a couple, checking their three-sixty views.

"We need to be lower," she said, after a minute. "And further east." She was holding the flash-image in her head, trying to make it match exactly to the screen's shifting views—the visual meshing of the psychic and the electronic could be a right pain in the ass. But...

"There, that's it." The image clicked like a key in a lock. "That's where we need to be—right where that layby is."

"*Roger that,*" Marshall said. She saw him glance down, and then point. "*Look, there. Why don't we take a stop at the old munce factory? We can eyeball everything.*" He paused, then asked her, "*How d'you know? When you have a... vision... like that? How do you know how to find the right place?*"

Anderson leaned into the corner, and they eased on through the traffic. "Instinct," she said. "You ever have a dream and then see the place you dreamed about? Freaks you out, doesn't it? It's kinda like that."

Marshall grunted, acknowledgement and curiosity. She could hear the faintest whispers of his thought patterns, almost intrigued: *Like déjà vu, I guess...*

Again, she shut him out.

But there, below them and riding straight from dream to reality: a familiar Brit-Cit bike, haring out from the Chris Barrie Block like every gruddamn nightmare was after it.

"That's him!"

Barking into the comm, she jammed a boot on the rockcrete

and slammed the Lawmaster through a sharp one-eighty. Rubber scarred the road, cars and lorries screeched and honked; she didn't care.

"Let's go!" she said. "We'll cut him off!"

The data-screen flashed options, routes and speeds. She hit the wailers, dropped the throttle.

Behind her, she heard the skid and roar as Marshall did likewise. And then they were away, thundering back over the top of the Expressway, and running parallel to the Knux-biker below.

"*He's fast,*" Marshall called over the comm. "*I'll give him that. Can you get an eyeball? See if he's got the kidnapped kid with him?*"

"He will have!" Now Anderson was here, she had no doubts about her premonition—the biker's movements felt *right*, like puzzle pieces falling into place. The colours and shapes were all dovetailing into one clear certainty: *this* was exactly where they needed to be. Mental spikes hit her through the traffic, mostly threats—*gruddamn jays*—but they were gone so fast, she didn't get time to focus.

And Marshall was right, that Knux-rider was *fast*.

As the routes began to merge, she could see him more clearly. He wore the same leathers and tinted lid as the previous night, but they were messed up, now, burned and scarred. He'd been in a fight, and—*yes!*—he had the blond kid with him, skinny wrists taped together. The kid was exactly as she'd seen him: cowering behind the Knux-rider's broad shoulders, just to stay out of the wind.

Anderson tore between lines of vehicles, an angry music of horns following her. Marshall stayed behind her, she could see him in the mirror; she watched as he swung round a suddenly-opened door.

Deliberate.

Bastard.

If they'd had longer...

But below them, the Knux member was still gaining ground, heading for the junction. The Lawmaster's screen flashed maps and blips and warnings; it told her to increase her speed.

Drokk it!

She pushed the bike as hard as it would go, made the engine scream. Cars and thoughts shot past her in a blur, too fast to see. If someone opened a door now...

And then, there was something else.

Three more bikes, Itsusuki Katas, by the look of them. They were lined up behind the Knux-biker: slim, high-end, and fast, all decorated in outlandish star-designs of blue and silver.

"Marsh!"

"*Boozters!*" One of the Eee-Zee Rest gangs. "*I got 'em!*"

She could only spare them half-an-eye, but she still saw the muzzle-flashes as the lead Boozter narrowed the Knux-biker's lead, draw his sidearm, and hosed the road with gunfire.

Windscreens shattered; rounds ricocheted. Cars screeched and stopped, slamming into each other. Metal dented, twisted. Alarms screamed. People raged, and shouted. A roadside advert exploded in a shower of sparks...

Why do they always *do that?*

One car had skidded to a stop at the outermost kerb. It hung, front wheels suspended over nothing, as its driver tried to scrabble out of the door.

A moment later, another spinning car hit it, sent it, driver and all, spiralling down to the roadways below.

Anderson winced.

It hit, crunched, teetered for a second, then toppled over sideways with a crash.

From streaming, orderly queues, the roadway below the Judges became chaos. Fights broke out, crowbars and spanners, accusations and fury. Side doors opened, people crouching behind them and returning fire—back at sector house, Chief

Johnson must be going futsie. And, around the edge of it all, the three Kata bikes glided like drokking dancers, barely bothering to slow.

One of the riders kicked at a side door with an outflung boot, crushing a shooter to the floor.

But the Knux-rider was good; he twitched to the left and right, avoiding the gunfire. His sheer skill made Marshall whistle.

"*Got some serious moves! If he's stolen that bike, Cass, I'll eat my miniguns, ammo and all!*"

The roadway was a tangle of horns and noise and fury; anger rose to the sky like the smoke of a stopped engine. The three Boozter bikes screamed clean round the edge of the mess, then took up the chase. She saw the front rider raise his pistol a second time—a D.R.H. Darkfisst, another costly piece of kit.

Whoever these guys were, they had one hell of lotta credit.

Never mind that now.

The Knux-rider glanced back, then threw his bike onto a sliproad and headed for cover—the car park in the base of the Norman Lovett Block, the home of the Holly Corporation.

A line of gunshots chewed up the rockcrete as he went.

"*Now we've got him,*" Marshall said. "*That car park's a dead end, he can't get out.*"

It seemed that the Boozters knew it as well. As they reached the entrance, one rider slowed and stopped, unslinging something from across his back. The other two didn't wait—they shot past the barrier and were gone.

Anderson could almost hear them, the echoes of engines in rockcrete.

But she didn't slow down. Wailers still going, both Lawmasters roared at full speed down the Expressway towards the block. Metal fences lined its outside; the jagged-edge Holly logo seemed like some sort of warning.

At the noise, the gang member at the door turned, raised the heavy rifle to his shoulder. But they were closing way too fast;

the burst went wide. As they passed, Marshall put a neat, single shot into the creep's forehead. The creep hit the floor, and they were through.

Wailers on low, ceiling tight overhead, they eased off on the throttle and purred forwards, listening for the—

There.

Not engines, voices. Shouts and threats and bursts of high-pitched sobbing—as they turned past the line of parked cars, they could see the Boozters had the Knux-rider backed against the wall. His bike lay on its side where he'd flubbed a corner; his leathers were gravelrash all up one hip.

But he still had the blond kid behind him, and he was armed.

Not guns; true to type, he had two heavy pieces of electro-steel, one over each gauntleted fist. They crackled, sending sharp shadows leaping round the walls.

But the two Boozters weren't coming close. They sat at pistol range, still astride their bikes, Darkfissts raised. They seemed to be shouting demands, wanting the kid turned over to them.

"Justice Department!" Anderson brought her bike to a halt; let the wailers give one final, dismal howl. "Hands on your heads!"

"Jays!"

The Boozters glanced at each other, then twisted to turn their guns on Anderson. They were young, their leathers painted and garish and studded with a hundred chrome designs. One had a chrome plate apparently bolted to the side of her head, the other had chrome spikes in his hair.

Anderson eyed the Darkfissts, but didn't bother drawing her own sidearm.

Kinda pointless, as the Lawmaster's miniguns' barrels spun up to speed, screaming at them.

In the tight grey of the car park, the noise was deafening. Not stupid, the Knux-rider raised his hands and put them on his head, the electricity shutting off; the blond boy was on the floor, curled into a ball. It looked like he'd peed himself.

But the two Boozters had other ideas. Unimpressed, they raised their automatics and opened fire.

Anderson was a sitting duck. Small calibre rounds spanged from the Lawmaster's metalwork and took bites out of her flak vest. The impacts made her wheeze.

But her guns were bigger.

Much bigger.

She spoke the order, and both Boozters vanished in a greasy red haze.

No fool, the Knux-rider had hit the deck. Marshall had his Lawgiver aimed straight at the biker's lid.

"*Armour-piercing.*" His command came clearly over the comm. Then, "*Don't drokking move.*"

Job done, Anderson shut off the miniguns and let them spin to a halt, barrels smoking.

"You," she said out loud, clear enough for the Knux-biker to hear it. She threw one leg over the fuel tank and walked over to stand with her boot on his shoulder. "You're gonna tell me what the hell's going on, or I'm gonna rummage round in your brain 'til I find it. And I'll drag out everything else you got—every crime, every denial, every regret, every fiction you tell yourself. Every last thing you still feel guilty about—right down to the time you lied to your grandma about running over her *cat.*" The kidnapped kid was whimpering, his mind a fog of terror, but Anderson's attention was on the biker. "What's it gonna be, creep?"

Still faceless, the Knux-rider raised his head enough to look from Judge to Judge—from Marshall's pistol to Anderson's badge. To one side, a mess of broken bikes and shredded flesh lay steaming with body heat; at the doorway to the building itself, a security guard stopped dead and tiptoed back out of sight.

Surveillance orbs whirred, but neither Judge looked up.
The Knux-rider said, "Looks like you got me."
The voice was female, but Anderson didn't care.
Hell, cuffs fit everybody.

Three

Victoria Elizabeth Xavier, aka 'Vex.'
   Age: 28.
   Height: 5'6".
   Hab: 303, Basement Quarter of the Eee-Zee Rest charity Hab Zone.
   Previous convictions...
   "Breaking and entering, GBH, dealing narcotics, armaments, illegal engine and droid parts, you-name-it..." Marshall stopped scrolling down his holo-screen and looked through the one-way window at the biker. "This one's a cut above your basic gang-thug, Cass. And one hell of a tek."
   Anderson nodded, but she hadn't taken her eyes from the woman in the holding cell. Part of the prep for a deep-scan was personal awareness, observing someone's attitudes and body language, and how they reacted to their surroundings. It could give you a strong indication of what you were likely to find—and how much resistance you were likely to encounter.
   But Vex—apparently—didn't give a stomm. She was sat in a metal chair in the centre of the room, her cuffed hands

secured behind her, her muscled shoulders bunched. Her head was shaved at the sides and her black-and-red hair was braided down her scalp and her back; she had a piercing in her eyebrow and a light-tattoo of a dragon down one side of her face. Not a gang-mark, by the look of it, just a serious piece of ink. The Department had taken her elektro-knux, her lid, and her jacket, and they'd left her alone.

She'd been in there for the last three hours.

Anderson sipped a caff and looked down her holo-screen, reviewing the info.

The kidnapped boy was one Julian Cavendish, seventeen years old, no criminal record. Her surface scan had shown nothing out of the ordinary: youth, wealth, naïveté, and want-my-Mommy fear. Anderson had wanted to go deeper, but the work had been cut short as Mommy herself had barged in, all expensive coat and pseudo-fur. Mrs. Cavendish had demanded a lawyer, found fault with everything, then taken Chief Johnson to strident task about the clumsy rescue of her darling. Johnson had hustled her into his office and slammed the door.

In short, Anderson thought, Cavendishes large and small had thrown up a double helping of 'drokk' and 'all.'

But hell, it had never been them that she'd wanted.

"You going in there?" Marshall asked her.

"Not into the room." Anderson took another sip of her caff. "I'll only speak to her if I need to lead her thoughts, for any reason—make her focus on particular memories. For now, I'm just gonna look."

She put the cup on the tabletop, steam curling in the air.

Beside her, Marshall shook his head. His thoughts were stretched like a web, hanging somewhere between admiration, apprehension and humour. Despite his previous claim, she knew she freaked him out too—she could see it—but—

Never mind him.

Focus.

Standing at the observation window, Anderson slid, very carefully, into Vex's inked, shaven skull.

So. What's behind Door Number One...?

The initial blur of surface images, the thousand random things that ambled through your forebrain during the day. A backstreet negotiation, a hefty gym-workout, a robo-pet, a broken brake cable. An argument, a new piece of engine. A bike Vex had seen, chained up for days—it was slowly falling to pieces as the local kids stole the bits.

Nothing out of the ordinary.

Except...

There was no dread. No reflexive fear of unpaid fines or stolen Chocco bars. Victoria Xavier had no fear of the Judges, of Psi-Div, nor of the scan she knew was coming.

The insight made Anderson stop. It had come with an image-echo: she saw herself, on her Lawmaster, riding just ahead of Vex's vision. They chased through the traffic, engines singing.

Vex had liked the adrenaline.

Liked the bike.

The flash of feeling was very strong: a bonding, a surge of curiosity and empathy. A flash of need. And it was exactly the opening that Anderson was looking for.

You trust me, Victoria.

We're the same, you and I.

Show me.

Past the pool of her surface thoughts and diving deeper. Following the nerve-impulses, the exploding flares of memories that spread from the image-centre like a fractal...

There: that same kinship. A focus on the bikes, and on the road. A feeling of shared interests; elation from the rush of it all, engines thundering in tandem...

And Vex *wanted* something.

She wanted something from Anderson, from the Judges.

The thought was subconscious, buried very deep—and even

as Anderson glimpsed it, a backwash of other images covered it up like a denial.

Bottles and crowbars, a kid with his face cut, a dark alleyway, the arc of a petrol-bomb. Crash and flare and heat. Silhouetted figures running in behind it, using it as cover. A very tall man, handsome and dreadlocked and dark-skinned; the flutter of his long black coat. Vex is boxing, a hard left-right, sweeping a leg to knock her opponent over, dropping and driving her fist, hard, into his face...

Raising that fist, the elektro-knux crackling...

Gang-stuff, pretty basic. Puzzled, Anderson pushed at it, past the surface, past the reflex defences.

We're the same, Victoria.

You can see that, you can trust me.

What is it that you need?

In the spark of electric knux-light, the image changed.

Loss and pain and worry. Livid fury. The same, dreadlocked man, his mouth open, his long hands wrapped over a belly wound. Blood oozing between his fingers. Vex in angry tears, her muscled shoulders bunched, her knux sending sparks across an empty car park. The man is being hunted; she needs to get him to safety. His mouth moves, but he can't—or won't—speak.

And under all of it, something else, something buried so far down it's barely even visible. A fear, but something so deep and so dark—

"Drokk!"

Startled, Anderson broke contact and stumbled backwards, lurching into the table, her fists to her temples.

Marshall caught the caff. "What is it? What's up?"

"I don't..." She shook herself, stood upright. "I don't know yet."

She took the caff out of his hand.

Drained it.

And then, annoyed, she opened the door.

*   *   *

"ALL RIGHT," SHE said to Vex. "Talk."

"Talk about what, Judge?"

Vex had tipped the chair onto its rear feet; she hung there, stretching her legs as best she could.

Marshall, too, had come into the room. He shut the door behind him and lounged, lanky and casual and arms folded, against the wall.

For the briefest moment, Anderson wished he'd stop being so protective—it was like being assessed all over again.

But she had other things to think about.

"Why don't we start with Julian Cavendish?" she said.

It was an opening gambit, an easy question to build up trust before they moved onto the harder stuff. And it was targeted, a device to immediately make Vex think about the subject.

But no surprises: the images were the same ones that Anderson remembered from Rikki, the boy with the BudJet Arms pistol. The bonfire, the graffiti, the fighting. They were clearer, this time—Vex was fighting the Boozters, and there were Cavendish and Rikki both, right in the middle of the mess...

Anderson said, "Where were you taking him?"

Another targeted query: a key, opening a door.

A tek-bay, large and draughty. Old bikes, bits of engine, a makeshift bar with a string of lights and a row of steel barrels. Bedrolls and cushions, a burning oildrum. Cavendish sits at one wall, his hands still tied, his face smudged with dirt and tears...

Vex said, "Home."

"He lives in a lux-hab."

Vex tilted backwards further, then smiled, one-sided and humourless. The light-dragon on her cheek coiled with the movement. "Yeah. The Boozters took him from his mommy. But his scrawny ass came with a ten-thousand-credit reward. I didn't kidnap the kid, Judge. I went after the Boozters to get him back."

That, at least, made sense—if Vex had busted Cavendish free from the Boozters, then held him herself for several hours... it explained the time difference between Rikki's memory and Anderson's flash.

More importantly, it meant Vex was telling the truth.

Marshall butted in, all nonchalance: "No trouble now, Xavier. Anderson, here, can unravel your brains like a length of soggy synthetti."

Anderson found a second metal chair, spun it around and straddled it, facing the woman. She had the simple stuff, now— Vex had answered honestly and trust would be easier, defences lower. It was time to take it up a gear.

"Victoria," she said, with absolute clarity, each syllable a nail pinning Vex to her seat. "Why did you follow me?"

Vex met her gaze, eyes narrow. She was amused by Anderson's chair—as if the Judge was hiding behind a barrier.

"I liked the bike," she said. "You Jays got some serious teks up here."

It was true, but not completely—and it wasn't what Anderson was looking for. No, she wanted to see that almost-hidden, subconscious need, that sense of kinship, that reaching out. It was fiercely buried, but Anderson could see it flickering in the depths, like flashbacks at an unwelcome—

Flashbacks.

Oh, you gotta be kidding me.

The pattern was familiar. She wasn't sure yet, but it bore a strong resemblance to her Academy descriptions of Post-Traumatic Stress.

...something dark and slavering and savage and starving-hungry, something huge and clamouring and greedy...

What the hell was going on here?

Moving carefully, aware that this was thin-ice territory and trying to remember the basics, Anderson touched at a passing flash, and tried to understand.

The dreadlocked man is screaming, his mouth stretched and soundless, his hands writhing as if he's reaching for something, yet can't touch it. Vex is holding him down, shouting for a medic; the man is banging his head against the rockcrete floor as if to dash his own brains out. Someone throws her a rolled-up blanket and she shoves it under his skull, but he can't stop, can't stop, can't stop...

LEAVE HIM ALONE!

Anderson rocked, mentally and physically, and nearly fell back off the chair.

Vex was staring at her, her face full of amazement, hate, horror, anger. "What the hell are you *doing?*" Her own chair was back on all four feet. Her hands were still cuffed, but she was struggling, shaking her head like she had a bug burrowing in her brain. "You leave that stomm alone!"

"What happened to him?" Anderson said. "You want me to help you. Why? What does he need?"

Vex's face was pale, the dragon standing out sharply against her skin. "What're you talking about?"

"Who is he, Vex? The man with the dreadlocks?"

"No," Vex said. "No, no, no." There was too much pain; her defences were sparking like her knux. Her voice rasped and broke. "You don't understand..."

"Sometimes," Anderson said softly, "your subconscious can access the things that you can't. Things stay in your mind, buried deep, and you face them only when you're ready— that's how people survive, how they... protect themselves. And sometimes, you'll get flashbacks, stuff like that. It's how your mind processes things that are too much for it. But it takes time. Years." She stopped, feeling oddly guilty. "I haven't *got* years, Vex."

She stood up, spun the chair round the other way, sat back down, the barrier gone. "Something's going on down at Eee-Zee Rest. I'm right, aren't I? This isn't just gang-wars, you and the Boozters. It's not just the kidnapping of some spoiled kid. There's something bigger, under there, something *hungry*—"

"All right, Anderson, that's enough."

Johnson had barged through the door, Mrs. Cavendish at his shoulder. The sector chief's face was a thundercloud, Julian's mother looked suitably self-righteous. Marshall stood upright, a smoke-billow of alarm rising from him.

"Sir?"

Anderson stood up more slowly. She could feel the sector chief's anger, rigidly controlled, underlain by a solid resolve. "Marshall, take Xavier to the cubes. Anderson, my office."

Vex tried to stand up, jarred to a stop, still cuffed to the table.

"Stay there," Anderson said to her. Then, "Sir, can you wait a minute? I'm right on the edge of something, here."

"I don't need your tricks, Anderson. Or your bleeding heart routine. Xavier's guilty of murder, arson, attempted kidnapping and enough traffic offences to keep her down 'til she's ninety. Young Cavendish has proven to be a solid witness, despite the trial he's been through. And his family are... ah... concerned about exposing him to further trauma."

Mrs. Cavendish radiated smug. Anderson quelled a desire to slap Johnson hard up the side of the head.

She said, "Sir, Xavier didn't take the boy. She saved his life—"

"That's not what he says."

"Then he's lying, sir." She looked from chief to mother and back. "Let me scan him properly and I'll prove—"

"How dare you, young lady." Mrs. Cavendish inhaled, drawing herself up to full intimidation. She had a chest like an inflated airship and her mind was saturated with indignance; clearly, she was used to being obeyed. "I don't know who you think you are—"

"Judge Anderson, Psi—"

"That's *enough!*" Johnson barked the words, and the room shook. Add another understanding, Anderson thought—

he didn't deal well with having his authority challenged. "Marshall, I gave you an order. Anderson, I said 'my office.' You two have caused quite enough chaos." He turned back to Mrs. Cavendish. "Leticia, my apologies."

Marshall caught her eye and gave a faint flicker of eyebrow. His thoughts said, very clearly, *Sorry, Cass. Play the game for now, and we'll see what happens.* He kept her gaze. *Can you hear me?*

She gave a fractional nod, and he came over to unlock Vex from the chair. Vex stood up, stretching her shoulders as Marshall refastened the cuffs. She shot Anderson one vicious, betrayed look—*you drokking bitch!*—then followed him out of the room.

Severely tempted to down one or both of Johnson and Mrs. Cavendish with a well-timed psi-blast, Anderson kept her mind still and her mouth shut. She said nothing; let the other two leave the room. Then she went out after them, and closed the door on the emptiness.

HALF AN HOUR later, when she re-emerged from Johnson's office with her ears still smoking, Marshall was waiting for her.

He didn't pause; he took one of her elbows and walked her down to the department tek-bay, where their bikes were parked. She shook off his touch, but listened as he spoke softly and swiftly, his eyes constantly searching the corridors.

"She's doing thirty," he said. "I think Cavendish wanted an example made of her. And she was pretty pissed—Xavier, I mean." He paused, his face troubled. "What the hell's going *on* here, Cass? What's all this about?"

Anderson waited as two Judges came the other way. Their suspicions were jarring and obvious—she wasn't wanted here—but she didn't care, she was getting used to it. "I don't know," she said, "But I think... Marsh, I think there's something hiding in Eee-Zee Rest. Something nasty."

"Did you tell Johnson?"

"He won't go down there." She snorted, the sound scathing. "He's just pulled the plug on the whole thing. He won't touch this Biggs character without three weeks planning and a colour-coded *map*."

Marshall said quietly, "Maybe he's got a point. I know this Sector, Cass—"

"Does he?" She rounded on him. "There's something *in* there, Marsh. Something big, with extra teeth, or I've gone proper futsie. Something that's scared both Rikki and Vex clean outta their minds—"

"Like what? Look, you gotta give us a clue here—"

"I don't know." *Dark and slavering and savage and starving-hungry.* "But I do know that it's so gruddamn terrifying that it's messing with people's memories. Whatever Eee-Zee Rest is brewing up, it's some seriously nasty stomm."

Marshall let out his breath. Eyed another Judge as he came past.

At last, he said, "Cass, I don't have your vision, and right now, I'm pretty pleased about that." He paused, then went on, "But I do know your record. And I know you tend to get in over your head. This is confusing the hell outta me—but one lot of gang-fights plus a kidnapped kid does not equal some fang-toothed monster."

Anderson shoved him back against the corridor wall. "You listen to me," she said, her voice low, "and I'll do you a deal. We go dig up every last piece of info we can find on the Knux, the Boozters, the Pink Chickens, Biggs, Eee-Zee Rest, the whole shebang. Everything. And if you still wanna leave it alone, then I'll leave it alone. We'll leave it 'til Johnson's filled out all his little spreadsheets and drawn all his little diagrams. Used all his multicoloured *pens*."

Almost in spite of himself, Marshall chuckled. "You think I'll give in. Don't you? You think I'll look at the evidence and we'll sneak outta here like a pair of kids, shinning down the midnight drainpipe."

"I think," she said, "that Johnson's assigned you to watch me because you understand Psi-Div. You've worked with us before, you said so yourself. And I think you know enough to trust my insights. And you'll do the right thing."

Marshall's chuckle faded into seriousness. "And I think, Cassandra Anderson, that you're playing me for a soft touch." His thoughts were reciting *onetimestwoistwo, twotimestwoisfour…* "You're appealing to my better nature."

She said nothing, waited.

"I'm a Judge, Cass, just like you."

She still said nothing.

Twotimesfouriseight…

He sighed, said, "But—fair enough—I guess you're not wrong. I do trust you." His gaze was shrewd, giving nothing away. "Deal."

She raised an eyebrow. "What're you hiding, Marsh?"

Twotimeseightissixteen…

"Nothing." His grin came back. "Plausible deniability."

Twotimessixteenisthirtytwo…

Slowly, trying to fathom what he meant by the tease, Anderson nodded. "You're saying we go?"

"We go," he said. "But no big drama. Okay?"

She returned his grin. "As long as we take Vex with us. She'll know where everything is."

Twotimesthirtytwoissixtyfour!

"Oh, Grud." Marshall rolled his eyes out loud. "Now there's a plan that can't *possibly* go wrong."

Four

"HOW LONG'VE WE got?" Anderson asked Marshall, over the comm.

Her Lawmaster had settled to an easy thunder, rumbling over the Hattie Hayridge Expressway towards the now-familiar pattern of lights. Anderson had miniguns deployed but not spinning; in front of her, Vex rode the old Brit-Cit bike with a certain upright tension, fully aware of the heavy calibre rounds that waited at her back.

Anderson didn't think Vex would make a break for it, but she wasn't gonna get this wrong.

"*Not sure,*" Marshall commented. "*With Johnson in the sleep machine, it was my call to make. But he'll wake up any minute, and he's gonna take a dim view of us busting a perp out the cubes. He'll come straight after us, and he'll be farting fire.*"

"Now *that*," Anderson commented to herself, "I need to see."

It was late, the sky was low and dark and the four Eee-Zee Rest buildings stretched up into obscurity. Few of the windows had internal lights; many of them were boarded over, or covered with nailgunned-down sheet steel, some of it bent open at the corners. It told the usual stories of poverty and street wars.

But this place was not usual.

Gruddamn funny-looking charity, she thought. As the lights came closer and she could see the blocks more clearly, she began to understand why Chief Johnson had not wanted to come out here.

Damn place gives me the heebies.

But there was no going back now; they'd already broken every rule in the book. They'd busted a surprised Vex out of her cube, walked her to the tek-bay and given her back her stuff— her jacket, her knux. Anderson was in this up to her ass, now, and the only way out was through.

Johnson'd have her badge for this.

Or he'll try.

A bellow of bikes approached them, headlights dazzling. Vex tapped her lid at the one in the lead and the figure nodded back, blatantly staring at the Judges. Anderson didn't need her psi-scan to read the confusion in his head.

But they passed in a roar, and vanished.

Yeah, all right, she thought. *I know how gruddamn crazy this looks.*

This was a hunch, a vision, pure instinct. The thing she'd seen was vague as nightmare: it had no form, no face, no name, no criminal record. She couldn't slap her cuffs on it and slam it in a cube. It felt more like an infection, a tide of *something* that had risen in the back of her head, bulging and seething and wanting...

But she'd done crazy stuff before—hell, she'd seen the Cursed Earth—and it'd all turned out okay.

This'd be the same. Wouldn't it?

An open-topped buggy was following her, a gang of teens hanging over the edges. They had an old-skool music system all racked up to eleven and, as they closed in, they began to whoop and catcall, whistling and making all-to-obvious gestures. She logged their ID, but quelled the temptation to retaliate—she had more important things to worry about.

Eventually, bored with her lack of response, they peeled off down the sliproad and were gone.

"*Heads up, Cass*," Marshall said. "*We're here.*"

EEE-ZEE REST.

Silent, its broken lights glimmering overhead.

They'd come in at ground level, and at the very end of the Expressway. In front of them, a dented sign showed the triple-Z logo and the slogan *Hope to the Hopeless*. Spraypaint had added the name *Slee-Zee Rest*. A heavy chain-link fence defended the perimeter, and a huge maze of roads wove outwards beyond the gate.

The whole thing was low, and grey, and dirty, and poorly lit; some of it was open, some under cover. Maps showed them four Blocks, and the absolute warren linking them—lock-ups and underpasses, gang-bases and warzones and dead ends. These were not the polite plazas and malls of the sector's centre, nor the open streets that bordered the Black Atlantic. This was the sector's underbelly, dark and full of questions.

And here they were, just gonna ride riiight on into the middle...

"*Slow it down,*" Marshall said. "*Eyes open.*"

"Roger that." Anderson had her data-screen on and the motion tracker activated. Blips danced, but they were a distance away, deep in the labyrinth that awaited them.

She felt her nervousness rising and quelled it, focused instead on the info Vex had given them.

On the walk down to the tek-bay, Vex confirmed a lot of what they already knew—that the Knux and Boozters had been fighting for years, and that the Boozters had access to some seriously top-of-the-range kit. As for Biggs, he remained both legend and mystery—the tale went that he'd been raised by dirt-poor parents and had used an amassed fortune to help others like himself...

But Eee-Zee Rest protected both him, and its secrets. People went in, they didn't come out. People in neighbouring streets went strangely missing. And those who were housed there frequently vanished; they just locked up their habs and were never seen again. Victims of the gangs, or so the stories went.

And, Vex had said, on top of all *that,* there were the occasional kids like Cavendish, the wealthy ones taken for their creds or potential...

The whole drokking place, she'd said, was as rotten as a day-old corpse—

Goosebumps chilled across Anderson's shoulders.

"Marsh! Company!"

A split-second after the psi-warning, the data-screen flashed the same thing—movement. There was a squat, rockcrete guardpost at the outside edge of the fence.

And it was occupied.

"*Gottim,*" Marshall said. "*This is still a routine visit, Cass. Don't—*"

"*Down!*"

She felt the spike of eager glee; saw the bipod on the windowsill.

Reacting by pure reflex, Marshall flattened his chest on the fuel tank and slid his Lawmaster sideways, almost going over with the motion. Vex did likewise, moving like a stunt-rider. Anderson, further back and with more warning, twitched the bars and let the missile streak straight past her, trailing fire.

It struck the side of a toona truck and detonated, the concussion hitting her like a fist. Salt water and stinking debris made her tyres skid sideways. She held hard to the bars to stop herself going over.

The sky rained fish-bits and burning metal.

"*That'll wake Johnson like his favourite drokking alarm droid,*" Marshall commented. "*Have some of this.*" He snapped the order and his miniguns opened up. They muzzle-flashed like fireworks; rounds chewing holes in the rockcrete and blowing chunks from corners and windowsills. Inside, the Boozter kept his head down. Then Marshall was past him and heading through the shattered remains of the gate.

"*Put him down, Cass,*" he called back, over the comm. "*Then RV first intersection, five hundred metres.*"

"Wilco."

Vex, her chest still on her fuel tank, followed Marshall. Their tail lights faded into the darkness and were gone.

Alone, Anderson slowed her Lawmaster. She was so intent on scanning that she missed the second Boozter completely. Her motion sensor blipped him at the last minute: a figure in the guardhouse doorway.

He had big, chrome shoulder pads, half a mask, and a hefty, five-chambered revolver, gripped hard in both gloved hands. As she pulled level, he emptied the thing, one shot after another.

The weapon was huge. It sounded like a succession of bombs going off—but it had a kick like a mule and he wasn't quite strong enough to hold it. It jumped, and the shots went wide.

Except the last one.

Struggling to keep the pistol under control, he'd jerked it downwards. The last round ricocheted from the roadway—and neatly took out her rear tyre. She felt the bike slew properly this time, felt the crumple of metal on rockcrete.

Her miniguns were pointed forwards. She couldn't turn, and she didn't dare draw the Lawgiver, she needed both hands on the now-rebellious bike. As the shattered tyre flubbed over and ever, as the wheelrim crunched and sparked, she slowed enough to launch a single psi-blast, hard, straight at the gunman's forebrain.

Revolver still in hand, he was trying to duck, but the blast was like a sunfire exploding in his head. He keened—horrible noise—and went over backwards, gun lost and feet kicking.

She watched him fall; saw two more stars behind him. They raised matching Darkfissts. Reaching for a random idea, a reckless impulse that came at her out of nowhere, Anderson threw the Fear right back at them.

Savage hunger. Seething and smothering. Your own nightmares, come screaming to life. They're coming for you, and they're coming for you now...

Both Boozters stopped dead. One toppled to the floor, holding his head and screaming. The other raised his Darkfisst and blew his own face off.

A ghost-image flashed at her, the last thing he saw. It was a basement, a halogen light, a large face with big, white teeth. Someone laughing, like a man insane—

And then she was past the doorway, and the image was gone. Her bike was handling like a bastard, its rear end skidding. It loudly protested the tyre... but it was still moving.

She was still moving.

She was in.

She checked for Marshall, couldn't see him, checked the holo-screen for the intersection.

Yeah, great, she thought. *Now what?*

Anderson shut down the miniguns and slowed the bike, trying to make sense of the map. The engine rumbled at her, growling like some huge and subterranean beast.

Where the hell's Marshall?

She tried her comms, got static.

The nest of streets was a tangle, a twisted knot of alleys, of metal grilles, of low, half-lit doorways, of failing neon flickers. There were bridges and underpasses, lights that offered everything from gambling and robo-dates to rounds of late-nite holo-golf. And there were people living here, laying on hardboard and wrapped in blankets, or slumping drunk against the wallsides.

Streets or tunnels, whatever these were, her headlight was a searchbeam, illuminating them to a passing flare of stark reality. Rodents squeaked and fled. People scrabbled to get out of her way.

Flashes of their thoughts flicked out at her—fear, desire, incomprehension.

The Judges... the Judges... the Judges...!

Down here, she was an icon, a faceless god-figure with authority on her badge, and an Eagle on her shoulder.

She was a target.

She slowed the bike even further, the engine lowering to a thrum. She'd lost Marshall and Vex both, couldn't hear them, couldn't see or feel them...

"Marsh?" *Marsh? Can you hear me?*

Nothing. Her comms fizzed at her, mocking.

In the back of her head, the sucking hunger-fear-whatever-the-hell suddenly rose, huge enough to drown out her every thought...

They've gone.

You're alone.

This was all a big mistake.

But still, she couldn't stop—she had to understand this. Her bike scraped and rumbled through the maze. Eyes stared at her; parents clutched children to their chests.

There were *children* down here?

They hid their faces as if she were some fable, suddenly dropped in their midst.

"Marsh?" The word was a whisper, and it fell onto nothing.

She passed under a crumbling archway, and, confused, brought the bike to a stop.

She'd hit a dead end.

What the hell?

She drew the Lawgiver, checked the map yet again. But she couldn't unravel the jumble of roadways, couldn't work out what was bridge and what was underpass, or where one road ended and another began.

She knew she should turn round, back up, but she stayed still, scanning the silence.

Around her was a derelict space, a rockcrete square that might once have been a shopping mall, now crossed by overzooms and all but lightless. A tall, faceless construct loomed at one side, silent and black—perhaps it'd once held advertising. An escalator sat rusting at the other. A spiral slipway led up to a balcony, and a building that might've been a bar.

And beneath its shadow, there was...

Oh, drokk.

...movement.

Her motion sensor caught it, but she felt it, heard it, saw it. From the square's edges came six, seven Boozters, all of them in chrome-studded leathers with their heads and faces covered. They carried no guns—but far too much in the way of glinting blades and lengths of chain. Their intent was obvious, and their thoughts... there were Judges here, inside their defences, and they wanted answers.

Wanted her dead.

Or worse.

They were blocking her exits. Carefully, Anderson got off the bike and used it to guard her back; let her tac-display give her crosshairs as she pointed the Lawgiver at the Boozster in the lead.

"On the ground." She aimed the pistol at his right eye. "I mean you. Hands on your head, nice and easy."

In answer, the Boozter spun his chain, hand-to-hand, in perfect figure-eights. It was slightly longer than his forearm and sported a heavy padlock on either end. As he came closer, his thoughts were clear.

You made a mistake, Jay. An' imma gonna drokk you up good.

She wasn't sure if the thought was aimed deliberately or just the usual streetrage—and she had about three seconds to pull the trigger before he introduced that padlock to her teeth. But...

Taking the risk, she flung a harsh, deep scan as far into his mind as she could.

This was not subtle, no gentle peeling back of images and layers. This was straight into his frontal lobe, where his short-term memories were still stored. It could be dodgy—going in without decent prep had a good chance of feedback or misinterpretation. If she botched it, she could give someone a heart attack, or flatline herself with the shock. But hell, she was alone, and she needed answers.

Badly.

The Boozter's recent recollections crashed into life.

Zipping up his leathers, looping the chain about his neck. He picks up a giggling little girl, spins her round and kisses her, and puts her down again. Their room is small, a dirty nest of blankets; a young woman watches him leave, her face etched in worry.

Further in, now, no time to waste—through into the hippocampus where his older memories waited.

A single, firelit room with a long table at the centre; he sits at its shoulder, listening to the woman at its head. He stands up, she hands him a glittering chrome badge—an award. But there's something he still has to do.

Rain on the windows. Now, he's in a penthouse, all polished floor and glass roof; the walls are pure, bright white, and there are images, seaside-blue holo-screens offering a dozen escapes. He can go anywhere, from this room.

Yet there's no furniture.

Unease flickers as he looks about himself for chairs.

A droid glides across the floor, sleek and elegant and faceless. It says, its voice flawlessly smooth, "Mistral, welcome. Mister Biggs will see you now."

Biggs's name like a punch in the gut—like Mistral's whole young life has been leading up to this moment. He turns to face the incoming Boss and stands tall, holds himself still against the tension...

...against something huge and clamouring and greedy...

With a violent mental shudder, Anderson found herself back in the plaza, gagging with the suddenness of the transition. Mistral's reaction had been instinctive and powerful—like the others, he'd just thrown her clean out.

The same thing! Again! Drokk it!

That same feeling of denial, of terror, of refusal. Every *time* she came close to touching or understanding it...

But she was out of time—Mistral was almost on her, now spinning his manriki-gusari hand-to-hand and round both shoulders. She caught his eye, held it, put pressure on the Lawgiver's trigger.

The rest of them were closing.

But she couldn't do it, gruddammit—he had a home, a wife, a daughter. Like so many people in this vast, sprawling hell, he was caught in a trap and had no control over his life.

Instead, she hit him with a psi-blast, straight between the eyes.

He went over backwards, kicking. The rest of the gang— six of them—stopped briefly in shock and then started to run, shouting.

She barked an instruction at the bike, heard the engine gun to life. The miniguns rose swiftly to full speed, but the Boozters were too smart to cross their line of fire. Instead, they parted to come at her from both flanks. They had every intention of tearing her to pieces.

And they might just succeed.

That thought sparked real fear, kicked in her adrenaline. She shot a second one in the upper arm, making him scream and drop his machete; took aim at a third and missed as he threw himself sideways, rolling neatly and coming up in a fighting crouch. She shot him again, straight through the knee—watched him fall, hollering for help.

Then they were too close; she holstered the Lawgiver, drew the daystick.

These guys were good. And she might be a Judge, but there was still only one of her…

Flash!

A spark of electricity in the dim, grey light.

She knew who it was before she even looked—the tight, focused temper was like a signature, familiar. Coming out from under the escalator, Vex took out one Boozter with a crackling-sharp left-right, then ran for a second, downing him with brutal face-punch efficiency.

Two left.

Caught now, between a Judge on one side and Vex's vicious elektro-knux on the other, they stopped. Anderson raised the Lawgiver to the face of the closer.

"I said, 'On the ground.'"

The young man—he was barely twenty—looked at her, his expression aghast. "Please, Judge," he said. "You don't understand."

She walked towards him. "Where's Biggs?"

The young man recoiled, mentally and physically. Like the others, the reflex-fear was a flood.

You don't know what he'll do!

She said, "What will he do?"

Vex had the last one on the ground, jerking spasmodically at the charge she'd shot through his backbone. As Anderson glanced at her, she unfolded to her feet and came over.

The body gave a last sigh and lay there, smoking. Now, only Mistral was still alive and awake, huddled on the floor with his hands over his head. Almost as an afterthought, Anderson tweaked him into unconsciousness.

He toppled over and lay still.

"Well, peejay?" Vex said. "You getting anything?"

"All right," Anderson said to her. "I've had enough of playing guessing games. What the hell is going on down here?"

Five

ANDERSON HADN'T WANTED to leave the Lawmaster, but Vex had pulled her away from the open mall and deeper under the cover of the rockcrete jungle. "We can't stay out here," she'd said. "Every Boozter in the place is looking for us, and you're gonna last about six seconds, Judge or not. I know you came here for answers, and I know where you can get them."

The surface scan was reflex; Vex cocked her pierced eyebrow, as if she knew exactly what Anderson was doing.

"I'm not trying to hide anything," she'd said. "And I owe you. Y'know, for busting me outta the cube." Her honesty had been clear, but there had been something else, something like dreadlocks and the flutter of a long black coat.

"C'mon," Vex said. "We gotta go."

Anderson set the bike's security system, and then followed Vex into the cold, grey tangle, all empty streets and endless overhangs. Black ash-marks indicated fires; walls were scarred with gunshots. Figures shambled past them, hunched and muttering. Vex didn't pause, but moved swiftly through it all, her thoughts focused and strong.

She knew exactly where she was going.

As they came to a second, more open space, Anderson caught her up and said, "Where's Marshall?"

Vex stopped. "I dunno. I lost him."

What?

Her dishonesty was complex—she'd made no effort to keep him in sight, or to go after him. Anderson caught her shoulder, spun her round, and stared into her face. Vex folded her arms and glared back, the dragon on her cheek glimmering in the light.

Her thoughts were ice-clear: *What're you looking for, treasure?*

Anderson's temper flared, but she held it down. "I need to reach the intersection—the one by the old mall—"

"That's the other way. We'll never get that far on foot."

"I'm not *leaving* him—"

"You don't have a choice."

"*Try* me."

"What's your name, Judge?"

The question was unexpected. It was about trust, not authority.

She said, without concession, "Cassandra."

"Then, Cassandra," Vex said, "You listen to me. We can't stay out here. I'll send one of my guys out after your partner, but right now, we need to get under cover. Before the drokking Boozters come after us in force."

Anderson said, "I'm not *leaving* him."

"We don't have *time*." Vex grabbed the neck of Anderson's flak vest and pulled her forwards until they were nose-to-nose. "Besides, I had a choice—it was him or you."

Again, that flicker of buried need.

Anderson paused, still glaring. She was tempted to tell Vex where to shove it, but the map on her belt-screen made about as much sense as—

Footsteps.

Still nose-to-nose, they both stopped dead.

Turned round.

There was a shadow at the end of the road, the angle making it stretch like some incoming mutie. It was rapidly followed by a second, a third. Laughter echoed.

"*We see you, peejay! We're coooming!*"

"Can we fight later and just get the drokk outta here now?" Vex said. "Before these guys get out the big toys?"

"Oh, Grud."

"Yeah. Come *on!*"

They ran headlong, like errant kids. Anderson had no idea where the hell she even was; she'd lost not only comms, Marshall and the Lawmaster, but *any* gruddamn sense of direction. She kept her pistol gripped hard in one hand, tried to follow the seethe of roads, but it was pure chaos—nothing she could unravel. Blips flashed as movement radiated around her, but she was moving too fast for a psi-scan, and she couldn't tell the Boozters from the desolate people that lived here. She dared not open fire without eyeballing the target.

Vex, however, didn't bother with maps—she headed through the maze with no hesitation. Her knux crackled occasionally, sparks that flashed the rockcrete to sudden brilliance and harsh, jagged shadow.

As she ran, her thoughts had a single dedicated emphasis—*safe house must find safe house*. She had considerable concentration, all completely untrained; she knew how to muster her awareness, how to narrow-focus on a task, and how to push herself to the limit. It was how she'd survived, how she'd become so skilled on her bike, and how she now navigated the streets in the almost-dark.

You know what? Anderson surprised herself with the thought. *She'd make one helluva Judge.*

"Here," Vex said. "Through there. And quick."

Vex gave her a shove and Anderson half-stumbled down a low flight of steps. She passed under an archway and reached a door, found a tall, dark figure looking down at her.

You!

The dreadlocked man, the man from Vex's memories.

Yeah, she realised a second later, *and that's the first damn thing that's made any kinda sense.*

The man nodded at her, but said nothing. He stepped back and let her pass. Behind her, Vex said, "Is the back room clear?"

The figure didn't answer, and Vex spoke again, "All right. You wanna come in, join us?"

Again, the figure made no response, but Anderson was already past him and into the main room...

She stopped, looking around her in surprise—and relief.

She'd seen this place before.

It had been in Rikki's memories, it had to be the Knux's base. There was a strong sense of homecoming, of familiarity; it smelled of steel and fuel, just like the tek-bay at Sector House. Bits of bike, like metal corpses, were littered everywhere, frames hunkered like skeletal shadows, awaiting their insides. A draft came from a shuttered roll-door. There was a desk, an old holo-screen, oil-stains across a rockcrete floor. There was a home-made bar, all steel barrels and synthi-hol, and decorated in strings of lights. Several tek-droids sat in the corners, all kinds of shapes and sizes—the closest one had three eyes and three arms, all pointing in different directions. Ignoring Anderson, it worked on one of the bikes, and clicked to itself like it was singing.

The place was a classic lock-up, and it felt like home.

It was also occupied.

At the arrival of the uniformed Judge, two dozen Knux had come to their feet, reaching for weapons. Their surprise and suspicion were apparent, their fears reflexive. But they held a deeper feeling, a common feeling, and something that came with a flush of newness.

Hope.

A Judge in their midst meant *hope.*

Anderson looked around at them and let her psi-awareness explore. The hope was strong, like a light; a flush of future, of freedom. She dipped from mind to mind, wanting to understand, but Vex had caught her up. With the tall, wordless figure still behind her, Vex said, "I'll explain. I'll explain everything." She pulled Anderson across the room to another door, yanked it shut behind the three of them, and bolted it.

Slam.

At the sound, all of the tension went out of her—this was her safe space, and she could finally relax.

"Thank Grud for that," she said. She flopped down in an old swivel-chair, and spun it to face the Judge. Behind her, a huge version of the Knux symbol was painted straight onto the wall, now worn with age.

"Glad to hear it," Anderson said. "And now, you're going to tell me what the hell's happened to Marshall. And who this guy is." She jerked a thumb at the dreadlocked man. "And what the drokk this is all about."

You're going to tell me why I'm here.

Why you want me.

The man had come to stand at Vex's side, his hand on her shoulder. He was lean and elegant, his long frame covered by that familiar, flapping coat. A surface scan confirmed that he couldn't—or wouldn't—speak.

It also told her that his mind was deeply scarred, a tangle of fears and horrors and flashbacks. But this time, it was subtly different—it was harsh, and recent. He met her gaze, though, and she realised that he, too, had hope.

Is this why I'm here?

To play shrink?

Vex gestured at an aged caff machine. "Help yourself."

"Just get on with it," Anderson said. "I'm fed up of chasing ghosts."

"I've sent someone after your partner—they'll bring him back here." Vex paused for a moment, then took a long breath and sat forwards in the chair. "Cassandra," she said. "Judge Anderson. This, this place"—she gestured—"it's my home. This lock-up, this mess, these blocks. This little corner of the Big Meg. I live here. I always have. And it used to be good. Not lux hab-good, but y'know—we did okay. The Knux could hang here. Safely. A bit of buying, a bit of selling, a bit of... well, you get the picture." Her mind flashed a collage of backstreet deals, a hundred trades of drugs and engine parts. "I was just a streetkid, like hundreds of others. The Knux raised me..." She tailed off, the dodgy deals flickering into childhood memories, all wit and thievery. "And then Biggs came."

The flash of fear from the quiet man was powerful, but gone before Anderson could understand it.

"Who the hell is this 'Biggs' character?" Anderson said. "No one knows who he is, what he even looks like..." She glanced up at the man, found his thoughts tumbling like rubbish blowing down the road. "Why's everyone so afraid of him?"

The quiet man had been watching Anderson, his expression curious. Flashes disturbed his mind like the charges of Vex's knux; as if to hide them, he walked over to the caff machine and gave it a kick. A cup rattled down and started to fill.

The acrid smell was strong.

Vex said, "This is Silence, the Knux's leader. He's the person with your answers. Silence was here at the beginning. He's been closer to Biggs than anyone, and he's the only one who's escaped... unscathed. Well, kinda. He's not spoken since."

"So *that's* why I'm here? You want me to cure him?" Anderson exhaled, genuinely daunted. "Listen, I'm a Psi-Cop, not a Doctor, and that's some pretty dangerous stomm."

He could go futsie. Or worse.

Silence handed the full cup to Vex, then kicked the machine again and poured a caff for himself.

Tension came off him like a wave—he understood all of this, and all too well.

"No, that's not why you're here," Vex said. "You're here because of Biggs. I need you... you need to stop him. Stop what he's doing. And Silence is the only one who can explain. He's the only one who's been down there and escaped, and the only one who can remember it clearly—"

"But he can't tell anyone."

Suddenly cold with understanding, with what they needed her to do, Anderson looked at the man.

He met her gaze, his dark eyes flickering with tension.

In his head, he said very clearly, *Please. I need you to reach it for me; I need to remember, to tell you everything. Biggs... has to be stopped.*

Hell. What other choice did she have?

SHE WENT DOWN, down past the voicelessness, down into the memories...

A penthouse.

Glass roof. Black sky, white walls, blue holo-screens. Perfect. If he wants, he can go to the beach and enjoy a 'real' margarita, play a round of dice, or go out for a walk with friends.

But he sits, with his hands in his lap, and he waits for the meeting.

Before he was Silence, his name was Robert Vantage—and he's nervous, but that's all. He's come ready to negotiate, and he's got all the info—his mind's full of maps, and presentations. And he has hope—the Block's new owner is wealthy, and the plans for the charity have been clear from the beginning.

This is a good cause, and Robert loves the area. This is home, and he wants to help—

Silence's mind baulked.

A dark flash; the impact knocked Anderson sideways. She fell against the wall as Silence, completely unconsciously, yanked his memories away from the image. It was the same thing, yet again, uncontrolled and pure reflex; the same denial that Vex had shown, that Rikki had shown.

Massive, horrific trauma. Something so terrifying that no one could remember it clearly.

Physically, Silence was shaking his head, his long fingers on his temples. His nervousness was climbing to a pure, dark fear, shot through with light like a storm. The denial in him clamoured, but Anderson stood upright and came to stand in front of him. She moved his hands and replaced them with her own.

He watched her, his eyes now dark as blood.

"You okay?" she said.

He nodded. *I can do this. I want to. I need to.*

Vex said very softly, "Is there any way I can help?"

"Offer him contact," Anderson told her. "Reassurance, physical and vocal. Your presence'll help him feel safe."

But she didn't wait to see Vex move, she went back in, past those eyes, under the surface, back to that place of storm and darkness.

"Mister Vantage, how lovely to meet you."

He hears the voice first: deep and strong and well-modulated, the voice of a professional performer. And it's faintly, oddly metallic, suggesting surgery of some kind.

But, as Biggs comes into the room—

The flare of shock that came from Silence came out of Anderson's mouth, "Drokking hell! *That's* Biggs? *That's* the Big Bad Boss?"

Reginald Biggs was legend, all right—he was a celebrity. Hell, she knew *exactly* who he was. Memories broke over Anderson in a flood like a sweat—Silence's memories, her own memories. Biggs's career and what'd happened to him had made all the Meg's major newslines...

Reginald Biggs was a Fatty.

Or he had been.

Screemsheet headlines flashed in her thoughts: they'd called him 'The Sheriff' and he'd been the absolute top of his profession, an elite sportsman, one of the leaders of his field. He'd held the title in this sector, and he'd competed at a city-wide level. He'd downed everything from food-platters to sofas to deprogrammed droids... Reginald Biggs had been massive of appetite, utterly fearless, and a world-class drokking champion.

Until his career had been sabotaged by a well-placed microbomb.

The detonation had taken out most of his lower intestine. The doctors had saved his life, but his injuries had forced him to retire, and left him on a liquid diet.

Looking through Silence's eyes, Anderson's thoughts shifted from shock to a sense of genuine pity.

Reginald Biggs was a Fatty no longer.

No wheel supported Biggs's belly—there was no belly left to support. From a titleholder of the Hundred Tonnes, Biggs had lost some nine tenths of his bodyweight and was now a sliding mass of folds, layer upon layer upon *layer* of loose, empty skin. A long, bright robe covered most of him, flowing down from still-strong shoulders, but she could see the creases where his flesh had overflowed his feet.

Reginald Biggs couldn't walk. He'd glided in on a hoverchair, his ringed hands crossed serenely over what remained of his stomach. And now he hung there, in Silence's thoughts, in the centre of his pure white penthouse... and he smiled, all big, white teeth.

"Bob," he said, his voice all easy confidence. "I'm so glad we got this chance to *talk.*"

No, no. Don't make me...

Silence's terror was writhing like a mad thing, twisting and turning in Anderson's mental grip.

That same sensation of a huge, craving hunger... and she could understand. A man with vast appetite, now forced to starve.

With shudder like goosebumps, Anderson realised that Biggs was insane.

The image changes, switching round on itself and falling as if from some vast height. From being in the Penthouse, Silence plummets, screaming. He hits a dirty floor with a crash, and lays stunned, his breath knocked from his lungs.

He should be dead.

But no, he's in darkness, the bright white and the holo-screens all gone. It's hot, the air is full and sweaty.

Not understanding, he kneels up, looks round himself in confusion—

Silence's thoughts balked again. A wall slammed up across the image, forcing Anderson back.

Briefly, she surfaced. She looked into the man's face; sweating in terror, saw the haunted look in his eyes.

"I want to help you."

Vex said to him, very softly, "It's all right. I'm here." Her hand hadn't left his shoulder.

I want you to help me. I have to tell you. I have to tell you how to stop him.

Anderson nodded; she was so close now. She went under again, clean through the wall, searching all those little tangles of cells, his memories all shifting and dancing. The thought-barrier grew and shifted, becoming a huge hand, sliding images aside, teasing her, stopping her from touching them, or from accessing the deepest ones.

And it was a lot harder to defeat.

Still, she could reach round it, grasp at its fragments like nightmares...

Find fear like a vacuum, black and open and starving.

With a twinge of nervousness, Anderson paused. This was the thing that Rikki had been afraid of—this was *exactly* the thing that she'd sought. And it was in here, in Silence's thoughts: that sense of yawning, craving need, huge as an auditorium. Physical need, emotional, mental. Terrifying.

…huge and clamouring and greedy…

She stumbled, and Vex's hand caught her.

The auditorium-image grows: it's a mouth, huge, engulfing. It's an empty belly and he stands in the very base of it, waiting for the flood of digested foodstuffs to break over and drown him. And when it comes, it's a wall of flesh, a mountainous, monstrous globule of skin and bone, a mounting flood of toxic waste. There's screaming, and eating, and things being smothered, and being swallowed whole. There's something in the block, something that lurks and slavers in the darkness of the basements, in the undertunnels, in the hearts and minds of the residents of Eee-Zee Rest—

White noise.

Silence's mind had shut down, gone so suddenly blank that Anderson shook her head to disperse the sparks in her vision. As she came back to the room, she saw that he'd fallen, his eyes rolled back in his skull. Vex had stood up and caught him in strong arms.

"Well?" Vex said. She was angry, but holding it back—she understood. "Did you get anything?"

"Yeah," Anderson told her. "I think I got enough."

Six

SECTOR CHIEF JOHNSON slammed both fists on his desk, making his senior staff jump and his coloured pens rattle.

"Who the hell authorised this?" He was puce in the face and raging. "Why didn't you tell me?"

The half-circle of Judges exchanged glances. One of them stepped forwards, her voice even. "You were in the sleep-machine, sir. The release was at Marshall's orders."

"Marshall?" Bob's response was scathing. "Marshall wouldn't pull something like this. That gruddamn mind-meddler's been in his *head*. Where are they now?"

"Sir," the woman glanced at her colleagues and kept going, "both their comms have gone down. Security orb reports show... they were last seen heading for Eee-Zee Rest."

"*Drokk* it." Johnson cursed at length, almost spitting in outrage. "They were given orders to leave it the hell alone." He shook his head, as trying to assimilate the info. "This isn't Marshall, he's been doing this too long to be this dumb. Baker, Wilson... get a catch wagon prepped. And I want a Manta in the air. Bradley, I want full schematics of the area, hab breakdowns, personnel, gang-history, the works. And you, Jones—get me Chief Ecks. I wanna have a *word*."

"YOU'RE TALKING ABOUT full-on gang war," Anderson said. "And in uniform or out of it, I'm still a Judge—"

"Don't get your badges in a bunch, Judge." One of the younger Knux glanced up from his bike and grinned, wiping his oily hands on a rag. "The gang thing's just a distraction and, officially, you won't know drokk-all about it. But we can keep the Boozters occupied—we've been doing it for years—while you go after Biggs."

Anderson sighed. She was sat on the edge of the lock-up's battered, knife-scarred desk, looking at maps on the holo-screen. One of the smaller Knux had lent her a set of Kevlar-lined leathers, a little big in the waist, but good enough. She'd kept both Lawgiver and daystick, though, and Vex had, very carefully, taken the comm out of her helmet and wired it to a simple earpiece. It was still picking up static, but Anderson wanted it with her.

They had not yet found Marshall, and she was worried about him.

The disguise was at Vex's insistence—a Judge was just gonna be too gruddamned visible, and every perp in the place was gonna knew where she was. So, along with the leathers, they'd scraped her hair back and combed it with boot polish... which stunk worse than the synthetti sauce she'd used last time.

First a redhead, now a biker. Next time, I'm gonna go with that nice blue rinse...

The thought almost made her snort.

But this whole mess was just too tense. Silence was still out cold; Vex had Kevlar leathers on and weapons fully charged. The Knux member stood by the desk with her brawny arms folded, her expression downright resolute.

Her thoughts were all too clear—she wanted to drokk something up. And badly.

"You sure you can do this?" she asked Anderson.

"Yeah," Anderson said. "I'm sure. From what Silence saw, I need to reach the basement. Whatever he's really doing, it's down there."

Across the warehouse, one bike engine started, then another. In the corner, two of the Knux were pulling the tarp off the quad-buggy with the minigun; a third had a single-use rocket launcher slung across her back.

Anderson wondered if Chief Johnson was still asleep—the one good thing about her radio being busted.

"All right," Vex said. "Let's do this. Mariah, you take the team and move out. First RV will be eleven-hundred between Craig Charles Block and Danny John-Jules Block." She tapped the holo-screen. "You know where you're going?"

A small, sharp-featured woman nodded, and turned to bark orders at the others.

"You not going with them?" Anderson said.

"I'm coming with you," Vex told her, grinning. "Like you hadn't realised."

THE HOLO-MAP HAD shown them their target—an ageing mechanical lift in the fourth citiblock, Robert Llewellyn, and the only basement access point they'd found. Biggs himself probably had a private lift or grav shaft, but it hadn't been on the schematics and they didn't have time to go hunting.

No, they were gonna have to do this the hard way.

Every time, Anderson thought to herself as they slipped back out of the lock-up. *Every drokking time! Just once, I wanna do something the easy way. Y'know, for a change.*

Behind them, the big metal roll-door rattled up. There was a sudden, chill draft and a hot surge of engine-noise as the gang massed up and headed out.

A couple of them had stayed behind to secure the base—and the hard slam of the rear door meant that they weren't messing about.

Anderson and Vex found themselves shut out, and alone.

"We head north-east," Vex said. "Robert Llewellyn Block is the one diagonally opposite this one, and we'll need to deal with the MidZone Plaza. It's floodlit, it's the Boozters' rallying point, and it's gonna be watched. So we go round, not through."

"Roger that." Anderson caught herself, said, "Yeah, I'm ready."

Vex indicated a route, out and under a rockcrete bridge all layered with growing weeds. To one side, a peeling sign said *The Multi-Coloured Chop Shop*; they passed it on foot quietly, and the engine-noise grew fainter as they went.

It began to rain, a thin, misty drizzle that made the air cold and the puddles flicker.

Vex glanced skywards and pulled a face.

Anderson turned up the collar of her borrowed jacket and hoped it wouldn't wash the polish out of her hair. She followed Vex carefully, letting the woman take the lead while she concentrated on her psi-scans.

"People, three o'clock. One of them's asleep, I think they're just homeless…"

"Delivery guy, he's lost…"

"Hostiles, going the other way…"

Vex nodded briefly each time. She carried no holo-screen, but she adjusted their course as they went, ducking through alleyways to avoid any contacts. Anderson could feel her fear, her hope, her worry about Silence, her concern for her crew. And on a deeper level, part of her mind was also trying to picture Biggs for herself, trying to force herself to look at what he might have done, what he might still do…

What was coming.

Remembering that sense of kinship on their chase through the city, Anderson found herself liking this woman more and more. Vex felt almost like a friend, someone with whom—

The crash of a huge metal footstep made them jump.

"What the hell was *that*?"

Vex pulled Anderson under an overhang. They waited, listening, shoulder-to-shoulder in the soggy shadows.

"I mentioned the big toys?" Vex said softly. "That's the Cry-10, the security droid. They call it 'The Cleaner.' And we can thank Grud it's going the other way." Anderson could hear it— it was going after the Knux's engines.

Rubble rumbled in its wake.

"How big *is* that thing?" Anderson asked her, but the image in Vex's head was enough of an answer.

As the stomping retreated, they moved on through the rain.

ANDERSON HAD NO radio, no screen, no outside contact. Boot polish was sliding thickly down her neck. It itched.

Ahead of her, Vex moved in a crouched half-run, occasional sparks dropping from her knux. It had taken them ten minutes to cover half a klick, but neither the psi-scan nor the scope on the Lawgiver had picked up anything more sinister than a lost droid.

Now, though, the roads were beginning to open out. The rain grew heavier, glittering in the flickering fluorescence of the old tube-lights. Anderson wiped her face with her free hand, grimaced at the shoe-polish mess, and wished she still had her lid.

"Down," Vex said.

She dropped to one knee and extended her scan.

A short distance ahead of them was another open space, this one significantly larger. Floodlights glared, casting stark shadows down grey side roads. Easing forwards, peering between the rockcrete pillars, the women manoeuvred themselves into line of sight, and stopped.

"MidZone," Vex said. "There used to be parties here. Sponsored floats and stuff. Recruiting for the corporations, or just showing off their credit. Biggs shut 'em all down. Siphoned off every last cred into the charity's 'critical work.'"

Anderson said, "Yeah, I bet." Then, realising why Vex had made the statement, added, "We will stop this."

Vex grunted.

The Plaza was big, a square of gently descending steps centred on something that might once have been a fountain, but was now full of trash. Empty storefronts looked blind across the rockcrete, their windows long-gone. And from the side of one crumbling building, suspended under the floodlight, flew a battered banner, its corners lifting in the chill wind.

It bore the Boozters emblem, chrome-on-blue.

And underneath it, MidZone was hosting a late-night rally.

"Drokk it," Vex said. "Back up, and slowly."

But Anderson said, "Wait!"

The Boozters were too far away for a clear scan, but the crowd was easily forty or fifty strong, many of them on the same sleek Kata bikes she'd seen before. They were armed, mostly with a glitter of melee weapons, a couple with the now-familiar DRH sidearms.

She watched them, trying to get a clearer idea of their purpose. Then the banner fluttered one last time and dropped away.

Stomm! She realised it with a shock: *That's him, that's Biggs!*

Beside her, Vex unconsciously echoed the curse.

He wasn't there in person, but his floating, seated form occupied most of a fifty-foot holo-screen. He wasn't young, but he had a powerful presence and a Grud-almighty grin, and a mouth so full of square white teeth that Anderson almost recoiled.

At his appearance, the crowd of people started shouting. The wave of righteousness that came off them was tangible, even from here.

But that wasn't all.

There, under the surge from the people, she felt it again, and now absurdly powerful—that hunger, that sheer, vast sense of *need*. It was so strong that it seemed to be actually part of the broadcast. And she understood it, understood that insatiable craving for sustenance, and that sense of loss so *huge*...

Biggs had been a city-class sporting champion—with all of the training and the motivation and the ambition that had gone with his achievements. And he'd lost his life's entire purpose...

What did you do, when your life ceased to have any meaning?

Again, she found herself feeling sorry for him.

But the Boozters were cheering him, now, whooping. They waved weapons, some of them inbuilt: many of them had replacement limbs, chrome and robotics, artificial hair, legs that unfolded like pistons. Their feelings surged with anticipation, with gleeful demand.

Biggs had made them promises. And now, they wanted them fulfilled.

"*My loyal friends,*" Biggs said to them. His face sagged at the jowls, but he still had good cheekbones and his voice was gorgeous, bass and deep and strong. The timbre of it made Anderson shudder. "*Thank you for coming out this late, for staying with me.*" He was pure charm, a showman to the core. "*I respect you, all of you, for everything you've undergone, everything you've survived. You know it's made you stronger.*" Cheers. "*You're the people who've made me welcome; the people who supported Eee-Zee Rest in its youth, and who still believe in the future it offers. The future of Mega-City One.*" More cheers. "*You've waited, my friends. You've watched. You've secured my streets and my towers. And you've secured your—our!—potential.*" The word had a sinister twist, something both hinted and horrific. Biggs paused, grinning. The crowd pressed forwards, their impatience rising. Something was coming, some announcement or revelation;

they hung from its edge, their hunger an echo of Biggs's own.

A flash of fear went down Anderson's spine. Not the nebulous hunger-fear, but something more immediate.

The crowd, turning...

The glare of halogen, a search-beam down the roadway...

"We need to get outta here," she said. "Now."

Vex didn't ask questions. She grabbed Anderson's elbow and they retreated, utterly silent and as quick as they could.

But it wasn't fast enough.

"*But still, there are those that would stop us!*" Biggs's voice was louder now, a clarion call. Music had slid in underneath his words, and was lifting the crowd to an early frenzy. "*Still, there those who would undermine the future we can bring to this city! Still, there are those who are traitors!*"

"Oh, stomm," Vex said.

Biggs's voice became a shout, "Find *them, my friends. Bring them back to me!*"

The rise of rage was tangible. The crowd began to turn, to eye each other, to look about itself for the guilty.

"*Find them!*" Biggs's shout was colossal. "*Search every roadway, every block! We're so close to realisation, my friends, so close to achievement... we can all but* taste *what we will become!*"

Taste.

The word was a tease, deliberate.

For one, brief second, Anderson wondered if she should just surrender. Send Vex back to her people and hand herself over. Demand to be taken to Biggs in person. After all—this was what she was out here to do.

No, not yet.

Not like this.

Not lifted onto the crowd like a sacrifice, not torn at by hands and greed, not with her hair pulled out and her face smashed in and her skin ripped and bruised. Not...

No, if she was going in there, she was going in there on her own terms, and in control.

"Run," she said.

They ran.

THEY RAN THROUGH the crazy, knotted streets, taking steps up to balconies and doubling back on themselves as they raced along the upper levels. In the distance, engines still roared, and there were staccato bursts of gunfire—the Cry-10 was still crashing and stamping after the scattering Knux.

At first, Vex didn't pause—her street knowledge was flawless—but still, there were Boozters everywhere, and she and Anderson were constantly ducking into alleyways to avoid contact.

"Three more, coming this way..."

"That corner, they're waiting for us..."

Soon, though, Vex began to falter; her thoughts starting to fray at the edges. She wanted to reach the lift, and was trying to still head that way, but her every route was blocked, one access after another. She was worried about Silence and her frustration was rising; it was the first time Anderson had seen her start to lose her cool.

Uneasy pictures bobbed to the surface of Vex's thoughts—a kiss, a long, dark body, that first morning with him at her side—

Anderson stopped looking—that was *way* more info than she needed.

And then, just for a moment, she asked herself how hypocritical that really was.

No time for *that* argument now.

They turned another corner, and another, the Robert Llewellyn Block now rearing over their heads. Huge, empty car park spread out at its feet, retreating down a ramp and under the building.

Down in the tunnel, white lights shone from the upper corners, and security orbs hung like eyes...

They had to go that way, and there was nowhere to hide.

"Anyone down there?" Vex asked.

Her scan was certain. "No."

"Then let's go."

They crossed the car park at a run, hugging the walls where they could, and they reached the top of the ramp without mishap. Backs to the rockcrete, they eased carefully down the slope.

At the bottom, the car park extended under the Rest, its white markings faded with age and time. On the far wall, a large painted advertisement offered the security and welcome of the BlueStar Mining Corporation; it had been sprayed over with an Eee-Zee Rest treble-Z symbol. Guard posts stood empty, and the lights flickered.

"Far corner," Vex said. "Keep going."

They stayed at the wallside, Vex's fists now clenched, Anderson's Lawgiver held fast in a clammy grip. Fear was stalking her now, sliding down her neck like boot polish. She could hear whispers, laughter, threats, promises, but nothing close enough to distinguish...

She remembered this noise—this had been the warehouse on the morning of their search-and-cleanse. She'd gotten it wrong that time, thinking that it meant an enemy close.

This time, she understood it better.

They were waiting for her, all right, just not here.

She said, "They know we're coming."

"Know where?"

"Not yet."

Vex's expression tightened. They kept on moving, around the car park's limit towards the cargo lift's metal doors. The light on the control panel was the only steady illumination.

Except...

Above the lift itself, a panel flickered into life, showing the number 204. As they watched, it counted down, 203, 202, 201, the numbers gathering pace as the lift descended.

Anderson stopped by one of the rockcrete bollards.

"They're on their way," she said.

Seven

Judge Marshall was not having a good day.

His eyes were covered and his mouth was stuffed with sock. Straining against the tape round his wrists had only twisted and bunched it, and left him covered in glue. He'd lost his bike, his lid, his radio, his Lawgiver, his daystick, and his drokking dignity.

And now, he was in here.

They'd trussed him to a cold metal chair, his arms caught behind him and his ankles taped to the legs. He strained, but didn't have the strength to break the tape, and if he rocked too hard, he was just gonna go over. Cable ties he could get out of—there was a knack to it—but this stuff was an absolute bitch.

Gruddammit.

He'd even tried calling her in his head, wondering, slightly stupidly, if she'd hear him...

Cass? You out there?

...but that had been a thin hope at best. If he'd been expecting a door-kicking-in rescue, then he was right out of luck.

At last, feeling faintly foolish, Marshall gave up, sat back and tried to think.

He'd made a mistake—a mistake, for Grud's sake! It was only when his comms had gone down that he'd realised he'd left her too far behind—and by then, of course, it'd been too late.

Cass. Where did you go?

Gang-figures, all armed, all popping up from cover like some holo-game. He'd slowed the bike, taken them down one after another—

The Boozters, however, had not been the problem.

Marshall felt the crash and stomp even as the Lawmaster's screen warned him—one oversized blip, heading his way. He saw the dust trickling from the rockcrete, saw the Boozters back hastily out of range...

...and the security droid.

And he stopped.

Ten feet at the shoulder, coming at speed and ducking the lower overzooms as it came, the thing was a monster. It was bipedal, a cobbled mess of black and blue flak-armour and the Boozters' classic superchrome. It had a humanoid head and mounted weapons—a shoulder-cannon, a 7.62 rifle along one massive forearm, and a hand that looked like the grip of an industrial crane. And it moved oddly, with an erratic, shaking gait.

Across its chest was spray-painted the legend, *Cry-10: The Cleaner*.

Marshall emptied both miniguns at the thing, barrels screaming, ammo cases tinkling around him. And when that didn't even make it pause, he tried for targeted single shots with the Lawgiver—optics, sensor arrays, feed-belts of ammo.

But the Cry-10 didn't care. It juddered, creaked, and aimed the forearm-rifle clean at his head.

"*Sir,*" it said, slightly apologetically. "*You're making a terrible mess.*"

Its grip-hand reached for the Lawmaster.

Swearing, Marshall threw himself clear—and just in time. The full-auto burst of the 7.62 missed him, chewing holes in the walls, but the hand had better luck. The Cry-10 seized the bike's front end, lifted it, and squashed it into artwork.

Marshall hit cover, breathing hard. He wondered where Anderson was, wondered how far her psi-scans could actually reach...

But it was too late—there were Boozters everywhere, and all of them armed to the teeth.

At least, he figured, he went down fighting.

HE WAS STILL trying to work the sock out his mouth when he heard a door.

A hand yanked the thing free, none too gently, and he spat out lint and foot-odour.

"You're pretty dumb, for a Judge." The voice was young and male, and carried an audible smirk. "Left your partner, came down here by yourself?" It chuckled. "Gonna tell us where she is? She's been calling for you, Jay, an' we can pick up her comms. And she sounds *cyuuute*."

Marshall snorted. "*Judge* Anderson can take care of herself."

"Yeah, just like you can." The voice chuckled again. "Thinking you can just... What? Walk in here an' chuck us all in the cubes? That might be fine for the street-gangs, Jay, but you can't pull that stomm down here."

"Game's over, kids," Marshall said, sounding weary. "You had your fun, but this is gonna come to an end, and re-eeal soon now—"

"All right, quit posturing." A second voice, sharp, business-like, female. "Boss wants him."

Marshall didn't need Anderson's senses to feel the sudden flash of elation—and the sudden flash of fear.

The young man leaned close. He smelled of cordite and cheap scent and faux leather. "It's your lucky day."

"Oh, goody," Marshall told him. "I hear the penthouse is quite something."

"Penthouse." The woman laughed aloud. "No penthouse for you, Marshall. Your kind get the basement."

THE CARGO LIFT hit zero with a distinctly chirpy *bing!*

And the big metal doors rolled back.

Anderson had been expecting more Boozters—the hostility was palpable—but as the doors clattered opened fully, the goons that deployed were not the ramshackle bundle of chain-wielding perps she'd pictured.

No, this was an elite force, professional. It was eight gunmen, moving in a tight, tactical formation. They split rapidly into two teams of four, alternating cover as they advanced into the car park and secured the area.

Not Street-Div, not City-Def... their jackets bore the triple-Z logo.

Biggs's private force.

Vex cursed under her breath.

But Anderson said nothing. She stayed behind the bollard, as still as she could, and studied them as they deployed.

The officer, a small, slim figure, pulled a holo-screen from his belt and moved it in a careful arc, scanning the area. It blipped evenly, lighting his visor in washes of green.

She ventured a careful scan. His immediate thoughts held a briefing room, a map, orders to secure the car park and seek out the hostiles... As the screen swept over her position, she barely dared to breathe.

But he'd drokked up...

He'd left the lift doors open.

She tensed, calculating the distance, her adrenaline rising.

They were too spread out for a single suppression spray from the Lawgiver, and she couldn't get all of them with a psi-bolt... but she could down that officer, which might just give her enough time...

As if he'd heard the thought, the officer turned to the figure at the rear. She heard his command clearly, though it was over his comms: *Shut the doors, you drokking idiot.*

Crap. She had about two seconds.

Okay, Cass. Go!

She hit him with the Fear, a sick, dark bolt of the terror and hunger and ambition taken straight from Silence's memories...

But the officer was good. He flinched and rocked on his heels, then raised his nine-mill SMG. As she came to her feet and started to run for the lift, she realised that he wasn't going down.

Drokk!

He opened fire.

She threw herself into a roll, one shoulder down and then over and back to her feet; bullets sparked behind her as she flung her body through the closing doors and into the lift. She caught sight of Vex, just coming to her feet with her knux fully-charged and belting the officer straight in the mouth.

Her thought, too, was crystal-clear: *Eat that, you bastard!*

The man fell, spitting blood and enamel, and the lift doors closed—

Didn't close.

The last goon, the one at the very back, had slammed both gloved hands in the way and was trying to force himself through the gap. Behind him, the remaining six grunts were fighting Vex with feet, fists, and the butts of their guns. Anderson saw her take down a second, wind a third, and then turn on her bootheels and run, ducking between the pillars as they raised their sidearms as her back.

She looked like she'd done this before.

But Anderson only had time for a glance. The grunt had thrown himself through the doors and let them slam closed behind him.

And the lift was moving.

Going down.

Grabbing her by the front of her jacket, he slammed her back against the juddering wall.

He said, "Got you, you bitch."

She smiled at him. "Maybe I've got you."

He blinked.

Her smile widened—but she didn't psi-bolt this one, she wanted him conscious. Instead, she threw a sharp, deep scan as far into the back of his head as she could. If these guys were Biggs's elite goons, he'd have all the info she needed.

She said, like a trigger, "Where's *Biggs?*"

And the images came.

THE BASEMENT, THE lift gently ticking down through the tower's floors and then fading into smoke.

The soldier's name is Caswell, and he's not been down here before. Rumour surrounds it, hints and whispers about what lives here, about what comes here and why...

Adrenaline. Tight, nervous fear.

It's dark and clammy down here; there's a hot breath of wind, fetid on his face. Sweat runs down his temple, itches between his shoulders.

He doesn't want to be here, doesn't want to have to do this...

But this is a privilege, right? Special? When they'd pulled him from the ranks of the Boozters, that was what they'd told him...

In the almost-darkness, metal creaks. Steel joints slide as something moves. He can't see it, his mind conjures phantasms. The air hurts as he breathes it in, like heat in his lungs. There's a hand on his elbow, steady, moving him forwards through the fear. The officer's voice says, "Caswell, you're the youngest person ever to be offered this trust. It's a huge step for you and your family. Biggs has made the promise personally—you'll never want for anything again." Caswell stumbles and the hand offers strength, reassurance. The officer says, his tone almost amused, "Not many people come down here and leave again."

Caswell doesn't want to understand what that means. He thinks about his family, about his parents, about their new lux hab. They have a real kitchen now. Windows.

His mind cries: But I don't want to be here!

And the air responds: Shhhhhh...

The hot wind laughs with a hundred voices. They come from all round him, teasing at his skin, plucking at his hair. His sweat dries cold, as if horrified. The floor feels all wrong, and he wonders what it is...

It makes him feel sick.

A voice says, "Come forwards, Caswell."

Biggs. Bass voice, strong and deep and calm.

Caswell can hear the faint metallic tang, the hint of Biggs's injury and the surgery that saved his life...

It sounds like a buzzsaw.

And he can hear something else, something metal, like something in the distance...

Biggs says: "Light."

Caswell blinks as his gaze is flooded, winces until his eyes adjust.

And then he starts screaming.

THE IMAGES ARE powerful, a blistering blast of complete understanding, a rush of horror so huge that Anderson had to cling to her sanity as it all broke over her at once. In a split-second, she understood Rikki's fear, Vex's denial, Silence's trauma, why they'd rescued Cavendish; she understood all of the missing cits and every single thing that'd been done to the members of the Boozter gang.

And she understood Caswell, the young soldier, understood what he was doing there. She understood, not only the hunger of Biggs himself, but what it had *become*...

Eee-Zee Rest was not a charity—they'd known that from the beginning. No, Eee-Zee Rest was the cover for Biggs's real purpose, the final assuaging of his craving for success...

Eee-Zee Rest was *fuel*.

Anderson found herself shuddering, right to her core. She wanted to throw up. All those missing kids, all those homeless and hopeless and feckless that Eee-Zee Rest had taken in...

The soldier, Caswell, had tumbled to the lift floor. His eyes were rolled back, his body twitching. Accessing the memory had overloaded him, and he jerked like a sparking droid, out cold.

But still, she could see what had flatlined his mind, see it as if it had been burned into her retinae...

The drokking basement was *alive*.

The floor was alive, seething and never-still. It had eyes, and hands. There were faces, still stretched in screams that would never be heard. There were parts of bodies, some still living, all driven way past the point of shrieking insanity. And there was a single, terrible consciousness somewhere behind all of it, a mind so big, so broken, so savage, that it had damaged every single person who'd seen it—damaged them enough to make them forget. The Fear, the brutal, horrific Fear that had haunted every mind she'd been into—she'd thought it was fear of Biggs himself.

It was more than that.

This consciousness was not human. It was something much, much bigger...

Oh, drokk.

It was the thing he'd been *building*.

Critically injured, deprived of his status and celebrity, Biggs had wanted a body to replace his own...

At least, that was how it had started.

Reginald Biggs was not an evil man—no more than any other regular cit. And at the beginning, his project had been something he'd needed—it had given him new skills, a new life, an alternative. The courage to overcome his injury, and to start again.

It had given him hope.

But his project had *grown*.

Slowly, as subtle as a caress, it had coalesced into consciousness. It had whispered to him, night after night. It had stroked his mind, enabled him. It had taunted and teased and tempted him; it had led him, by the leash of his own thwarted ambition, to exponential need, and to more and more excess.

And now, it was completely outside his control.

BRIEFLY, ANDERSON CONSIDERED dropping the leathers for the uniform of the downed guard... but she didn't have time.

The lift stopped, and the loud *bing!* announced her presence to the consciousness beyond.

The doors clattered open.

And the hot air hit her like the breath of an incinerator.

She gagged. The stench had not come across in Caswell's thoughts—memories from different senses are held in different parts of the brain. Now, as she stood in the lift's light, looking out at the darkness beyond, the reek of rotting flesh was overwhelming.

She pulled the biker's borrowed neckscarf up over her nose, but it wasn't the smell that scared her.

No, this place was one huge, living, breathing super-consciousness, one vast and sucking mire of pure and naked need.

And it knew she was here.

It was *watching* her.

Anderson cleared her thoughts. Breathing steadily, four beats in, four beats out, she shut out the smell, the Fear. She closed her own terror down. With an effort that made the muscles jump in her jaw, she forced herself to visualise the blue light that the doc'd taught her—to fill her head with it.

You can't touch me.

Everything's fine.

Everything's…

When she was sure she was in control, she stepped out of the shelter of the lift.

Immediately, the sense of space became vast—not just a car park, this was more like a hangar or tek-bay, or like some huge underground base. Yet the air was hot, hot like a lover's breath.

It brought her out in chills.

She felt the seethe of emotions scratch at her, raw and savage; she felt them call up an echo of emptiness in her own belly. Despite her focus, her own fear curled like smoke. She could *feel* the floor through her boots; feel imaginary hands grasping at her ankles. Silence's visions haunted her, Caswell's thoughts—this creature's slavering and craving, never satisfied. It yearned for sustenance, and the more Biggs had fed it, the more its yearnings had clawed at him, and all the time it had been swelling in power, and promising him the fulfilment of his dreams…

And she could *feel* the compulsion, a peculiar lure to surrender. Something in her wanted to sink to the floor and to let it embrace her, to let it slide over her and pull her down, to feel like she was a part of it and would never again be lonely or worried or hurt or lost…

Get out of my head!

With a shudder, she exhaled the fears and the phantoms, and she concentrated on the light. She remembered Marshall's *twotimestwoisfour*—basic, but effective—she remembered the very earliest training that she'd undergone at the Academy…

Breathe… keep your own thoughts separate…

I am Judge Cassandra Anderson.

I am in control.

The inhuman hunger retreated, and let her think more clearly.

Lawgiver gripped like an anchor, she moved carefully forwards, out into the dark. She was unsure what lay at the centre of all this; she wanted a torch, wanted to shine a light and see the final secret, the thing that Biggs was building. She wondered what had happened to Marshall, and to Vex…

It laughed at her, like claws through steel.

You doubt yourself, little one.

You are not enough. You know that.

Come to me.

She banished the temptation, focused on the blue light in her mind.

I am Judge Cassandra Anderson.

I've walked in the dreams of monsters.

I've seen the Cursed Earth.

I've seen love and madness, and emerged sane from both—

The fear-hunger-greed rose at her, jab-scratch-pound, and she faltered…

This is drokking crazy.

I'm going to die in here.

She stopped, her mouth dry, terror breaking over her skin in a fresh wave of sweat. She was having increasing trouble trying to work out where she ended and the consciousness began…

Come to me.

Sink into me, and let me hold you.

You'll never want for anything again…

She raged back at it.

Stop it!

You're nothing!

You can't touch me!

Forcing herself to focus, she started forwards again. She found Caswell's memories filling her head—she could be stepping on faces, on living hands outstretched for help. They could be clawing at her ankles, desperate for her to stop and save them. She could be standing on the everyday cits of the Big Meg—the homeless and the hopeless who'd just come here for help and food and shelter—and she couldn't even see them, couldn't even hear their thoughts as they were lost in the—

Come to me.

Let me love you.

Nothing will matter when you let yourself give in...

She stopped, calming her breathing, clinging to her focus by sheer stubbornness.

And then, something moved.

Eight

THE SOUND WAS familiar, like the after-echo of a dream...

The anti-grav hum of Biggs's chair.

Across the darkness, his voice said, "Judge Anderson. Your courage is remarkable."

He spoke a command, and the basement was flooded with light.

Pure white halogen, stark and harsh. She blinked, then, reflexively, looked down...

And really wished she hadn't.

Caswell's memories had been tainted by his fear—the floor was not just flesh. There was flesh there—a discarded slide of unwanted bodies, a morass of seething and struggling—but it was overlaid with myriad lines of cabling, as if it were being held down. This was not just the Sector's unwanted, this was a deliberately focused layout of connections and servos and hawsers and implants.

All leading inwards, upwards.

To a central node.

Oh, you gotta be kidding me...

Anderson stopped, staring, caught by fascinated horror. She knew she should follow the lines to their heart, to Biggs's construction, whatever the hell it was, but she was rooted to the spot, horrified by the mess in which she stood.

By her boot was a ball-and-joint socket, moving through an endless, hopeless circle. Beside the other, sticking up through the layers of cable, was the steel half of a replacement skull, its optic roving blind. There were hints of robo-platings and of artificial limbs; there were piston-muscles and the shreds of flesh that still clung to their outsides.

And the whole thing made a dreadful sense. The Boozters were cyber-enhanced and they were the ground-force with which Biggs had controlled and secured his base. They'd been here from the beginning, just like the Knux. So, he must've bought them. Seduced them with promises of enhancements, with equipment, with status and power and wealth…

With *lux* habs.

The eyeball roved blindly, unphased by the light.

Thinking of Caswell, she took it a step further.

His successes had gradients. And there were a few, like the soldiers in the lift, that'd adapted fully—and who'd become the elite. Perhaps because they'd better withstood the onslaught of the Fear, perhaps because they'd been stronger to start with, perhaps because they'd just accepted their transformation…

He'd *bought* them, all of them, to the last man and woman. And he'd been—or the *consciousness* had been—playing with them ever since.

His chair whirred again, close.

"Few are those who come this far without faltering." His tone was respectful, elegant and polite, yet something in it made the sweat slide hot down her back. "And fewer still those who make it out again."

He moved in front of the light, and she looked up.

But not at him—not yet.

She looked up for the node, for the centre of the cables. She needed to know what he'd made.

And as she did so, the vast, rumbling hunger came at her again, rising and suffocating like hands locked round her throat. It tangled with her own terror—she shouldn't be down here, she would never leave this place. It was better that she surrender now...

Yes. Come to me and feel no pain...

The thing was *huge*.

At the far wall, harshly lit by the halogen glare, the endless cables snaked up into a titanic steel frame. Within it, haloed by the seethe and flare of glittering metal, a colossal, fifty-foot humanoid figure, all nested and sleeping. It looked like an avatar, like a golem, like some vast, enshrined robo-deity...

And the call of its temptation was impossible.

Now, little one! Now, you bear witness!

Let yourself go, my pretty one, sink to the floor and you will never be lonely again. Never feel doubt, or fear, or hate. You will be free from the thoughts of the outside, know only love...

It filled her head; she could hear nothing else. Not Biggs, not the hum of the chair, not her own thoughts. It teased her—like the delicious fear of watching a horror holo-flick through parted fingers. It undid her discipline, her training, as if she were a child. She was tiny and alone, dwarfed by this creature, by this massive construction of cable-crawling madness.

You know me, do you not? You've known me all along. I am the Boozters you've chased and fought, I am Silence's fear and the thing Vex fights. I am the Cry-10 that conquered your colleague. I am the guard who brought you here. I am Biggs. I am myself. I am you. I am all of you. I am in all of you. And you cannot resist...

The thoughts came in concepts, rather than words—an amalgam of images, of skin and steel and need and lust and hope and fulfilment...

And I am waiting, and my time comes soon.
Behold!

Through the dazzle of the light, she thought that its eyes were open, staring out at the empty chamber. It wanted her to look into them, to see further into the mind it had woven for itself...

Grown from Biggs's loss.

"Cassandra." Biggs's voice rumbled like the distant call of thunder. "You have no need to be afraid." The words had a sinister, coaxing inflection. "We can make you very welcome."

She tore her attention from his creation, and made herself look at him.

Her voice rattled harshly as she said, "What *is* it, Reg?" Terrors wove round her tone. "What did you *make?*"

"You really need to know?"

Her mind was too full to read him properly, but she still could see flashes, teasers so strong that she thought they were deliberate—the medical tables, the implants, the successes, the failures. He was mocking her, provoking her, letting her see only what he wanted her to see.

It was vivid, and horrific, and it came with *all* the noises.

She tried to hang on, tried to untangle her mind from the steel-and-flesh thoughts of the monster. "You can't scare me. I think you need help."

Her voice sounded small, even to herself.

He laughed, rich and deep. "You? Help *me?*" His words echoed the thoughts of the consciousness. "Your type just—blam!—blast things." He made a scornful gesture with his ringed fingers, still smiling. "Judges." The word was a snort. "Carry the Law between your ears."

No. It's not that simple, it's never that simple. I was trained to...

Trained to...

Yes, I remember...

Somewhere in the core of her mind, she was recalling herself.

She was remembering the breathing exercises, and how to clear her thoughts. *Four beats in, four beats out.* Remembering the basics, how to stop someone reading her. *Twotimestwoisfour.* Remembering the doc and the blue light, and standing on the top of the overzoom...

The Law between your ears.

My training has been my life!

She found anger. It's a strong force—like fear, it can drown out everything else. It can be cleansing, drive back the tentacles. It needs to be controlled, but there are times its flood is as good as a purge.

Anderson turned on the beneficently floating figure that was Reginald Biggs.

Oh, no, you don't...

And she threw herself into his mind.

A DINNER PARTY, some sort of celebration, with plates and plates and plates of food. He's its guest of honour; conversations flow over and round him. People approach him with deference, offer him sponsorships, opportunities, enough credits to keep him in luxury—

No, that wasn't what she needed.

Deeper.

Past his public persona, to things darker and more hidden. Older memories—his need to win, his craving for adulation, the fathomless ambition that'd driven him.

She needed to understand *why*...

If she was going to stop this.

Cheering crowds. Screaming tension, banners lining an arena. It's down to two of them now, the city's star, the one-and-only 'Sherriff Fatman', and his rival Virginia Hardup, the woman the screemsheets call 'the Deceptor.' Virginia's charming and grey-haired, she wears cardigans and pearls. She acts like a larger version of your grandmother, but you didn't turn your back on the bitch. There's a sofa, cushions and all, his mouth is full to overflowing, he barely needs to chew, he swallows bulk that would choke a lesser man—

The micro-detonation rocks him, and he falls, rolls. He can't get up. The tiers of people are on their feet, pointing, screaming, shouting, waving; the ref is bellowing into the mike. The Deceptor doesn't stop, she's still gobbling and grinning, no thought and no mercy. She's shovelling everything she can find into her maw, fragments of it falling from her pink-painted lips. But he's on his side, now, helpless, blood soaking between his fingers. His support crew—they're Boozters, of course they are—are all round him, barking into radios. The pain is horrific. He struggles to understand.

Can he hear sirens?

Amazingly, stubbornly, he keeps his consciousness. He has to get up. He can't lose this! He can't—

Anderson found herself flung out, landing on her mental ass like a cast-aside robo-pet.

But the images had been powerful, and they'd cleared her head further—the clamour of the monster had retreated to an external yammer.

She said to him, meaning it, "I'm so sorry."

Reginald Biggs glowered at her, no longer the urbane and public charmer—now, he was angry, and the broken tilt to his sanity was much more obvious, like a bone's sharp edge poking through the flesh. His face was red to the jowls, and the colour had spread down his folds of neck.

And—she caught it, though he tried to hide it—he was *scared*.

He was scared of *her*.

Of what she could do.

Carry the Law between your ears.

Hope sparked like a petrol-bomb; her heart pounded.

I can do this.

I can do *this!*

But he'd shut her out like slamming a door. "You ever consider," he said to her, his tone flat with fury, "that entering someone's mind without consent is a violation? That people's memories are *private?*"

"I'm a Psi—"

"That's not an excuse." His anger was solidifying now, and, just like hers, it was a powerful defence. Strong emotions tended to rule almost every other thought. "You can't just go rummaging about in people's minds like that. You don't have the *right.*"

"I want to *help* you." She held his gaze, held her own fears down, tried to focus on her flare of hope, to follow it to its genesis. "Why didn't they operate, Reg? Build you a new intestine?"

For a split-second, he faltered. A memory flashed—*a med-unit, he's laying on the floor as there's no bed or gurney big enough to hold him.* "They tried," he said, his bitterness like acid. "But my body rejected it. I never competed again." His voice shuddering with rage and vast bitterness, he said, "They confined me to a *liquid diet.*"

The loss in him was staggering; it rang heavy, and human, and real. And she was so close to him, now, so close to understanding this properly—if only she could get that little bit further. *Let me in,* she said to him silently. *Let me help you.* Aloud, she said, "And that's why you came here." She was still trying for that core sense of self, trying to reach the man within the trauma, trying to really touch him. "Why you learned your new skills, learned how to do... this."

"I had to do *some*thing." He was back to being angry, shoving her compassion aside. "To *build* something, to *make* something..."

To be something!

Voice and thought melded, and he stopped, his gaze now

drifting up to the sleeping monster. She followed his look, and realised that a certain, avid eagerness had started leaking from the outer edges of his mind.

Piping falling away, fluids cascading to the floor. The thing breaks free of its flesh-bed and stands strong. Ready.

Oh, yes, I have been waiting for this...

The premonition was powerful, but not unexpected; she was losing him. She reached out, put her hand over his.

His gold rings were cold.

"Reg," she said. "You need to understand: that thing's *alive*. I don't know if you can feel it, but it's taken your need, your loss, your ambition, and it's turned it into something terrifying." She looked back into the warehouse, the ooze of flesh and steel that slid across the floor. "All this time, Reg, you've been feeding it—and it's been growing. All those people, all the names here, lost and forgotten, all the fuel it's consumed—it's taken it all in. Soaked it up like a sponge. Its sentience is colossal. And when it wakes up fully—"

He laughed at her, laughed like a madman. "You think I don't know that? I *made* it to carry me! To carry my mind!"

His thoughts were ragged now, his rationality breaking up as the monster began to stir. Its consciousness was moving to full wakefulness and it was whispering at him, *stop this need now must be free must feed must walk and let them see let them all see...*

Biggs's mind was teetering, becoming a tangled, sliding mess of his own memories, of the creature's invading thoughts and of his own. But within him, maybe, she had planted a tiny iota of doubt...

She couldn't give up hope. She had nothing else.

"Please," she said to him, a last attempt. "This isn't the answer you think it is." She studied him, searching. "When it wakes up fully, you won't be in control—"

Then a strong hand gripped her shoulder.

* * *

SHE'D BEEN SO caught up in her attempt to reach Biggs that she'd not felt him coming. She tried to turn, reflexively raising the Lawgiver...

Stopped dead.

Oh, no....

She didn't need the scan, she could see immediately what they'd done to him—see the emptiness behind his eyes, the utter, sucking absence of identity.

Mockingly, his badge and Eagle had been left intact.

Marsh?

He stared at her, blank. Fighting a strong urge to chuck up, Anderson frantically fumbled in her head for something—anything—that would help her reach him.

"Marsh?"

But there was nothing, he couldn't hear her. He was dead, but still living, unconscious, but still moving. The monster's hunger had taken him, had swallowed him completely.

And it laughed at her horror.

Yes, you will all come to me...

You know you'll succumb, in the end...

"Marshall." It was barely a whisper.

He said nothing, thought nothing, yet his grip on her shoulder was merciless and powerful. It was a demand, she knew that much. And she should stop him, shoot him—hell, she'd be doing him a favour—but she just couldn't make herself pull the trigger.

Oh, Grud...

When he applied pressure, forcing her to walk towards the towering sanctum of the monster, she didn't fight him. Her mind told her, bizarrely, that this was how a perp must feel, walking to the cubes...

She had a sudden flashback of Rikki's fears, right at the beginning.

Put in a box, alone.

The thing was overwhelming, too *big*. She could feel the consciousness stray back into her mind, just as if it crawled in through her eyes and ears...

Never alone, never again.

Come and touch me, taste me...

Be a part of me...

"Little girl," Biggs said. His tone was darker now, on the very edge of stability. "When I fell, the audience bayed. Like animals. They cheered for the Deceptor; they *celebrated* what she'd done. When I fell, they *laughed* at me..."

"So—what?" She threw it back at him. "This is just a revenge kick? The city mocked you, so now it must pay?"

"It was my *life!*" Biggs's thoughts flared and sparked like a faulty engine; the last of his rationality was failing. His chair rose and hovered gently over to where the monster loomed. It was beginning to twitch. "When I begin, not even the Judges will stop me."

No, don't do this—

Desperate, she threw a psi-bolt at him with everything she had. No finesse, no fine-tuning; it was pure pain, and she buried it in his core of his mind and let it detonate, just like the microbomb had done in his flesh. But he knew about pain—he'd survived it before, done this before. His chair wavered, but he didn't falter. Instead, he reached out one huge hand, the skin hanging from his lower arm, and he pulled at the first set of cables.

Fluid spouted. Anderson felt the consciousness shudder with anticipation, felt it begin gather like an incoming tsunami.

Biggs's chair rose higher—he reached for another set of cables.

She could feel his exultation, the final realisation of his years of planning. He would be free, he would be completely restored, and the city that had mocked him would be sorry.

But you'll be lost! She thought it at him, cried it aloud, "You don't understand!"

He didn't care. The fluid was draining from the tubes, the thing was moving. The consciousness was rising like a wave. She held herself still, Marshall's hand on her shoulders, holding her fast as if he could not let her go.

Almost in slo-mo, she watched a third handful of cables drop free, a fourth, a fifth.

And she felt it as Biggs's sanity finally broke, and as the consciousness came to its full manifestation.

His chair tumbled to the floor, his empty body with it.

And the monster started to move.

Nine

ON HER SHOULDER, Marshall's hand was thin and cruel. His grip was hard as a cargo loader; his fingertips dug through her borrowed leather jacket. The thought of what'd been done to him made her knees nearly fold.

But she had no time to help him. Above her, the creature was pulling itself free from its bed of steel cables, yanking the last of the piping out of its flesh. Fluid gushed round her boots, drowning the mess on the floor.

The blindly roving eye drowned and winked out.

This, she told herself sternly, *may be the stupidest gruddamn mess you've ever gotten yourself into.*

She took hold of Marshall's wrist in both hands, bent her hip into his body and flipped him clean over her shoulder. He landed on his back with a splash and lay there, stunned and gaping like a beached fish.

A twinge of concern—she didn't want to leave him. But Biggs's creation, outlined by the harsh light, was now fully free. Almost fifty feet tall, a perfect blending of need and flesh and machine, its eagerness loud as a shout, echoing in her head like a drum. She wasn't sure how the hell it was gonna get out of the basement, but, as soon as it did, it'd be stomping through the sector and gleefully smashing stuff up…

And—at a guess—it was going to start eating.

She still had no radio, no way to reach for help…

Crazy or not, this was down to her.

The monster lumbered forwards, still unsteady, liquids sloshing round its feet. With its freedom, it'd lost its interest in her; she seemed too small to bother it. Instead, it thumped at a big red button with one massive fist.

Klaxons blaring, one end of the ceiling began to move, descending, hydraulics hissing, to form a ramp. As the thing lurched towards it, heading for the oblivious cits of the sector, Anderson raced after it, the splashing fluids under her boots giving way to the solid ringing of the metal walkway.

You're crazy! she told herself. *How the hell're you gonna do this? How the hell—?*

Her thoughts verged on flatline panic. She forced them down, made herself focus.

To tackle Biggs the monster, she had to find him. She had to locate his final spark of humanity, give him back to himself— she'd done it before, but never on this scale.

Judges!

Your type just—blam!—blast things.

No, we don't. I'm a Psi-Judge, and I know how you think!

She knew his memories, the signature of his mind—and she knew she could still find him.

Save him.

Reckless, she threw herself at the monster's lower leg. Clinging to the flesh-buried pipes as it strode up, she climbed it like a gym-wall. As it headed up into the open, she reached its knee, its thigh.

Her presence nudged at its awareness. She felt it look down.

Notice her.

Still there little one still so stubborn soon you will cease to matter everything will be changed…

It was pure concepts—there were no real words. And it crept back into her brain like an overgrowth of weeds, tugging at her.

She recited basic Academy lessons, criminal codes, parking violations, anything to keep her own panic under control, and to stop this thing from reaching into her and yanking her mental insides out, just like it'd done to Marshall.

Feel need want love trust rest be complete…

To keep it from swallowing her whole.

The monster reached the top of the ramp. The drizzle touched Anderson's face, and she tried to focus her thoughts on the sensation, on the strain in her muscles. As it came out into the open, she found the hollow at the small of its back, and she stopped there and hung on. They were at the entrance to Eee-Zee Rest, at the guardhouse that she and Marshall had come past on their Lawmasters—it felt like a year ago. But the thing didn't care; it kicked over the building with one massive foot and kept walking, grabbing for the overzooms at it went.

Rockcrete tumbled past her and smashed in the road.

If she was going to stop this, then she had about ten seconds.

Because the screaming was already starting.

IN A BOARDED doorway, Vex skidded to a breathless stop.

She'd lost them, she was pretty sure of that—elite goons or not, she knew the roads and alleys of Eee-Zee Rest better than almost anyone. She could run the bastards ragged, keep them guessing for hours.

She wondered what had happened to Mariah, and the rest of her Knux crew.

But she had one last thing that she needed to take care of.

And *this* was something that she'd been looking forward to.

Beside her, a pair of wide eyes looked out of a piled-up trash-heap—a lined, filthy face watched her fearfully.

"Sorry, man. Here." Vex held out the creds she had on her, and a gnarled hand appeared and vanished again. The figure grunted a thank you and buried itself once more.

Leaving it alone, Vex eased carefully to the edge of the wall. She glanced outwards, listening.

She could hear the thing, though she couldn't see it—hell, it wasn't exactly stealthy. But it'd been drokking up her crew for far too long, and she'd been waiting for exactly this chance.

The Boozters had gone—all busy, chasing Mariah and the rest of the Knux. Vex had already made a right mess of Biggs's elite squad. And if that blonde Judge was any damned good, she'd keep Biggs himself out the picture—or at least occupied.

This was the moment Vex had been waiting for.

Her chance to take down the Cry-10.

THE PLATING WAS easy to find. She could hear it, rasp and grind and stamp, as it chased a pair of red tail lights through the depths of the Eee-Zee Rest compound.

Vex's crew were good—the quad bike was leading the thing back and around towards the Knux's base, to the dead ends and blind alleys that would give them the best chance of taking it down.

But that quad bike was fast.

And Vex was on foot.

She began to run.

She raced along an upper expressway, half of it broken and falling to the streets below. An old chain-link fence marched along the road's edge; in places, the posts had toppled but still hung, half-suspended, held in place by the links. Vex ran past them, her attention on the heavy figure ahead of her. The faint, misty drizzle was getting in her eyes and making her knux fizz like a damp pylon.

As she grew close, the quad bike zipped a sharp one-eighty with its four-wheel drive and then stopped, headlights bright, engines revving and rumbling.

Vex grinned.

The Cry-10 stopped, the shoulder-mounted cannon swinging up and over from its backrest and locking—snap!—into place. A red laser designator picked out the bike.

It said, "*Sir, madam, I do not wish to do this. But really, the mess you're making is quite intolerable...*"

The quad sat where it was, driver at the wheel, gunner at the ready. Vex could hear more engines incoming.

But the gunner wasn't waiting for that cannon to load and fire. Roaring defiance, he pulled the trigger and hosed the thing with heavy-calibre rounds.

The Cry-10 juddered, but didn't go down. Rounds spanked against its black and blue armour, denting it to artwork.

They didn't stop it.

"*Really,*" it said. "*I must object.*"

As two more bikes screamed into the alley and took up flanking positions, the cannon coughed into life, firing a single, twenty-millimetre shot that would take out a rockcrete wall.

The quad screamed into reverse—just as a crater blew out of the roadway.

Vex knew this bastard all too well—and gunfire alone was not going to put it down.

No, it needed a more... personal touch.

"*Justice Department. Stay where you are!*"

Anderson heard the familiar loudhailers, and she wanted to shout with relief. Floodlights slammed on, silhouetting the monster in a glare of rain-glittering white.

Quietly, she thanked Grud that Sector Chief Johnson had apparently found his balls.

The monster, though, didn't give a stomm.

It bellowed, inarticulate and furious, and broke into a jerky, shambling run.

Anderson hung on as Johnson thundered orders. *"Section one, on my command. Target areas two through five. Section two, fall back to secondary potion, and hold. Sections three and four, I want that basement secured and on the double. Now: FIRE!"*

Lawgivers barked on full auto. Sheltered by the creature's massive torso, she still felt its shock, a tidal backwash of pain, betrayal and outrage, then a furious rush of sheer, bloody-minded determination. It was going to smash these tiny, toy Judges that dared get in its way, to crush every vehicle, every tiny spark of resistance. It had been waiting too long for this, and nothing was going to stop it.

Puny so small think you can face stop me…!

She felt one foot rise and slam down, heard the mangled crush of metal. She felt its arms come up, saw them slam into the closest of the overzooms and bring it down in a rain of rubble, cars and all. Still clinging on, thirty feet above the ground, Anderson could hear people screaming, feel the faint flickers of incomprehension and terror…

What the stomm is that thing?

This can't be happening!

Why don't the Judges bring it down?

Dude, this is, like, sooo some holo-movie set…

Hell, she hadn't liked Johnson very much, but the fact that he was out here, and this gruddamn organised…

Seemed his obsessive compulsion wasn't just about his pens.

A second volley of shooting, a second vehicle crushed. The monster raged, heaving with fury and hurt.

How dare you can't stop me too small tiny people toy pop-guns crush all crush will be free will be hahaha…!

But its pain was having another effect, somewhere in the core of its psyche. Like a memory trigger—like a beloved place or a familiar smell—the pain was reaching Biggs. It was caught up with his own pain, with the microbomb that had ended his career.

And somewhere, it was bringing him back to the surface.

Reg! She could see him, could almost reach him. *Can you hear me? Reg!*

The beast was in among the Judges, now, stamping and raging. Johnson was ordering a retreat, while the second section gave covering fire. He was also shouting for the Manta, but Anderson had no idea how close that might be.

Vex had given Anderson her radio back, but it was still all white noise—she had no way to tell them she was here.

Drokk this. Think!

A third volley of shooting made the monster judder. It bellowed—but every shot, every bullet, every flash of pain brought Biggs's thoughts closer to the surface.

Reg! Again, she tried to reach him. *I know you're there! You have to stop this! And I can help you…!*

It was taking too long. This thing would break out past the Judges' cordon and then all merry drokking hell would break loose.

There was only one thing left.

Still clinging to her precarious perch, still using the recitation of the Department's codes like some sort of demented lifeline, she did the only thing she could do.

She gave in.

She let the monster consume her.

And she went completely into its head.

VEX RAN ALONG the overzoom.

The alleyway was too tight for her team to keep playing dodge-'ems. Smart enough to realise this, the Cry-10 had folded back the cannon and had raised the 7.62 rifle on its forearm.

A single suppression with that thing would make soup out of the lot of them.

Vex reached the broken end of the roadway, judged the distance and jumped.

She heard Mariah shout for the Knux to hold their fire, and she landed with a clang on the Cry-10's flank. One of its arms was caught using the rifle, and the clamp-hand on the other was too big and slow to reach for her. It tried to grab, but she clambered quickly and sat herself on its empty shoulder.

Now I got you.

A quick scan, looking for the cover, for the location of Cry-10's Central Processing Unit—for the chip that made it work.

There. As she'd suspected, back of the neck.

The thing twitched and twisted, trying to throw her free, but she hung on with the determination of a rider at the holo-rodeo, with the resolve that had allowed her to outrace a Judge, to rescue Cavendish, and to secure help for her silent and traumatised partner.

This one, she thought, *is for everything you've done to us, all down the years.*

Vex tore off the cover, then slammed her fist into the CPU and shot it with five hundred volts.

Then, numb to the shoulder despite the insulation of her gloves, and whooping all the way, she rode the thing down to the floor.

DARKNESS. INSANITY.

A swirl of colossal inhumanity, of utter incoherence. A cyclone of images tumbling one past another, a sucking whirlpool of pure need.

Will not stop must be free must be seen must be free must be seen must be...

She saw the earliest stirring of its consciousness, the first screaming lives, the dissolving and the amalgamating of flesh and mind. She saw the Fear that it generated in those who witnessed it. She saw Biggs's initial work, a med-bay at first, and his experiments to learn critical new skills...

They can't fix me. I'll do it myself!

I'll show them who's beaten!

But down the years, that had all gone. His initial motivation, his skill, his equipment, his victories, his public recognition, had all faded into memory. The creature's rising had swallowed them all; they'd been lost in its growing, surging need as it swelled outwards through the basement.

And it had grown in Biggs's head like an infection.

Anderson was lost, too small; she was swamped by it. She found herself stumbling, a child in a vast and tumbling darkness. She was looking for him, calling for him.

Reg! Where are you?

But he made no response—if he'd heard her, he said nothing and her shouts echoed hollow in the buffeting wind. She walked onwards, lost and alone, through halls of mirrors at insane angles. They were all around her, all showing the same images. The Boozters on the med-bay tables, screaming. Bodies struggling, vanishing below the seethes of cables, dissolving into parts and memories. Rich kids stolen for their blood-types or their genetic heritage; homeless people used as experiments or fuel. Every way she turned, more and more mirrors showed her the horrors.

The same things, the same things, the same things...

Dimly, she was still aware of gunfire, of metal and rockcrete, of the strain in her shoulders, of Johnson giving orders. She could feel herself, still hanging on. She could hear the static of her comms, and now, the broken fragments of words that occasionally came through it.

But all she could see were the mirrors.

Free must be free must be seen must be free must be seen...

They were too much. She turned from another mirror, and another, and another, as they began to close in upon her, piling one on another. She'd lost the recitation of her Academy lessons now, she was just being buffeted, helpless, staggering from one image to another as if the corridors between them were filled with a raging gale. And the wind was in her head, her ears, her heart—it filled her with the same horrific fear that she'd seen, right at the beginning...

Dimly, like a dream-call, she heard Johnson in the radio, "And...son? D... zzz... copy? Marsh...?" but it was too far away. Too unreal.

The mirrors were close, all round her, boxing her in. The wind was caught in her skin, tearing at her from the inside out.

Reg!

But the images were shifting now, shifting as if he'd heard her. They showed her Biggs as a young man, and the sheer ferocity of his teenage training. His ambition, even then, the dedication with which he'd driven himself...

He was competitor born—driven to win.

More images, earlier than that, the inevitable school cloakroom.

Biggs surrounded by older boys, mocking. They pick at his shabby clothing and make remarks about his size. But he doesn't care—he's very strong, and he's not afraid of them. He can put them on their asses, all right...

And then, even earlier. *An empty house, semi-derelict, vanishing under heaps of trash. He's little, and he's hungry, but there's nothing to eat in here, and his parents are sleeping. They're always sleeping. Sometimes, they sleep all day. Other times, they shout and scream at him, and he doesn't even know why...*

And earlier still. *He's crying. He's very little, now, standing at his parents' bedside. They stir, his little heart leaps. But his mother screams at him, she sweeps him up and takes him into the corner. With her foot on the pedal, she lifts the lid on the thing he fears the most, the dreaded thing, and she drops him into it. The lid slams shut.*

No! He screams and screams for her. He bangs on the metal walls. Don't leave me in here, please, please, not again…!

But he hears her turn away, and then the creak of the bed as she falls back into it.

No!!!

Everything is dark. His parents are out cold. Again. The last time, he was in here for hours, and hours, and he cried himself to sleep…

Bereft.

Alone.

Ignored.

The images fade, leaving only one behind. There, in the smallest mirror, Anderson could see Biggs the man. He was in his penthouse, his chair floating and his robed body reposed and calm. The wind was still blowing, but it seemed to pass over her—she could barely feel it.

The single image was reflecting all round her, possessing every mirror.

Reg!

She'd found him, found the core spark of his mind.

"Why?" she says to him. "Why did you do this?"

In the mirror, he smiles. He speaks, his bass voice rich and quiet. 'I just wanted to be noticed. The acceptance, the recognition. I wanted the security of celebrity—people to know who I was. I wanted people to see me.'

Another reflection says, 'My parents were addicts. I ran away when I was seven. I was so determined… I was going to make something of myself. Never end up like them. Never again be sealed in a dustbin for hours at a time.'

Anderson says, like a dream, 'I'm sorry.'

'Not many people would forgive me, Judge.'

'I'm not forgiving you, Reg. I just understand.'

She'd reached the real heart of it now, the centre of the consciousness—its node and origin.

Somewhere, her radio was crackling with urgency, but it wasn't important.

Biggs glances at it, as if he realises what it means. The gunfire is taking its toll on the monster and he knows—this will all be over very soon.

'I'm sorry,' she says again. 'I wish this could have ended differently. But you know you can't do this. This isn't recognition, Reg, this isn't the accolade you wanted. This is... it's just another dustbin.'

He nods sadly. 'I never meant it to go this far. You were right, I lost control, and it took on a life of its own. I think I lost... lost what it all meant.'

'It's easily done. Very human.'

He sighs, looking suddenly exhausted. 'I'm glad about that.'

Anderson nods.

'All right, Judge,' he says. 'Get it over with.'

Then she drives a fist into the mirror, and everything breaks into shards.

Ten

ANDERSON REGAINED HER consciousness in the bright lights of the Department med-bay.

The air was clinical, clean. Droids hummed quietly. Her bed was warm, sheltered by a pull-around curtain. And beside her, Chief Johnson sat with his head bowed and his hands in his lap.

He had a strip of speed-heal across one side of his face, and his hair was burned to stubble.

As the tumble of mirror-images came back to her, she wondered what the hell had happened.

But she didn't have the energy to scan the Chief's thoughts, surface or anything else. Instead, she sat up, groaning, and he turned to look at her.

"Anderson," he said. "How you feeling?"

"Like I've been chewed up and spat out." Dream-fragments lingered—her last view of Biggs in the creature's mirrors, his understanding and his sheer, bone-deep weariness. She sat up further, trying to piece the images together and wanting to know the end of the story.

Johnson held out a hand to steady her. "You've got a broken leg, blondie, you fell one hell of a way down. And there's enough drugs in you to stun a body-plating. Best you stay still for a bit."

"How long have I been out?"

"A day or so. Enough time for us to get the clean-up detail underway."

Tension flickered. "What happened? What—?"

"Drokking mess." Johnson shook his head. "Whatever that thing was, we put it down. Took out two of my people, put six more in med-bay—but civilian casualties were minimal." He looked like he was going to say something else but thought better of it. "Reginald Biggs is dead, they found his body in the basement." He glanced sideways at her. "And I have cubes all full of Boozters." He flickered something that might've been a smile, then drew in his breath. "You did this Sector a favour, Anderson." It was an admission, and the remark that followed it was barbed, "In the end."

She winced, understanding the reprimand. But another thought was uppermost in Johnson's mind, and she had to know the truth. "What about Marshall?"

His expression gave her the answer even as she picked up the mental picture—a bed like hers, him lying there, empty, staring at the ceiling through eyes that saw nothing. He was physically undamaged, but motionless. There was no one home.

"Grud," she said.

Johnson paused for a moment, his sense of loss very human. His next words came with an effort, "It wasn't your fault." There was a complex dishonesty to him—he was doing the decent thing for her sake, though he didn't entirely believe what he was saying.

Chief Johnson, it seemed, was not a bad guy after all.

"Sir," she said. "You know he chose to come with me—"

"I realise that, Cassandra." His use of her name was deliberate—it was affectionate, and there to make his words sincere. "Marshall was a good man, and a good officer, and I'm sorry to lose him."

"Maybe, if he came back with me to Psi-Div…?"

"I've asked Chief Ecks," Johnson said. "And we're going to try. There may be someone who can help him."

She nodded, feeling a flash of Biggs's accusation, *Your type just—blam!—blast things.*

"Can I see him?"

"Of course. When you feel up to it, we'll find you a chair and a medi-droid to take you. And Anderson…"

"Sir?"

"You do know why he let you do all this?"

She was going to say no, and then she realised what he meant—and realised that she'd known it all along.

It was why she'd kept shutting him out.

"Yes, sir," she said quietly. "I know."

She found a more recent memory—Judge Montana. He, too, laid out in a med-bay cubicle. She pushed it aside almost the moment she thought of it—Montana, she'd been able to save.

But Marshall…

Twotimestwoisfour.

She wasn't responsible for his feelings, or for the decisions he'd made because of them. But still…

Problem with having drokking partners, she thought. *It never ends well.*

Johnson said nothing else. They sat there in silence for a long moment, then he suddenly stood up. "But," he said, "There's someone here to see you, if you're strong enough for visitors?"

Knowing exactly whom he meant, she nodded.

VICTORIA ELIZABETH XAVIER had a new leather jacket slung over her shoulder, and the kind of upper arms more usually found on a bodybuilder. She'd outfought a squad of Biggs's elite guard and taken down the Cry-10 almost single-handed. And she sat, grinning, on the edge of the bed to tell Anderson her part of the story.

Still somewhat woozy, Anderson did her best to take it all in, nodding at the right moments.

"I think I did pretty well," Vex said, as she came to the end of the tale. "Considering."

Anderson grinned at her. "And how're your crew?"

"Good," she said. "Take more than chrome-dome thugs to slow those guys."

The grin widened. Anderson wanted to ask about Vex's partner, but the woman's thoughts were already overflowing with him—Bob Vaughan was back on his feet, and looking at a whole new life. He couldn't speak—not yet—but perhaps, in time, he could heal enough for his voice to come back.

Suddenly, though, Anderson thought of something else. "Vex and Silence?" The drugs must be still raging round her system, because she found herself giggling like a lunatic. "Vex and gruddamn Silence? Oh, you gotta be kidding me..."

Vex chuckled in return, the dragon shifting on her cheek. "He's taking over Eee-Zee Rest. Got a helluva mess to sort out, but he's the right man for the job. And we've got the team to do it, so hey—we can turn the charity into everything it was supposed to be. Everybody wins. Thanks to you."

"So... I guess they're not throwing you back in the cubes?"

"Good behaviour," Vex told her. "You know how it is."

"My butt." Anderson laughed at her. "We're Judges, we don't let you out for that kinda thing."

Her response made the woman laugh aloud, the sound odd in the stark tiles of the med-bay. "Listen," Vex said. "You need to rest, and I know you gotta go back to Psi-Div. But if you ever come through this way, Cassandra, me and the Knux—we'll throw you a party or something."

Anderson nodded, but there was still something she needed

to ask, a final question. "Vex," she said. "Why'd you get me into this? When you first followed me—what the hell were you trying to do?"

Vex frowned, and dropped her gaze, her sudden guilt both complex and obvious. After a moment, she said, "You're a *Judge*, Cassandra. You have any idea what that looks like, from the outside? You're... omnipotent. You've got absolute power; you can do whatever the hell you want. You can walk in anywhere, take anything. Everything. And even more than that, you're Psi-Div. You can read people's thoughts, pare them down to the bone, get all the things you need to know. No secrets, no mysteries. And you can put people down with a..." she gave a mock-mystical gesture "...flick."

It was uncannily close to Biggs's words: *Your type just— blam!—blast things.*

Anderson managed to laugh. "It really isn't that easy," she said. "People are complicated things. They have secrets for a reason—you can't just go stomping about in there and yank this stuff out. Not really."

"Not even the stuff about my Grandma's cat?"

"Not even the stuff about your Grandma's cat."

Chuckling, Vex shook her head. "But still, Judge or not, when you were riding over the Expressway, you looked just like me, just like one of my crew." She paused then said, "Human." She shook her head. "I guess I followed you, Cass, because I really needed your help, but I didn't know how to ask for it. Didn't know how to approach you, or trust you." She grinned, half-ashamed, looked up. "I do, now. And I'd like to call you my friend."

Anderson said nothing, looked down at her hands on the cover. She had a pretty good idea of what friendship meant to a gang-member, and she could feel Vex watching her, feel her searching for that bonding, that kinship that they'd almost shared...

But somewhere, there were Eagle eyes upon her.

She said, "Thank you, that means a lot." Then, with an effort, "I'm glad... that you and your team came outta this intact. Glad that Eee-Zee Rest is in good hands. But... but I won't be coming back."

I can't. I can't do this.

Vex sat still, her gaze still searching, but Anderson didn't want to read her thoughts. She felt like she'd uttered a betrayal.

Awkward now, the quiet stretched out between them.

And then snapped.

Vex got to her feet, gave a slightly stiff apology. "Guess I overstepped the mark, there. Sorry. Look... ah... Bob's still not quite himself... I should go. Gotta lot to do. You know how it is."

Anderson nodded, searched for some farewell, something to reach back for that sense of kinship, to summarise the trauma they'd shared, their impossible success... but any words seemed somehow trite. She said, "Yeah, I know how it is. I'm glad the Sector's, y'know, in good hands."

"Yeah."

"Yeah."

Vex watched her for a moment, then ducked out of the curtain. Anderson stayed sat up, looking out through the chink she'd left. Droids had appeared to check her readings, and look at the dressing on her leg. Their hum was soft, and oddly soothing.

She spared a thought for Marshall, for Montana, for the Doc that'd been supposed to partner her through the Big Zero Six...

Friendship.

I can't do this.

All gone now.

One day, maybe, she'd get used to it. To everything she was expected to be, and to deal with—to see, to hear, to find, to understand, to fix, to break... and to everything that she couldn't allow herself. Things like trust, and kinship.

Your type just—blam!—blast things.

The droid cheeped, a pleased noise that meant that she would mend.

One day, maybe.

But it wasn't gonna be today.

About the Author

Danie Ware is a single working Mum with long-held interests in role-playing, re-enactment, vinyl art toys and personal fitness. She went to an all-boys' public school, has a halfway decent English degree, and spent most of her twenties clobbering her friends with an assortment of steel cutlery. These days, she juggles raising her son and writing books with working for Forbidden Planet (London) Ltd., where she runs their events calendar and social media profile – and has the original Judge Anderson inspiration-image behind her desk (no kidding). In those rare times when she's not writing, working, or on manoeuvres with her son, she usually falls over exhausted.

Danie is the author of the critically acclaimed Ecko series, out now from Titan Books and *Children of Artifice*, an urban fairy story, out from Fox Spirit Books. She also writes *Sisters of Battle* for the Black Library, and has short stories published in numerous anthologies. She lives in Carshalton, south London, with her son and two cats.

You can find her online at danieware.com or @danacea.

DEVOURER

LAUREL SILLS

To my Auntie Chrissy—
the strongest woman I know.

**MEGA-CITY ONE
2101 A.D.**

Prologue

Psi-Judge Turner froze, his pulse thudding loudly in his ears, his eyes scanning the deserted street. He held his breath as he waited to hear the child's voice again, straining his psi-sense for that tiny, panicked, chirping call.

This was a Shine district, towering blocks of GlamCo living where the 0.01 per cent of the Mega-City One population lived out their lives in shimmering force-field-protected security. Turner craned his head to gaze up at the tiny sparks caused by floating debris hitting the shields. He had a fleeting moment wondering what it would be like to breathe that filtered air before he shook himself and focused.

He closed his eyes and opened his thoughts to the night. The roar of consciousness threatened to overwhelm him, the teeming, collective mass of tumultuous thoughts from the concentration of humanity above whirling him into a state of vertigo. He had to try and sift through it if he wanted to pick up the kidnapper's trail, but he'd never been good at wide-scale processing.

A scream stabbed into him, savaging his open mind. Stupid.

He slammed up his barriers, braced himself and zeroed in on the echoes of terror.

A hand pressed over his mouth, rope biting into his wrists, pain as his small body is dropped onto the ground, gravel crunching as it bites into his back, a bag pulled off his head to reveal a leafy manicured garden, the shimmering wall of the tower in the background.

He ran.

A wide ramp traversed the side of the tower, narrowing as it wove through a holo-leaf-lined arch towards the pleasure garden, ending in a tall reinforced metal gate, sparkling with the filter-field. His helmet projected a Justice Department code and the door swung open on soundless auto-hinges.

Pulling out his Lawgiver, he stepped in, senses reaching to identify the child and her abductors. He paused as he emerged into the garden of his vision, white gravel paths snaking into lines of ornamental hedges and lush flower beds. A feeling of quiet awe washed over him as he realised that most of the plants were real, only bulked out in places by swatches of holo-plants.

A crunch of gravel sounded from the depths of the garden, with no thoughts to accompany it. He frowned, concentrating as he trained his Lawgiver on the sound.

"Identify yourself," he barked, his footsteps sounding unnaturally loud as he moved towards a bend in the path. "That's a Judicial order; the sentence for disobeying is three weeks in the cubes."

"Judge Turner."

An immaculately suited man was seated on a stone bench in a clearing, the high hedgerow encircling him like a cage. He sat with his hands clasped loosely on his lap, a calm silence emanating from him, lapping at Turner with a bullying insistence.

Turner shook himself. How did this man know his name?

"Where is the girl?" he demanded, feeling instantly stupid. He could sense it now, an absence of fear, of tension; the distress call he had followed snuffed out like a light. "What have you done to her?"

The man smiled, his teeth perfectly white, his pale blue eyes stark and cold beneath the silver hair swept artfully back from his weathered brow. "I wanted to speak with you, Judge Turner. The call was designed specifically for you. You felt her panic, did you not? You *yearned* to help her."

Turner felt sluggish, and realised with rising alarm that he could not read the man.

"You should be mindful of your weaknesses, boy. They can be used against you." The stranger gestured to the bench beside him. "Sit, please."

Turner sat.

"Weakness?" Turner pushed the word through numb lips. "I am *protecting* the weak."

"Noble sentiment, *Psi*-Judge Turner." The man sneered as he spoke the syllable, and shook his head. "But it is a falsehood, to think that you are what you are because of your own wishes. You are a tool, Turner. Your gift has been taken and controlled by the Judiciary, twisted and warped to use for their own ends. This gift of mind we have, Turner, do you really think it was meant for such tawdry use as this?"

We have. It made sense now, why he couldn't read him, and this feeling, this *haze* that had suddenly come over him. This man had psi abilities, strong ones, blocking Turner from using his own power. Turner fought it, sending out feelers into the psi-fog pouring off him.

"Tawdry use?" Turner murmured, exaggerating the dull edge of his voice. Keep him talking; make him think he had control.

"It is abhorrent." The older man stood, his shadow looming larger as it fell across Turner. His casual tone belied a raw, barely contained rage. "It is *sacrilege*."

The tendrils of mind Turner had been carefully working into the miasma of control were suddenly gripped in an iron vice, and the white-haired psi smiled. Turner fell forward from the bench onto his knees as agony exploded within his skull.

"Oh, Turner, no. You cannot refuse us."

Two figures stepped out from the shadows, dressed in grey robes remnant of the vestments of long-dead religions. They had deep hoods that hid their features, and from the darkness beneath came a flood of psi-power. He could almost see it as it streamed towards the white-haired man, where it refracted like light in a crystal.

"This gift is sacred, Judge," the white-haired man said, stepping forward, "a gift only to be used in the service of Karlul."

Turner was paralysed in the onslaught of psi-energy cascading from the man's lips.

"And you are not worthy, Turner, not worthy at all."

The two figures stepped in to hover behind the smiling man.

The Psi-Judge began to tremble as he realised he was too weak to resist them.

"Say it with me, Turner. I. Am. Unworthy."

Turner opened his mouth, shut it, bit his tongue, hard.

"*SAY IT.*" Spittle flew with the force of his words.

"I am unworthy," Turner whispered.

The words echoed, bouncing against the walls of his mind.

"I am unworthy," he said with more force, looking up at the figures, squinting into the glare of their power.

"I am unworthy." His tongue had found the shape of it now, rolled and repeated it without effort. And he knew, then, that he *was* unworthy. "I am unworthy, I am unworthy, I am unworthy."

As he felt himself begin to dissolve, there was only one, uniting force that held the pieces of him together, the threads of him thrumming on the brink of snapping. A certainty, an all-encompassing conviction, a whole and final truth, penetrating the whole of his being.

"I AM UNWORTHY."

One
THE KID

ANDERSON SWEPT HER gaze across the narrow street, bathed in the orange glow from the chop shops on the lower twenty or so floors of MacDemarco block, full of jostling citizens as they haggled at the food stalls. Locust, Beatlo and maggot dealers nestled beside Noodle-Os and Mexi-vans. She shouldered her way towards a Burriburger stall, which had the benefit of being at the end of the row, with big old rockrete walls cosying up on two sides. Taking an empty stool, she leant back against the rockrete and ordered a Burri-Loco Burger.

She was on a precious few hours of down time, but there was no such thing as an off-duty Judge, even if they did have to stop and eat every now and then. Taking a breath, she did a cursory skip-and-dip, skimming the minds around her to make sure no one was planning a quick jump on a distracted Judge; she didn't want to have to get physical with her mouth stuffed full of loco-burger. Picking up a few gang-bangers, some guy frantic for something he'd lost, and some black market Fat dealers, she settled back to wait for her food. These lowlifes were lucky she was hungry. Maybe they'd be out of here by the time she was done, maybe they wouldn't.

Easing her psi-sense back from the crowd, she became aware of someone watching her. Leaning casually against the counter, she let her eyes drift again until she pinpointed her stalker: a ragged girl, skinny, barefoot and covered in dust, peering out the mouth of a narrow alley.

Without letting the child know she'd rumbled her, Anderson did a quick screen to see if she was a gang spy, but the only thing she picked up was how hungry the kid was. Jumping off her stool, Anderson started towards the girl, but the little brown eyes widened and she darted away down the alley.

"Hey! Wait!" Anderson called. *Drokk it! I wasn't gonna hurt you, kiddo. I just wanted to buy you a drokking burger!*

The child stopped suddenly and turned around, as if Anderson had said it out loud. Holding her hands out placatingly, Anderson lowered herself into a crouch.

"Hey, kid, you're not in trouble. It's just I don't like eating alone." She gestured to the stall behind her, where her loco-burger had just been placed enticingly on the counter. "Wanna come warm up the stool next to mine? You'd be helping me out."

The girl took two steps forward, and then narrowed her eyes, as if trying to see through Anderson, before visibly relaxing and nodding. The two of them left the alley and hopped up onto the stools. Anderson pushed her burger towards the child, whose eyes were pretty much boring a hole in it already, and ordered another.

Watching her tear into the food, Anderson considered her next step. That girl had performed some kind of mind screening on her. She could have blocked it easily, but she'd decided to let the kid have a root around, making it clear to her that she knew exactly what she was doing.

"Handy, sometimes, isn't it? Being able to see if someone's lying or not."

Swallowing, the girl kept her eyes on the food and nodded, before taking another bite.

As the second loco-burger was presented, Anderson ordered a side of cheezo-fries and a sweet-shake for the kid. How had she been missed at screening? She should be at the Academy with the other psi-cadets. And by the looks of it, she'd be a lot better off there too.

"You got a name?" Anderson asked, taking a cheez-laden bite of her loco-burger.

Drokk, this stall's good.

The girl looked up at her for the first time since they'd sat down, and grinned.

Anderson smiled greasily at her, projecting how much she was enjoying her food, and the girl in turn shared her pleasure in the crunchy fries and the HotHot sauce. She seemed more comfortable communicating mind-to-mind than she did verbally. In fact, Anderson hadn't heard her voice yet at all. She decided to just eat with her in silence for a little bit.

Instead of pushing for her name and information on her parents, Anderson brought up images of the Academy. Of other kids the girl's age playing psi-games. The clean, comfortable uniforms, the dormitories with their crisply made beds, and the food hall, complete with the smells of freshly baked bread, cakes and cheezo-fries.

The girl grew very still.

"That's where I grew up," Anderson said. "What's it like where you live?"

The instant she asked, she knew it was a mistake. The kid threw up her walls, shut Anderson out, and reached for the shake.

She was *strong*. To have got here all on her own was impressive, especially for one so young—Anderson guessed the girl was around seven or eight.

"You know, there are a lot of people like us where I grew up. It's sort of like a home, for special people. Special people that can tell if people are lying or not."

"Special?" the kid murmured, eyes fixed on her hands. Her childish voice sounded almost out of place coming from her serious little face.

"Yes, kiddo. Very special. Not everyone can do what we do."

The kid took a deep breath, then looked up at Anderson. "You're like me, aren't you? That's why I was watching you. I heard you feeling about in people's heads."

Anderson smiled and nodded.

"Do they—?" The girl trailed off.

Fighting the urge to push her, Anderson finished off the last bite of her burger instead.

"Do they make you listen to the bad men too?"

"What?"

Without thinking, Anderson dipped into her mind.

A figure, bloody and twitching on the floor. A fat, shadowy little man, leaning back in a chair with his feet up on a packing crate.

"Brat, he telling the truth or not?"

A deep focus on the man on the floor, her stomach heaving, her heart thumping. She can feel the pain, the panic, the fear.

"Brat! You gone deaf on me?" The man stands and lunges at her, and she feels a sharp pain in her cheek. "Is he telling me the truth?"

Clenching her little fists, she shakes her head. No, the man on the floor was lying.

She flinches away as the fat man swings back his shiny black boot and kicks the man on the floor hard, in his stomach...

Anderson saw red. She clenched her own fists to control herself, so as not to scare the kid. She hadn't been missed in screening—she hadn't been screened at all. Those gang-bangers had probably bought her as soon as she'd shown signs and kept her for their own ends. It must be *real* useful having a pet psychic around.

The kid was looking at her with wide, outraged eyes.

"*I didn't want to look at that,*" the little girl said through gritted teeth.

"I'm sorry kid, but—look. What they're making you do— that's not right. At the Academy no one's gonna make you look in the bad men's heads." *Well, at least not till you're older,* Anderson thought, making sure her walls were up. "And no one's gonna hurt you like that. They'll take care of you, teach you."

Trying to gauge what the girl was thinking, Anderson encountered walls every bit as impenetrable as her own. The kid was looking at her intensely.

"Because we *are* special, kid. But what we can do, it should be used to protect people, to stop the bad men, not help them."

Her little brow furrowed, and she looked from the empty burger wrapper to her hands. Suddenly she sat up, stock-still.

"He's here."

Anderson picked up a familiar panicked thought; the frantic man she'd sensed in her skip-and-dip earlier, now flooded with relief as he spied what he'd lost.

"There you are!" A meaty hand shot out and engulfed the girl's skinny arm with scarred, tattooed fingers.

Anderson rushed to her feet, her stool clattering to the rockrete.

"Step away from the child, citizen."

The gang-banger was huge, a dusty leather-clad mountain with a square, tattoo-covered face, topped with a shiny, tattoo-scrawled scalp. A chop shop thug by the look of it. But which gang did he belong to?

"She's my girl, Judge. Little squirt ran away when I sent her to her room for talking back. Ain't that right, sweetheart?"

The girl looked at him blankly, but projected to Anderson exactly who this was. The kid had been kept in a little dark room with a harsh, chemical smell. There were bad men here—one of them in the slightly comfier room outside of hers, guarding her as always—but below her, she could feel the misery of hundreds of children, the pain of burned fingers and tortured breathing emanating through the floorboards, a constant accompaniment to her life since she had been moved here. *A drug shop*, Anderson realised.

There was a deafening bang, and suddenly the girl was writhing on the floor, screaming along with those torn apart by an explosion downstairs. By the time she'd managed to get her walls up to block out the agony, she realised the room outside of her own was empty. She listened to the minds of the gang-bangers as she made her way through the warren of corridors, eluding them in the confusion, and made her escape.

"Citizen, you are guilty of kidnap and child slave labour violations, as well as violating psi-screening regulations and aiding and abetting a drug shop—the sentence is thirty years in the cubes."

With a speed she wouldn't have thought possible, he snatched the kid around the waist and ran into the crowded street.

"Grud-*damn* it!"

Her Lawgiver was no good with so many people around. Drawing her daystick, she launched herself at the tightly packed crowd, which had closed in behind the fleeing thug and his struggling captive. "Stand clear!" she yelled, shoving through milling citizens.

It was no good, too many people separated her from the girl. Leaping onto a stall counter, she swung on top of a grub-van, leapt across to a call-box and jumped at where she saw his blue-stained skull pushing through the crowd. Rolling as she hit the ground, she cracked her daystick against his ankle with a satisfying crunch.

"You Grud-damn *bitch*," he roared as he pitched forward, dropping the girl but catching her by her neck before she could make a break for it.

Anderson moved in, kicking down on his knee and swinging

her stick into his groin. He turned, shielding his gonads as he slammed his fist into her jaw. Tasting blood, she pulled her Lawgiver out and leveled it at his head. This close, she could be sure of her aim.

She had him, there was no way he could fight her off and still hold onto the kid.

At that moment she felt a sharp impact to the back of her head. Pitching forward, she caught sight of a pair of booted feet making a speedy escape. By the time she had staggered back to her feet, the girl and her abductor had disappeared.

She frantically craned her head around, panting and reeling. Where the drokk had they gone?

Suddenly her mind filled with images of a side street, flashes of broken glass and trash littering the ground, and Anderson sped off towards the tip-street that the stall-holders used for their rubbish. The kid was showing her where they were.

Then her comm buzzed, a dry voice crackled into her earpiece.

"This is a code 198. All Psi-Judges to report to headquarters immediately. Repeat, code 198. Attendance is mandatory. Tracking engaged."

Anderson stopped in her tracks, torn. If she didn't go back now, she was in deep drokk. But what was she supposed to do, abandon the girl?

Kid, she tried, reaching out. If she could send a psi-dart, she could come back for her later. But there was no answering mind.

The girl was gone.

Two

PARTNERS

ANDERSON WAS DIRECTED to one of the cadet amphitheatres —there was no way every Psi-Judge in Mega-City One would fit into a standard debriefing room. The aisles were full of bristling Judges, most of them furious at being dragged back like this. She expected she was probably wearing the same grim look as her fellow Judges.

Judge Adjonyoh was sat slumped near the back with her arms crossed, her knees resting on the chair in front as she tried to accommodate her long legs. She nodded as Anderson slid into the seat beside her.

"You heard anything?"

Adjonyoh shrugged. "Something to do with Turner, I think."

"Turner? I heard he'd lost it."

She nodded. "He's not the only one. There's something messed up going on."

There was a hush as Judge Aline Verastegui walked to the podium. Adjonyoh whistled through her teeth.

"Must be some serious drokk if one of the Council of Five shows her face."

Anderson couldn't help but agree.

She'd never seen Judge Verastegui up close before. Perps had always underestimated this woman, thanks to her diminutive frame and her huge, intense eyes. Coming in a little over 5'2" with her thick greying black hair plaited neatly and pinned on top of her head, you'd be forgiven for taking the Street-Div veteran for a sweet grandma. But this little lady held the record across Mega-City One for gang-banger sentences. She took down the Blood-Sucker mob pretty much single-handedly. Word was that hidden in those pretty plaits were razors, ready to slice into the grubby fingers of anyone who took it into their head to grab her by the hair. She was a legend, and someone Anderson had looked up to since her cadet days.

"Right, Psi-Div, I don't want to waste your time and I don't want you to waste mine, so let's make this as quick as we can."

The murmuring voices fell silent and all eyes turned forwards.

"It won't have escaped your notice that every active member of Psi-Div is present, and, apart from myself, not a single Judge from outside the division. That is because the grave matter I am about to disclose concerns Psi-Div and only Psi-Div."

If it wasn't for the high level of training of every Judge in the room, Anderson would have been flooded with frustration as the Judges again bristled under the order. But Psi-Div was the only place in Mega-City One that Anderson could relax into the silence of her own brain. Not only was it an offence to dip into the thoughts of another Judge, but Psi-Judges had been trained to shield their minds from the stray leakages that a lot of people with low-psi ability often projected by accident. Emotions stayed where they were supposed to: inside the minds of each individual in the room. Anderson enjoyed the novelty of relying on facial expressions and body language.

"Before I get to the pressing issue of the psycho trying to kill us all today, let me give you a little history lesson. Forty-two years ago, back when Psi-Div was little more than a handful of weirdos trying to figure out their asses from their elbows—

and screening was disorganised to say the least—the Cult of the Devourer nearly put an end to the division before it had even properly formed."

Adjonyoh met her eyes and mouthed the word, as every Judge in the room sat forward. *Devourer.*

It was a kid's story. The psychic demon from an astral plane bent on breaking down the dimensional barriers to suck the psychic life force of every sentient being. A monster come to break the world.

"The Cult of the Devourer believed that your psi-abilities are a gift given by the demon they call Karlul, a gift that should be used in its service, and only in its service. That Psi-Div is perverting something sacred.

"It started small; the trial screening programme was yielding low results, until we discovered that those found to have the abilities were often vanishing, their results doctored.

"Things escalated quickly after that, with Judges disappearing, some showing up again as babbling idiots, their minds turned. By the time we figured out what was happening, the cult had numbers to rival the budding Psi-Div. It was a dark time, Judge turning against Judge as you battled your own, mind-to-mind."

She paused to let this vision sink in. Anderson looked over the crowded auditorium, a shiver running over her at the idea of having to face down her fellow Judges.

"At the cost of too many lives, not to mention minds, we prevailed. The Cult of the Devourer was wiped out. Done. Finished.

"Or so we thought."

Judge Verastegui turned to the huge, wall-spanning screen behind her as it flickered to life. A picture of a man strapped to a hospital bed was revealed, straining against his bonds.

"Judge Turner was found last night wandering the streets of Shine District."

A collective gasp swept over the hall as people recognised the young Judge.

"We cannot know for certain what turned his brain, but one thing we do know. A psychic did this, one with enough power to burn a thought brand into his brain like some old-time cowboy searing his name onto a heifer."

Anderson held her breath as the audio came on, the sound of Turner's raving, ragged, broken voice echoing across them all.

"*I AM NOT WORTHY. I AM NOT WORTHY.* I AM NOT WORTHY."

Adjonyoh's knees slid from the chair back and she sat up straight, her knuckles whitening as she clenched her fists.

"This is not an isolated incident," Judge Verastegui continued. "We would not have gathered you here in such force if it was just one errant brain-warped Judge."

She took a breath and dropped her gaze to the tips of her reinforced boots.

"'I. Am. Not. Worthy.'" She drew the words out, emphasising every syllable. "It could have been mere coincidence that these words were the same words burned into the brains of Judges that the cult couldn't turn forty-two years ago. That's what we thought, anyway, when Psi-Judge Singh was found three months ago in the same condition."

"I knew it," Adjonyoh muttered.

Singh had been Adjonyoh's buddy at the Academy. Seeing him like that couldn't be easy for her. Especially as everyone thought he'd been killed.

"And then there was Peters, and Dewit, and Nellis," Verastegui continued as the screen split into a grid, showing Judges strapped to beds like Turner, all straining and raving. Drokk, there must have been nearly twenty of them. How had they kept this under wraps?

"Last night the decision was made to make this Psi-Div's top and *only* priority. We believe we're dealing with a copycat. The fact that there is someone out there with the strength to take on a Psi-Judge is not acceptable. The possibility that they are organised and growing in number is a threat we cannot allow to build."

With a nod to the back of the room, the screen went dark, and she typed something into the podium's data pad.

"You will be receiving your reassignments to your data-holos now."

Anderson activated her holo as the room lit up around her, glimmers of light appearing as everyone checked where they were being sent. Anderson frowned as she read hers. That was odd.

"All active case-loads will be passed to your non-psi partners. I want you to understand something here, people: this is your *only* priority. I don't care if you're on the tail of a serial killer, a child-napper or mutant-smuggler. You will drop it and trust in us, your non-psi comrades, to deal with it. Because, as important as you may think you are, we handled this city quite well without you before this division was established. If you break orders and stray from your assignment, it's a year in the cubes for you."

There was a lot of hissing and shifting in seats as the Judges took in the threat. Sometimes Anderson wished they had a bit more carrot and a bit less stick, but then, this was Mega-City One, and they were Judges. If anyone understood the importance of discipline, it was them.

"Dismissed."

Judge Verastegui swept out of the room before the Psi-Judges could get to their feet. Anderson stayed in her seat as Adjonyoh uncoiled her long body to tower above, her mouth a fine line.

"I got a quad," she said as she squeezed past on her way out.

"That's good. Think of it as a break from chasing perps and cracking skulls." Anderson tried to sound like she believed what she was saying.

Adjonyoh shrugged. "Cooped up in a room with three other Psi-Judges scanning the city? Gonna get intense."

Quads mind-linked to amplify their ability. They'd be carrying out grand-scale skip-and-dips and filtering the dross from the cream, passing on anything useful to the street sweep teams.

"You on clean-up or quad?"

Anderson bit her lip. "Neither. I'm supposed to stay back and receive my assignment now." She swept her eyes over the room, noticing other Judges making no move to leave. "Looks like I'm not the only one."

"Well, that's something at least. Good luck." Adjonyoh nodded goodbye, leaving Anderson in a rapidly emptying hall.

Psi-Chief Smee stepped up to the podium, back straight and eyes narrowed as always, her short dark bobbed hair counteracting an otherwise stern appearance.

Good; Psi-Div were being left to get on with it now. It felt better somehow to receive orders from one of their own.

"Those of you remaining will come down here where I can see you."

Tramping down the narrow steps towards the front rows were those who Anderson recognised as Judges high levels of psi-ability, known for getting the job done. She pushed down a little thrill of pride. She also noticed a lot of grey and balding heads scattered throughout. All of the senior Judges, including the cadet trainers, were present as well. It was strange to see them at a briefing. They were normally either behind a desk molding young minds or in the gym cracking young heads.

"Okay. Those of you remaining have been selected for investigative tasks. As we just heard, this looks likely to be connected with the Cult of the Devourer. Fortunately—or unfortunately, depending on how you look at it—we have a number of senior Judges who have first-hand experience of this grud-awful excuse for humanity. They were among the Judges that overcame it the first time around, and you younger Judges, no matter how cocksure and bright-eyed you are, have no drokking idea what you are up against. Each pair will feature one senior and one junior. Together, you're going to be given a quadrant to turn upside down until you find these insects, and together, we will stamp them out."

She flicked the podium data-pad and everyone's data-strips flashed incoming. Activating it once more, Anderson's stomach sank as the name flashed. She looked up to see a pair of hooded, furious eyes staring back. The eyes belonged to an older Judge in her mid-sixties, her dark hair peppered with grey and shorn into a practical short-back-and-sides. She was seated in her usual hunched posture, her short stocky body belying a surprising strength for someone her age. Anderson knew this because she had been on the receiving end of this strength during training. Renowned for her crotchety impatience and her dismissal of anyone under the age of forty as useless, she was a formidable partner to say the least. *Judge Mei Yin. Lucky me.*

Judge Smee wrapped up by assigning quadrants and dismissing the pairs. Anderson pushed herself out of her chair and approached Mei Yin.

"Psi-Judge Mei Yin, it's an honour—"

The older Judge brushed past Anderson without acknowledging her, and strode up to Smee before she could leave.

"This is drokk and you know it," she said, squaring up to Smee. They were about the same height, both with the same old-world Chinese heritage, but the younger Smee looked momentarily fragile as Mei Yin bore down on her.

Taking a deep breath, Judge Smee put on one of her famous *don't-mess-with-me* smiles that stopped just short of her eyes.

"Mei Yin, I don't have time for this right now. You know how serious this is."

"Damn right I do. Which is why you shouldn't pair me with this baby. Send me out on my own. I don't do well with partners, you know that."

Anderson realised she was holding her breath. Watching a Judge talk back to a superior with such reckless abandon didn't come around every day. This was a feature show, and she had a front row seat. Smee was their chief, but she'd probably been knocked about the practice mat by Mei Yin just like everybody else.

"Judge Mei Yin, you have been given an order, and I expect you to follow it."

The room was now empty save for the three of them. Probably just as well for Mei Yin. A big public showdown would not go in her favour.

Mei Yin opened her mouth to say more, but Smee cut her off.

"I know how you feel about partners, it's why you've been given a pass on buddying up for this long. But we need you now, out there, on the streets. And we need you with young blood and strong backup. Anderson is the Judge for the job. Understand?"

Mei Yin whipped her head around to glare at Anderson, nodded once, then stormed out of the room.

"Well, that went well," Anderson said before remembering where she was. "Drokk, did I say that out loud?"

Smee raised an eyebrow at her, but there was a definite smirk hiding behind her cool facade. "No need to thank me," she said, moving towards the door.

She looked back when Anderson didn't move. "Well, what are you waiting for? Go. Get to work with your new partner."

Three
THE SOUL TREE

ANDERSON HURRIED AFTER Mei Yin as she strode down the hall, her shoulders drawn up as if fending off a blow. She turned into the suit-room and Anderson entered quietly on her heels, feeling it prudent to keep her mouth shut for now.

Mei Yin shrugged on her armoured jacket and adjusted her Lawgiver in its holster. She rolled her shoulders and stretched her neck to either side with audible clicks. "All right then, *cadet*, let's get to work."

Anderson was still trying to form a reply when Mei Yin pushed past her and she had to almost run along to keep up.

"Cadet?" she muttered under her breath. She'd worked drokking hard to shed that title.

"Excuse me, Judge Mei Yin?"

The woman didn't falter in her charge towards the vaulted entry hall with its body scanners, squawking perps and implacable street squad Judges getting on with the day-to-day.

Anderson picked up her pace, and, without thinking, reached out to grab the older Judge's shoulder.

"Mei Yin—"

Her hand was grabbed and twisted with breathtaking speed

149

as Mei Yin pushed her up against the wall, just out of sight behind a thrumming body scanner.

"What the *drokk*, Mei Yin?"

"Listen to me, cadet," Mei Yin hissed through her teeth. "I do not do partners. You understand? If we're stuck together by the powers that be, then so be it. But you'll keep your mouth shut and follow along like a good cadet—"

"My name is *Judge* Cassandra Anderson," Anderson said, finally giving in to the temptation to twist herself easily out of Mei Yin's grip. "And you will gruddamn call me that."

The two women stood staring at each other, breathing heavily from the confrontation. Mei Yin grunted and turned on her heel, leaving Anderson to decide whether or not to follow. Shaking herself, she released the fists she didn't realise she'd been making, shut her mouth, and followed like a good cadet.

THEIR LAWMASTERS WOUND their way around the evening traffic as a sickly orange sun fell behind the city blocks. Mei Yin had given her the coordinates so she could 'tag along,' but Anderson wasn't letting her out of her sight; she wouldn't put it past her to give her the wrong destination.

They took the bypass over Septic Town and sped through the backstreets of the 'Forest,' a district known for the Woodolin factories, producing quality fake wood for the slicks in Shine District to pretty up their apartments with. The place stunk of whatever drokk they used to make the useless, highly flammable stuff, and Anderson sighed as Mei Yin pulled up outside of what looked like a junk shop, the dark, dusty windows full of Woodolin oddities. Relieved at least that Mei Yin hadn't lied about where they were going, she parked up and entered the shop to the sound of a tinkling audioclip, alerting the proprietor that they had customers. A wrinkled old man pushed through a beaded curtain behind the counter.

"What can I do for—"

"Herm. It's been a while." Mei Yin picked up a tiny, intricately carved tree—of the pine variety, if Anderson had remembered her history right—and studied it closely before looking up to grin at the shopkeeper.

The old man's face fell as he recognised his visitor. "I thought you'd be dead by now," he said, pursing his mouth as if he'd smelt something bad. Which was saying something in the Forest; Anderson was trying to breathe as little as possible.

Mei Yin let out a low chuckle. "I just had better things to do than talk to your scrawny ass."

"Oh, yes," he harrumphed. "Miss high-and-mighty-mind-reader, so much better than the people she left behind."

Mei Yin let out an audible sigh and leant on the dirty glass counter. "I didn't come here to reminisce. I need information."

"I don't know anything! I'm just an old man selling my work—all legal—and minding my own business."

Mei Yin lurched over the counter suddenly and grabbed him by the scruff of the neck. "I don't have time for this, old man. There isn't a carver wipes his own ass you don't know about in this district."

Anderson stepped forward—surely two Psi-Judges could question one tiny man without having to resort to physical force. Also, it sounded like this guy knew Mei Yin. That was shaky ground. Back when Mei Yin was recruited, they were picking out psychics of all ages; she was probably a teenager when she entered the Academy. Far older than anyone nowadays and with strong community ties that would have been harder to break.

"Listen," she said, aware that this was the first time she'd spoken since they'd arrived, "let's just dig the intel out of him and get on with it."

"Okay, then," Mei Yin said without taking her eyes off Herm, who was bent uncomfortably over the counter top. "How 'bout

I ask the questions and you read the answers, kid. Easy as that, right, Herm?"

Herm remained silent, his eyes narrowed in what seemed to Anderson like intense concentration.

"Herm, I wanna know about any folks going missing. To be more specific, I wanna know about kids due for screening."

Anderson took a deep breath and slid into Herm's mind, ready to pick out anything triggered by Mei Yin's words. She was presented with the image of a real, living version of the miniature tree Mei Yin had picked up, now towering against a grey sky, its bows green and bursting with life, the air heavy with moisture, beads of water gathering on the ends of the needles. She shook her head and opened her eyes.

"How is he doing that?"

"Huh. Something that *Judge* Cassandra Anderson hasn't come across in her two long years since graduating?"

Anderson inwardly rolled her eyes and braced herself for Mei Yin's smug explanation.

"You're getting better at that, Herm." She let him go and he collapsed briefly onto the counter before pushing himself back out of reach of a quick lunge.

"Does he have psi-abilities?" Anderson demanded.

Mei Yin shook her head. "Just a trick of concentration. They used to call it 'meditating,' that right, Herm?"

She reached behind her and picked up the carving again. "A majestic pine? Really? I always thought your core would be a dried up wasteland shrimp—something like that."

Herm smiled grimly and Anderson tried again, in case his focus had shifted, only to be met once again by the calming vision of the tree.

"So we can't read him. Fine. Thanks for the demonstration. Are you going to get on with whatever it was you had in mind instead?"

Mei Yin dropped the little carving on the floor and stomped

down on the delicate thing, crushing it to splinters. Herm flinched, but didn't move.

"I'm not asking for much, Herm. I just want to know if anyone's gone missing."

"What's in it for me?"

"How about an obstruction of justice charge?" Anderson said. "That's what, four months in the cubes?"

Mei Yin picked up an intricate piece depicting some sort of winged human—a mutant of sorts, Anderson thought.

Herm's lip twitched.

Mei Yin lifted it above her head and sent it crashing into the counter, which exploded in a shower of glass. Before he could react, she'd leapt over the devastation and grabbed him by the neck, shoving him against the wall.

In the same moment, Anderson detected a flare of fear. She zeroed in on it, confirming her suspicion that it didn't come from Mr. Pine Tree.

"Hey," she said, causing Mei Yin to freeze for a moment. "He's not alone."

She strode behind the counter drawing her Lawgiver, pausing outside the beaded curtain before swooping in on a young teenage girl, crouching behind a half-finished carving of a reclining cat. She held her chisel shakily towards Anderson.

"Hey, kid, put that thing down before you hurt yourself."

Eyes wide, the girl pushed herself up against the wall without relinquishing her weapon. Anderson heard the curtain stir as Mei Yin dragged Herm in with her.

"Jespa, meet your great auntie," he said dryly.

Definitely shaky ground. This was how Mei Yin treated her family?

"This is your *sister*, uncle?" the girl sounded incredulous.

"Jespa, huh?" Mei Yin interrupted before he could reply, her eyes darting to Anderson suggestively. "Who's gone missing round here recently?"

"*Focus*," Herm said sharply.

Anderson shot into the girl's mind and was faced with not one, but a forest of majestic broad-leafed trees, a gentle sun filtering through their rustling bows.

"Sure is pretty inside your head, kid."

The sunlight flickered as she felt Jespa's concentration break. Suddenly, standing beneath the green canopy was a ragged little boy, a little younger than Jespa, and then he was gone.

"He a friend of yours, Jespa?" Anderson pressed.

The sky darkened and for a moment a vision of the boy laughing flashed in and out of being.

"Why don't you want to help us? If he's missing, tell us who he is. Maybe we can find him."

"Because we don't help you mind-suckers," came the angry retort from Herm. "You're all mutant abominations. Just because you're useful, some jumped up Judge gets to decide you don't count. You're nice, friendly monsters—"

His tirade ended in a grunt as Mei Yin planted a solid fist into his stomach.

"That friendly enough for you, brother of mine?"

But Anderson didn't care about him. She was in the beautiful centre of Jespa's soul. And now she was looking at the boy again. She stepped closer to him as he began to shiver. *Who are you?* she thought fiercely. *Jespa, listen, I don't want to hurt him, I want to find him. Wherever he is, I think he's in grave danger.*

The broad gnarled trunk of the tree he was standing in front of began to smooth itself as a number formed on the bark: 2390.

"Don't tell her anything, Jespa," wheezed the old man.

Anderson opened her eyes and stepped forward, taking the chisel from the girl's limp hand.

"That's his door number, right? 2390?"

Jespa bit her lip.

"You know I'm telling you the truth, don't you?" She let a

wave of genuine determination hit the girl, a determination laden with the drive to find the kid, with all of the anxiety pinned through it, the real fear that he could be in the hands of a demented cult.

"Which block?" Anderson said softly.

Jespa looked at her feet, her sleek black hair hanging in a curtain to cover her face.

"MacDemarco," she murmured, almost inaudibly.

"Thank you," Anderson said. She heard a grunt from behind her as Mei Yin let her brother go.

"Well, Herm, it's been good to catch up." Mei Yin was already halfway across the shop.

"Don't let your uncle give you a hard time," Anderson said as she left the girl scowling at the ground.

Swinging onto her Lawmaster, she looked hard at Mei Yin, who was bringing MacDemarco block up on her data strip and projecting an image of it into the air between them.

"It's mostly chop shops," Anderson said. "No clear gang affiliation. It's been a sort of neutral zone for the past decade or so. Gang-bangers go in to get their mods. The block's got a strong union; any violence and that gang are banned."

"Must be some union if they can keep the gang-bangers out."

"You haven't met Abdullah, have you?"

Mei Yin huffed in dismissal. "You're pretty familiar with it," she said, squinting as the building plans peeled back, floor by floor.

"Strangely, I was over there this morning. Actually, there was this girl—"

"Right, then. Let's stop wasting time in this stomm-hole."

Anderson huffed in frustration as Mei Yin's Lawmaster churned up a cloud of acrid dust and sped off, leaving Anderson to follow, again.

A feeling of *déjà-vu* came over her as she pulled up outside of MacDemarco for the second time that day. She was satisfied when Mei Yin pulled in a few seconds after her, bringing up the schematics of the building again.

"Apartment's on floor fifty-one, fourteenth column."

"We'll go there after," Anderson said, swinging her leg to the dusty ground. "First, we speak to Abdullah, see if she knows anything about any missing kids."

To Anderson's relief, Mei Yin nodded. There followed a frozen, disorientating moment until Anderson realised that Mei Yin was waiting for her to lead the way. She turned to set her Lawmaster to monitor anyone who entered and left the block.

"Well, get on with it then, take me to Abdullah. I haven't drokking had tea with the old witch before, have I?"

Anderson allowed herself a small sardonic smile. There she was.

"AND YOU'RE SURE this girl was telling you the truth?" Abdullah asked, scrolling through a long list of minor crimes reported over the last month, with a few major arrests, and one skirmish with a gang-banger pushing happy pills that turned into an all-out brawl before the union reps could deal with it.

"As far as she knows, he's disappeared," Anderson said.

"Could be he just didn't want to see her any more," Abdullah mused, running her fingers through long, grey-streaked hair.

Anderson shrugged. "We just want to confirm it either way."

Mei Yin was looking over the union HQ with interest. It was a converted apartment: the kitchen and living room had been knocked into one large space and lined with desks, manned by fourteen or so operators tapping industriously away or talking into earpieces.

"Some organisation you have here," Mei Yin said, a hint of approval in her tone.

"I have no reports of kidnaps or any missing kids." Abdullah tapped the apartment number Anderson had given her in and three cits came up on the screen: Cevca Cruz, sixty-three years of age, retired; her daughter Ava Cruz, thirty-two, technician, and Jonjo, fourteen years old, her son.

"That's him," Anderson said.

Mei Yin stated the obvious. "Well, he doesn't appear to be missing."

Then every screen in the room started flashing a red alarm, and a deafening siren blasted through the room.

"Report." Abdullah tapped her earpiece while the room exploded into frenzied action.

"There's been an explosion in the fourteenth column," reported a heavyset man from his station.

"Let me guess, floor fifty-one?" Mei Yin said under her breath.

"Squads fourteen and seven are closest," a younger woman called over.

"Send 'em in," Abdullah ordered, pulling on a bullet-proof vest and grabbing a Phase-9 blaster from the drawer of her desk.

"Don't worry, Your Honours, fully licensed." She winked at them as she made her way to the door, the two Judges hot on her heels.

Mei Yin put on a burst of speed to outdistance Anderson and grabbed hold of Abdullah's shoulder. "Leave this to the Judges, citizen," she said.

"We are a fully trained response team with a superior knowledge of this block and its inhabitants. I respectfully suggest that you—"

Anderson pushed past both of them and sprinted to the service elevator, which had speed settings to shoot straight to whichever floor her data holo told it to.

"*Anderson!*" Mei Yin barked.

"Catch up when you two have finished chatting," she called back as the doors snapped shut. Mei Yin may be her superior, but they were *partners* now, not trainer and cadet. Anderson was tired of following her around.

As the doors opened, smoke billowed into the lift, and Anderson flipped up her breathing kit as she flattened herself beside the door. The hall was dark, lit up by a low, pulsing red emergency light. Casting her awareness out, she was relieved to find only one angry, buzzing, hopped-up mind guarding the lift. The smoke provided excellent cover as she crouched low, out of his line of sight. As the tip of his blaster edged through the open doors, she grabbed it and smacked it into his face, hearing the crunch of his nose above the sound of a curse. Dragging the blaster around, she pulled him into a chokehold, squeezing until he passed out. Then she shoved him through the door and fell into her crouch, setting her Lawgiver as she made her way towards the blast zone. She could sense a confusion of activity up ahead.

Her foot snagged on something, and she looked down to see a body sprawled out on the floor. She saw with dismay that the stiff—she didn't need to check the vitals to know it was definitely dead, the smoking hole where his chest should have been confirmed that—was wearing a response team uniform similar to Abdullah's.

There were three gang-bangers up ahead, shooting around a tight corner with their backs to her. The hall branched left and right, and they seemed to be holding off the response team to the right, which suggested that apartment 2390 was to the left. She crept up behind them as their attention was occupied and shot the first at point-blank range in the back of his head, kneeing the second in the balls as he turned towards her in surprise. The third took a step back, covered in the bloody pulp of the first punk's brains, and was taken out by one of the response team's blasters.

She grabbed the guy currently clutching his groin and moaning by his tufted bleached white hair, and dropped into his mind. There were five more of them holed up outside of the apartment. The explosion had dented but not destroyed the door. Since Abdullah took charge, every apartment had been fitted with blast-proof titanium doors, designed to hold until a response team could come and wipe out whoever was trying to attack one of her tenants.

"You are in violation, on multiple counts, of sections 2, 10 and 14 of the Municipal Code. Sentence: life in the cubes," she said as she cuffed him.

Four response team members joined her as she finished up.

"We have three men down," grunted a grizzled, brown-skinned man, who was clearly in charge.

"Four," Anderson corrected him, "found one of your guys by the lift."

He swore. "What can they be after? The people on this level are just families, not gang-bangers."

"They want them to keep their mouths shut, is my guess. And two Psi-Judges just showed an interest in them. No one can keep a secret long once we show up."

But how had they known? They must have been monitoring Abdullah's systems. Maybe they even had a sneak in her team.

At that moment the emergency lights went out, and Anderson kicked herself for not having any night vision kit on her. "Stay here," she ordered, and turned back to the pitch-black corridor, backing her way towards the sound of an angle grinder screeching against metal.

A blast exploded the plaster near her head and she ducked back into a doorway, sensing terrified citizens cowering inside. That had been close.

Testing a theory, she ran across the hall blindly to the doorway opposite, reaching its relative safety as a volley of shots barely missed her. She might not be able to see, but the gang-bangers certainly could. Closing her eyes—out of habit, they were useless anyway—she slid into the mind of the guy on guard as two others attended to the door.

She dropped lightly into his sensory system, and the world lit up in ultraviolet. She could see herself as a purple smudge at the other end of the hall.

Mei Yin, she projected, locating the older Judge coming down with Abdullah in the lift.

Report. The response was sharp and tinged with fury.

I'm in the east corridor facing down three punks, I need a distraction in the south hall.

No response, but moments later the whole scene lit up in shocking white as a flash grenade was flung from the south hall.

Snapping the mind-to-mind connection as the punk began shooting blindly into the light, Anderson ran towards him and flung a low sweeping kick to knock him down, jamming her armoured shoulder into his face. By the time he was down and the emergency lights were back on, the other two gang-bangers were dead, Abdullah was shouting orders and levelling her blaster at the last punk alive, and Mei Yin was glaring at her with unconstrained, venomous scorn.

Anderson grinned at the two women while catching her breath. "Glad you could make it."

Four

DRUGSHOP

Cevca and Ava Cruz had a standard two-bed apartment, with an open-plan kitchen-living space, and a closet-size bathroom. Despite the violence outside, their home remained untouched. Anderson wished more low-income blocks were like this one. This sort of security was normally reserved for the rich and influential, not chop-shop workers or retirees.

Abdullah was rummaging in a cupboard while the two tenants sat wide-eyed on the couch. She filled two glasses with water and emptied a sachet of white powder into each one—probably one of those sugar-based placebos peddled on the street to relieve shock—and passed the glasses into their shaking hands.

"Drink that up."

Anderson guessed that whatever bonus block-leaders normally pocketed bought everyone security doors.

What blocks like this *really* needed was an Abdullah.

"Thank you," Cevca said. She was a sturdy-looking woman, with fine grey hair pulled into a loose ponytail. She took a sip, and then, noticing her daughter just staring at her glass, touched the younger woman's shoulder gently, before putting her hand over hers and guiding the drink to her lips. Ava sipped dutifully, took a hitching breath, and seemed to gather herself. She was very like her mother when you looked past the close-cropped hair: the round face and large brown eyes were the same.

"I know why you're here," she said then, looking up at Mei Yin, who was standing and watching the scene patiently, much to Anderson's surprise.

"Something to do with a squad of professional murderers trying to blow through your door?"

The woman smirked fleetingly. "And I also know that you coming here just nearly got my mother killed."

Cevca tutted at her daughter. "There is no hiding anything from these Judges," she said, glancing at their badges.

"It's true," Mei Yin said, almost softly, "but I'd rather you told us what's going on, rather than having to sift through every corner of your mind to get it."

Ava nodded, and took a larger swig of her drink. "I appreciate that."

"Is it true, Ava?" Abdullah interrupted. "Is Jonjo missing?"

Ava's lips pressed into a thin bloodless line, but she nodded.

"Why didn't you report it?" Abdullah demanded, and was about to say more before she caught a withering glance from Mei Yin.

"Did you notice what happened when two Judges showed an interest? Imagine if we had reported it. What then?" Cevca said, sitting forward. "They came to Ava's work and told her that Jonjo wouldn't be coming home. And they told her what would happen if we reported it. And they keep their promises, I can say that much."

"I would have kept you safe. We *did*," Abdullah said.

"Yes, but what about tomorrow, or the next day? What about when Ava goes back to work? Are you going to protect her 24-7?"

Abdullah opened her mouth to speak but Mei Yin cut across her. "Who came to your work? Who took Jonjo?"

Ava smiled bitterly. "Jonjo? And the rest. There must be ten kids missing from this block alone, and you had no idea. How can we expect you to protect us?"

Abdullah went pale, shaking her head. "What are they doing with them? Ava, we need to know. Who's taking them? These are Judges. You have to tell them. They can help."

"And you'll be breaking the law if you don't," Mei Yin added.

Ava sighed and collapsed back on the couch, the anger going out of her. "The Gasser Gang."

"The Gasser Gang?" Anderson said. "They operate around here," she clarified to Mei Yin. "Drug runners mostly. But they're small-time. What do they want with a bunch of kids?"

"Not so small-time any more." Abdullah leant back against the worktop. "They've gone into production. I heard they had to expand fast."

"Yes." Ava nodded, as if affirming something to herself. "Might as well tell you now, it's too late for us anyway. I know what they are doing with our children. And more importantly, I think I know where they are taking them."

ANDERSON SHIFTED IN her crouch twenty-two floors up on the air-filtration service platform, her arm hooked around the rail as she held her binoculars with her free hand. The wind tore at her hair as it whipped down the walls of Cash Block, which had a clear view of the huge double-door service entrance of Axel Block below.

"This is bull-crud," she muttered into her com. "Let's just get in there and see what's going on."

"*No,*" Mei Yin's voice was tinny through the helmet speaker. "*The second we go in there, they could send out a psi-alert. We're not ready to deal with these creeps in force yet.*"

"That's if this has anything to do with the Cult," Anderson said for the sixth time.

"*Stop complaining and concentrate.*" Was that a hint of humour in her voice? Mei Yin was enjoying this.

"You're not the one freezing her little ass off up here," Anderson muttered.

At that moment she got a warm-edged image of a quiet cafe and a steaming mug of Bug Broth being raised just high enough to enjoy the acrid aroma. "*I always enjoyed stake-outs,*" came Mei Yin's smug reply.

Anderson's muscles cramped as she watched a service lorry drive towards the doors. Her binoculars identified the guard leaning in the van's window to chew the fat with the driver as a perp, a Gasser Gang member with an illegal blaster slung over his shoulder. Her training itched to sentence him to ten years in the cubes immediately, but it also kept her rigidly perching on her lookout. What was really going on in there? Was the gang being used as a front for the Devourer cult?

As he waved the van through, she got a clear view through the back windows, the tinted glass no match for her Judge-grade binoculars.

It was full of children.

"Mei Yin, we gotta move. A van full of juveniles was just driven through the back door. We have to get in there now."

"*Drokk!*" Mei Yin swore. "*How many? That doesn't seem right.*"

"You think every kid they got here has psi-abilities?"

There was a pause. "*It doesn't add up. We can't be missing that many in the tests. And unless our genetics are going haywire, there just* aren't *that many of us out there.*"

"So what, this hasn't got anything to do with the Cult?"

"*I didn't say that. They could be using them for anything…*"

"Then we have to find out what that is." Anderson rose to stand, rolling her shoulders with a crack.

"*Okay, but we do this my way,*" Mei Yin snapped. "*We're quiet, no blasting our way in. We cover our psi-badges and we don't read people. A Devourer may be skilled enough to pick it up and we can't risk it.*"

"Sure thing, *partner*," Anderson said. "Anyone asks, we're just a couple of street Judges, looking into some missing kids."

"*Meet at south-east corner entrance.*"

TWENTY-FIVE MINUTES LATER, she was following Mei Yin down a narrow corridor on floor minus-three, her psi-badge hidden in a zipped pocket and her Lawgiver out and ready. She could sense people moving above and below them, a teeming mass of minds concentrated four floors beneath. She itched to read what was going on in those minds, but Mei Yin was right, it was too risky. She didn't much fancy a hundred powerful brainwashed psychics bearing down on them right now. Best to slip in and slip out without causing a stir, and to come back with reinforcements. If this *was* the Cult's base, it would be no simple matter of calling for backup; they'd need a coordinated attack by the whole of Psi-Div. It was imperative not to raise any alarms.

Mei Yin paused before a corner, sensing—as Anderson did—a consciousness around the bend. With a speed Anderson was still amazed by, she vanished out of sight, followed by the sound of a hard *thwack*. By the time she'd caught up, Mei Yin was gagging and cuffing an unconscious Gasser. There was nowhere to hide him in the hall, so they dragged him to the heavy metal door at the end, opening onto the east emergency stairwell, which this guy had probably been guarding.

This block was pretty ancient by Mega-City One standards, the design based on old-world apartment blocks, with huge resyk chutes along the back wall.

Tempting. Probably shouldn't shove a live perp in there,

though. They settled on burying him under the detritus of trash that had been discarded around the chutes instead.

Two floors down and they were close to the mass of misery they'd zeroed in on. There was also a sharp chemical smell hanging in the air.

The door opened onto another corridor, this one lit with a flashing blue fluorescent light—looked like the kind used to remove contaminants before working in a sterile environment. Interesting.

They took the left fork this time—the building schematics told them this level mirrored the one they had descended from, but there was a pair of doors that shouldn't have been there, leading... well, that was the question; the schematics didn't seem to go that far. Almost as if they'd been erased. Behind the heavy steel shutter she could sense three bored minds. Guards.

The Judges positioned themselves to either side, and Mei Yin counted down on her fingers: *three, two, one.*

They burst through the doors, Mei Yin propelling her small body with devastating force as she smashed one punk's teeth out with her daystick. The other two stood quickly, upending the table they'd been sat at, spraying cards everywhere as they reached for their blasters. Anderson shot one through the eye, while Mei Yin snapped a spinning kick at the third's throat.

The first guy started groaning through his pulped mouth.

"Sentence for attacking a Judge," Mei Yin said, drawing her Lawgiver, "death." She finished off the two writhing bodies and stood panting, looking at the devastation they'd just caused. Meeting Anderson's eyes, she grinned. "It's good to get out from behind the desk every once in a while."

Anderson felt her mouth quirk before training her eyes on the second door, the one they'd just killed three men to get to. A large glass panel showed a small antechamber with plexostrip hygiene filters. No contaminant was getting through to whatever was making that chemical stench on the other side.

She was hit by a moment of *déjà-vu*. She was in a small dark room filled with a fainter version of this caustic stench.

The little girl.

"This is where they were keeping her," she said out loud.

"What?" Mei Yin paused, her arm outstretched to push open the door.

"Earlier today, just before we got smacked with a tracking order? I was in the middle of chasing down a punk who had this kid. She's psi—*strong*. Some gang-banger hid her from screening. This smell—it's the same one she showed me, mind-to-mind. They're using her as their own personal lie detector, and they're keeping her here."

Mei Yin's face froze. "Why didn't you gruddamn tell me that this morning?"

"I tried, you cut me off."

"You were in the middle of chasing down some guy kidnapping a kid with psi powers. One they'd hidden from us. What do you think we've been doing all day?"

"Yes, I get that. But the gang-banger was just a norm, your garden-variety scumbag. Not a Devourer—"

"He could be working for them. *Think*."

Anderson bit back a retort. Mei Yin was right. She should have made the connection.

"Okay. I should have mentioned it sooner. But at least we know this is the right place. Let's get out of here and contact the chief."

"Wrong again." Mei Yin opened the door and held it wide for Anderson to enter. "We still need to make sure this is psycho headquarters before we mobilise the whole of Psi-Div."

And again, she hadn't thought it through. She was feeling more and more like a cadet by the second. If they pulled all the Psi-Judges away from their work and it was the wrong call, well, they'd be in deep drokk. Who knew what leads their counterparts were following?

The stench through the doors was so bad they pulled on their breathing kit. A sickly yellow light oozed through the window on the door at the far end of the hygiene blast.

It opened onto a huge vaulted warehouse. They were on the top level: the door opened onto a metal walkway with stairs leading down into an enormous workshop.

When she saw what was below them, her heart sank.

Hundreds of children filled the space below, busy stirring steaming vats, laser-combing powder at cast tables under heat lamps, using huge funnels to sort it into slabs. They all wore thin white jumpsuits and cloth face guards. An inadequate nod to safety gear against whatever toxic substances they were handling.

A drugshop.

"This isn't it," Mei Yin said under her breath. She sounded a little relieved.

"No, but it's one hell of an operation. We have to stop this. Now."

Mei Yin shook her head. "We'll call it in, but that's all we can do."

"*Come on.* I know we're not supposed to work any other cases, but we're here *now*. This was a lead that led to a massive illegal operation. We have to—"

"Were you in that briefing? We can't, Anderson. It pisses me off too, but we have to leave it to the street Judges. Look: we'd have to have backup anyway. We can stick around and keep an eye on things until reinforcements arrive. But that's it."

At that moment Anderson's attention was caught by a door opening in the far wall. The tattooed punk entered, and behind him followed the tiny figure of the kid.

"That's her!"

The man and the girl began to walk towards them along the walkway.

"Let's go," Mei Yin yanked her by the arm.

"We just have to wait here. We can take him. Get her out of here."

"*Now*, Anderson. That is an order. We may be partners, but I am still your superior. Understand?"

Breathing hard, Anderson clenched her shaking hands into fists, and let Mei Yin lead her out of that miserable place.

THEY STOOD IN a side street with a view of the access road, waiting for a street Judge to relieve them. The raid was planned for the following morning: they'd know by now that someone had been inside killing punks, but there was no way they could pack up the entire operation and leave in less than a day without the Judges knowing about it. If they started to come out in easy-to-capture groups, then so much the better. They'd never suspect a pair of Judges would leave without at least attempting to shut them down, so the best-case scenario right now was that they were just increasing security. Worst was that the top brass would flee, bringing the kid with him, but if that happened, they'd just nab him and that would be that.

A Judge turned up in under thirty minutes. Mei Yin filled him in on the specifics and told him to look out for the girl.

"She's about eight," Anderson elaborated, "unkempt curly hair and mid-brown skin. They'll be keeping her close. It is really important that she's taken into the Psi-Div junior home. They'll be expecting her, so—"

The Judge held up his hands. "I'll do my best. But there's, what, like a hundred squirts in there? We need Psi on this. How am I supposed to—"

"You won't get Psi-Div on this," Mei Yin interrupted. "So make sure you get it right. Come on, Anderson, let's get back to HQ and see what's what."

Five
WORTHY

THE ATMOSPHERE AT HQ was tense as they walked through to file their report. They were under strict orders to only work this case, so they needed to explain what they'd been doing all day. Groups of street Judges eyed them even more suspiciously than usual. They could tell something big was going down.

They'd find out soon enough, if the Cult of the Devourer had their way, along with every other living soul in Mega-City One.

They went to the infograb lab and downloaded the data streams from their holos, recording a brief audio report. As they were leaving, they bumped into Judge Chilton on his way in to the lab. He'd been partnered with Palmer earlier, Anderson remembered.

"Any news?" Chilton asked Mei Yin, leaning his broad-shouldered frame against the wall. A senior Judge, and only a few years younger than Mei Yin, he carried his age well; hair shaved off where it had started to thin, with a strong jaw and a rugged, worldly air to him.

Mei Yin shook her head. "We thought we were onto

something, but it turned out to just be a massive child-slave kidnapping ring."

He smirked. "That all?"

"We couldn't even stick around to lead the raid," Anderson added bitterly.

Chilton nodded sympathetically. "Them's the breaks." He shrugged. "But what can you do?"

At that moment they all staggered as a massive psychic wave shot through the building, bringing the Judges to their knees.

NOT WORTHY. NONE OF YOU. NONE OF YOU ARE WORTHY.

She slammed her psi-walls up and the attack faded to a lament, like a distant wail coldly lapping against her consciousness.

"They're here," she said, looking up to see the other two Judges had managed to overcome the onslaught as well.

"No, not quite," Chilton said, meeting Mei Yin's eyes.

"A Trojan horse?" Mei Yin asked, pushing herself to her feet.

"Think so. Come on, let's find out which poor idiot they've got to this time."

The sharp sound of blast fire echoed down the hall, and they ran towards the processing hall.

It was chaos. Norms with low-level psi-ability were writhing on the ground; the baselines were staring around them with incredulity, daysticks and Lawgivers drawn, trying in vain to figure out what was attacking their colleagues.

From the far side a door was flung open and four Psi-Judges—a quad—led by Judge Adjonyoh stumbled through, clearly using all their strength not be reduced to crawling on the floor.

"What the drokk is going on?" shouted a street Judge as Anderson, Mei Yin and Chilton skidded to a halt.

"He's through there," gasped Adjonyoh, the only member of the quad who hadn't slumped against the wall. "He just, he just—"

"Okay, Judge, we'll take it from here," Mei Yin said. "You—"

She turned to the street Judge who had spoken up before. "Get these people out of here, as far away from that corridor as you can. Now!"

Without waiting to see if her orders had been followed, she ran in the direction the quad had just fled from.

As they ran towards the source, Anderson could feel the power of the onslaught grow. All three of them began to slow their pace as they reinforced their barriers.

The quad chamber, with its padded scanning bays and small psionic amplifier, had a deep, throbbing, darkness of mind pulsing from it; they must be using the amplifier to project the attack. It felt as though she was pushing against a billowing wind. Chilton made it to the door first and took a step back in alarm.

"Palmer. Gruddamn it, no!"

Mei Yin gripped his shoulder as Anderson forced herself to take the final, agonising step to the door.

Palmer had both hands on the amplifier. His head was flung back, eyes wide and staring, his face a rictus of agony.

Without pausing Mei Yin crossed the room, pulled out her daystick and smacked him solidly across the temple. Anderson staggered as the pressure broke, the air snapping clear, leaving her panting in the silence that enveloped her. Palmer crumpled to the ground, unconscious.

Chilton was shaking his head.

"Impossible. He's been with me all day. How did they get to him?"

Mei Yin took a deep breath, and looked him in the eye. "I'm going to have to scan you, Chilton."

Anderson gasped. It was a deeply personal, deeply painful process to be scanned. A process that was only carried out under order of the Chief, and only ever in the direst circumstances, by an expert in the procedure.

"I'll go find the Chief," Anderson said, turning to leave.

"No," Chilton barked.

Anderson froze. Was Mei Yin right? Had they gotten to him?

"Do it now." He looked at Mei Yin. "There isn't time to go through the proper channels."

Anderson let out her breath as he took one of the quad bay seats. Mei Yin nodded grimly and went to stand in front of him, placing her hands on either side of his forehead.

"I'll wait outside," she said.

Chilton managed a small, grateful smile. "If these bastards are in my head, I want to know about it."

The minutes ticked past as Anderson took up a position in the hall. What sort of psycho mind game were they playing? And how had they planted such a sophisticated mind bomb in Palmer? Was there a chance that if, as Mei Yin feared, Chilton had something similar in his brain, she would accidentally set it off in the scanning process?

She shivered. The reality of Judge against Judge was finally hitting home. There would have to be a Division-wide scan after this. How were they supposed to function if they couldn't trust each other?

"He's clean," Mei Yin said as they left the room; Chilton looked pale and shaken, and Mei Yin not much better.

"They must have got to Palmer before the briefing." Chilton rubbed his face with both his hands. "He had that thing lying dormant within him all day."

"Maybe the amplifier was the trigger?" Anderson suggested.

Mei Yin nodded. "That makes a lot of sense. No point it going off unless he could cause maximum damage."

"Well, it didn't work," Anderson said. "Not how they wanted it to. We got to him in time to just make it a truly disturbing experience for all. But it was just a warning."

"Don't be so sure," Chilton said. "We better check on the norms affected. They may have had just enough psi ability to allow for an imprint. We may have lost some good Judges today."

* * *

IT TURNED OUT that twelve Judges needed to be sent to the med ward, and three had fallen into comas they might never wake up from. Chief Smee warily ordered a Division-wide scan, starting with the Judges on the scene. Lucky Anderson. At least she could get it over with, and the specialist wouldn't be worn out from carrying out too many of them yet.

Even so, it was just as gruddamn awful as she remembered. Like the complex pattern of her mind had been unraveled, pulled apart, scrutinised and thrown on the floor. She felt raw and exhausted as she stepped out of the med ward.

Judge Adjonyoh walked out behind her, looking pale.

"Gruddamn it, I hate those scans," she said, rubbing her temples.

Anderson nodded. "When was the last time you ate?" After what they'd both been through, some company would not go amiss.

Adjonyoh shrugged.

"Come on, let's get some grub."

Six

IMPLOSION EXPLOSION

ADJONYOH TOOK HER to her home turf near Nouvelle Block. There was a place that specialised in replica Old India food, and Anderson's mouth watered at the idea of a Bombay-Locust Pie. They sat out on the chipped, battered tables outside and waited with a couple of lassi shakes.

"These things used to be made with real bovine milk," Adjonyoh said.

Anderson grimaced. "Can't get over the idea of drinking another species' secretions."

Adjonyoh grinned and shrugged. "Well, whatever the hell they use to make it now, it tastes okay."

Anderson sat back as her spiced mealworm fritters were set down in front of her, and both of them were quiet while they ate. She really needed this—she hadn't had anything since before the briefing.

"Crazy about Palmer," Adjonyoh said, mopping up some sauce with the last of her chapatti.

"Mm." She didn't really want to think about Palmer.

"He was coming by to see Judge Devlo, wanted to check in

to see if we'd picked up anything in the quad. Always was too chatty, that guy."

Anderson smiled and shoved another fritter in her mouth.

"Then his eyes clocked the amplifier and he just—he just switched. It was like he'd been possessed." Adjonyoh shook her head.

"It's hard to believe something so powerful could have lain waiting in his mind to take over for so long." Anderson grimaced.

They were both silent for a moment.

"Well," Adjonyoh said, sitting back and stretching. "I hate those scans, but I'm sure as hell glad to know I'm clean."

Anderson felt something tug at the edges of her consciousness. Taking a slow breath, she leant her elbows on the table and rubbed her eyes.

We're being watched, she projected, training her frequency to a quiet, private dart.

Adjonyoh went completely still as she confirmed what Anderson had already picked up. *He's outside of that tech shop, about three doors down behind you.*

Anderson nodded.

"Well, I'm about done. If I don't get some sleep soon, I'm gonna pass out. Shall we walk off this food a bit first?" *Let's find out what he wants?*

"Sure, let's take a wander around the holo park, make sure everyone is behaving themselves."

As they passed him, he looked intently down at his data pad. He was young, probably a few years younger than Anderson, with very thin, lank brown hair, white-cheeked and pale. They felt his subtle psychic scrutiny as a tingle in their backs. He followed.

As soon as they had rounded the corner, Adjonyoh peeled off down a side street and Anderson slowed her pace. When she heard his foot scuff, she rounded on him. He froze, panicked, and turned to flee just as Adjonyoh showed up behind him.

Anderson felt him fling out a psychic field that made Adjonyoh stagger, and he ran. Anderson sighed and sped off after him, Adjonyoh close on her heels; Adjonyoh's longer stride let her lope past Anderson and gain on him.

"Wait!"

As soon as Adjonyoh got too close for comfort, he hurled another psi-dart at her. She faltered and fell to all fours as Anderson ran past her, whipped out her daystick and smacked him sharply around the back of the head, just as Mei Yin had dealt with Palmer mere hours ago.

The psychic pressure disappeared as he fell, and Anderson grabbed him by the collar, dropping her daystick and unclipping her blaster, forcing it up under his chin. She'd hit him hard enough to stun, but not to knock him out.

"If I sense so much as a psi-twitch, I'm gonna blow your head clean off—got that?"

He stared at her with wide, frightened eyes, and nodded.

"I'm charging you with evasion of justice: six months in the cubes. But I suspect we may be dealing with something a bit more serious than that, aren't we?"

She heard Adjonyoh calling for a catch-wagon to come pick up a suspected Devourer.

"Why were you following us?" She reflexively tried to dip into his mind to get the answer, but was met with an impenetrable wall. "I guess we'll have to do this the old way. Judge Adjonyoh, if you wouldn't mind?"

While Anderson held the blaster firmly under his chin, Adjonyoh whipped out her daystick and rammed it into his stomach. He cried out, gasping and struggling to breathe.

"Who are you?"

Another *thwack*, accompanied by a *crack* as Adjonyoh broke one of his ribs.

Anderson tried dipping into his mind again. This time the pain caused a chink in his armour.

He was supposed to follow them, nothing more, not until he could get her alone and call in more Devourers. Adjonyoh was their next target, due to get the full Palmer treatment.

Adjonyoh had seen it too.

"You drokking little—"

"Wait!" Anderson stopped her from delivering a killing blow to his temple at the last second. "We have to take him in. We need to juice him for every little detail he has on these sickos."

By the time the catch-wagon was there, Adjonyoh had calmed down a little, cuffing his hands behind his back.

It wasn't *his* hands that were the danger. Anderson's own hand was getting stiff from holding the blaster under his chin, her senses straining for the tiniest bit of psi-energy from him.

"Finally," she said to the driver. "This guy is a dangerous psychic. We need to get him dosed and out of it before we can think about moving him."

"No!" he sputtered. "Don't. Not drugs."

Ignoring him, the Judge moved in with a hypo spray gun ready to inject a high dose.

At that moment a change came over the Devourer. His gaze grew intense and beads of sweat began to form on his forehead.

"Hey!" Anderson shouted. But she couldn't feel him projecting anything. Whatever he was doing, it was only going on within him.

Suddenly, his eyes rolled back and his back arched, forcing Anderson to drop her blaster and try to hold him down. He strained, his jaw clenched, and then went limp.

"Woah, what *was* that?" Adjonyoh said.

Anderson strengthened her mental defences and plunged into his now-unconscious mind, trying to figure out what had just happened.

But it was no use.

"I'm not reading any electro-activity whatsoever." Anderson

looked up at Adjonyoh. "He's just performed a mental shutdown. He's completely braindead."

GOING BACK TO HQ was the last thing she wanted to do right now, but they had to accompany the body of the Devourer and make a report.

"That's one hell of a self-destruct," Adjonyoh said after they were done.

"Yep." Anderson felt flat. They'd come so close to gathering some useful information on these creeps, only to have the lead die in custody. It didn't look good. Chief Smee was livid, but she'd held back from blaming them.

They now had knockout drugs on them, to be carried at all times just in case they should happen upon catching one of the Devourers again. Anderson was skeptical. Lightning rarely struck twice.

"Right, Anderson." Adjonyoh gripped her shoulder. "Go and get some rest. You look like you need it."

"Thanks," Anderson replied, swinging her leg over her Lawmaster, "so do you."

Rest, she thought, as she drove away in the yellowing dawn. All she wanted to do was stumble into her sleep machine and shut the world out for a few sweet minutes. But that perp slipping through her fingers had left her wired and ready to do something *useful*.

The strike at the drugshop wouldn't have even happened yet. She turned off the highway and headed towards Axel block. So she wasn't supposed to be working any other cases. Well, all right then. She just wanted to passively make sure, in her down time, that they got that kid out and safely to the junior Psi-Div.

Seven

DART

SHE PULLED UP just as the team was moving in. They had a unit on the roof, two in the closest blocks and surrounding streets, and a hit team entering from all forty-seven ground-level entrances. Should do it.

As the doors were breached three huge catch-wagons and med-wagons pulled up, the drivers getting out and reporting to the Judge coordinating the raid.

"These for the kids?" Anderson asked him when he'd finished giving his instructions.

"Psi-Div?" he said, eyeing her badge. "Thought you guys were steering clear of this one."

"I'm not really here." She winked at him. "I called this one in. I just wanted to make sure you found that kid okay."

He nodded. "We got her description with every Judge currently barreling through that drugshop. No kids have left the building since the report came in. We'll get your girl."

Anderson thanked him and went to wait it out on her Lawmaster. The minutes ticked past, and she had to reign in her impatience: she should be in there, getting this done right.

That was a toxic warehouse, packed full of children. For all she knew it was highly flammable—probably was, going by the girl's memory of an explosion—and there was about to be a blast-fight going on over their heads.

BOOM.

Right on cue. But that hadn't come from the lower levels. The windows blew out on the fifth floor, flames billowing into the yellow night in a shower of broken glass.

No! I don't want to go with you!

The kid. Someone was using the blast as a distraction to get the kid out. Revving her engine, she shot past the commanding Judge, who barely noticed her in the commotion, and sped round the corner to where the call was coming from. Skidding to a halt, she fired up her cannons as a group of men and women ran out of a door in a cloud of black smoke, a struggling girl flung over one of their shoulders.

"Hold it right there!" she called, putting her lights on full beam to blind them. "Drop the kid and hit the dirt."

At that moment she was hit by a bolt of psionic energy, like being punched by a metal fist from the inside of her brain. In the second it took to recover and reinforce her defences they were gone, running towards a small black van with open doors. They dived in, and it started driving before they had shut the doors behind them.

She shot after them in pursuit.

"I need air support!" she yelled into her comm. "I'm tailing someone who just nabbed the kid I was after."

"I'm sorry, Judge, but I am unable to fulfill your request. All units are kind of busy right now. You'll have to deal with your one little girl by yourself."

"Gruddamn it, this is important. I think I'm dealing with"—she cut herself off before she told him about the Cult—"with the gang boss here."

It was a lie, but she needed the backup.

There was a pause. "*Okay. They're locking onto your comm signal now.*"

A blast exploded the rockcrete right behind her. Someone was leaning out of the back with a blast cannon aimed right at her. She couldn't return fire, not if she wanted to get that girl back alive.

She aimed her cannons at the overpass they were coming up on. It collapsed in a cloud of rockcrete dust and the van skidded to a halt.

She heard the distant whine of the sky-copter, but it was too far away.

"Give me the girl," she said through her voice-thrower.

The driver doors swung open and two figures emerged from the van. The instant she locked eyes with one, she realised her mistake. As three more figures stepped out of the back, she felt the pummeling force of their collected psi-energy barreling for her.

"Submit, Judge Anderson." It was a man with pure white hair in an immaculate suit. The scariest thing about him was the calm, almost gentle look on his face, destroyed by the cold madness of his eyes. "I've had my eye on you. You're strong. Ever so strong. But not strong enough to withstand us." He shook his head sadly. "It is a great shame. The things we could have achieved together. But we've learnt our lessons the hard way. There is no recovery from the brutal programming you suffered at the Academy. No, the only kind thing to do is to disable you."

A small, scared face stared at her from the darkness of the van. Her eyes were big and her brown skin was streaked with soot.

Help me! she screamed, mind-to-mind, before the white-haired man turned to her.

Anderson was driven to her knees with the weight of the psychic energy as the five Devourers all focussed their abilities on her. But they weren't *doing* anything with her. It was like they were holding her down. Ready for the white-haired man to—do what?

The kid was silently crying now, her head held in her hands.

"What... did... you... do... to her?" She forced the words through her clenched teeth.

"Quiet," he snapped. And she felt her tongue clamped painfully between her teeth. "She is safe now. Safe from you. Exactly where she should be. It isn't too late for her. Unlike you—"

He turned to her, then, and she felt the talons of their minds begin to tear into her. She thought she screamed, but she couldn't be sure if it was out loud or in her mind. It was as if they were pulling her apart with their bare hands. She couldn't withstand it. This was it, this was how it ended.

Light flared and a harsh wind washed blessedly over her as their attention was drawn to the sky. Backup. She slumped to the ground as she felt them let her go.

"She's done," she heard his crisp tone declare.

Was she? She couldn't feel her body, the raw pain of her ravaged mind was the only thing she was aware of as she slipped into darkness.

No. You've killed her!

The kid. She heard the doors slamming, the engine rev as they backed up and drove around her bike.

Kid! From the recesses of her failing self she flung out a psi-dart. But whether or not it hit its mark was out of her control. She hadn't the strength to guide it.

And then there was only darkness.

Eight

SUNKEN CITY

SHE WAS COLD. Her arms were, anyway. And thirsty. Really, really thirsty. She blinked her eyes open and shut them again quickly. It was too bright.

"She's awake."

Where was she? The last thing she could remember was the blinding light of the sky-copter. Had she passed out?

The kid. They were getting away!

Squeezing her eyes shut against the glare she tried to push herself up, but her arms were caught in something.

"Kid... I gotta get her. They're taking her away."

"Anderson?"

Drokk! What the hell was Mei Yin doing here? Had she followed her? She was in serious trouble.

"Go after them. Tell the 'copter to follow the van—"

"Anderson, they're gone. It's over. What the hell were you—?"

"No! You can't let them have her. You can't—"

"This is too much. I'm putting her back under. I won't have her this distressed."

Who was that? Not Mei Yin.

"Listen. *Listen* to me." She tried to open her eyes again. "Gruddamn it, tell that sky-copter to shine its lights somewhere else."

"There's no sky-copter, you thick-skulled idiot."

Mei Yin had such a way with words.

But it didn't matter. Nothing mattered. She was flooding with calm.

"We're lucky she *has* such a thick skull," the other voice said.

So relaxed. She sighed, and fell back into oblivion.

"OKAY, IT'S TIME to wake up, Anderson. Prescribed rest period over."

Anderson opened her eyes to Mei Yin's scowling face looking down at her.

"Wha—?" She tried to reach up and rub her eyes, but couldn't. Looking down, she saw that she was on a med-bunk, her arms and legs strapped down.

"What the—?"

"Just until you're ready for a scan. Grud knows what they left in that screwed-up little head of yours."

"What happened?"

"You were found unconscious next to a destroyed overpass. Meds on the scene assumed you'd had a blow to the head, but they've ruled that out now. It was a psychic that did this."

Hence the restraints.

"What in the name of the *Law* did you think you were doing going back there? Do you realise you've explicitly disobeyed a direct order? You went to work on another case, and now you are useless against the Devourers. You could get time for this."

"They were there. I was on the case."

Mei Yin huffed.

"That's what I told them, and Chief Smee has graciously deigned to agree, so you're off the hook. *This* time."

Anderson nodded gratefully. "They knew she was there. Must have got it from us—our coms—or maybe they have spies in Street-Div. Gruddamn it, we led them straight to her."

Mei Yin's lips became a hard, thin line.

"We should have been on this as soon as the first Judge went nuts. They've already got their putrid tentacles into us."

Mei Yin was right. If their superiors had been quicker to admit this was the Devourers, maybe it never would have got this far.

"I'm ready."

"Ready for what?"

"The screening. I have to get out of here. They have her, and we don't know what they're doing with her."

"Screening? You're not ready for that yet. You're too weak for anything. Disobeying an order might not have led you to the cubes—this time—but it sure as hell rendered you useless to me."

Anderson took a deep breath, closed her eyes, and focused. *There!*

"I can find them."

"Sure you can. Especially now you're strapped to a med-bunk."

"I got a psi-dart out to the kid. I can follow the link. She'll lead us right to them."

Mei Yin looked genuinely lost for words. Then a slow smile crept over her face.

"Good work, kid. I'll go fetch the head doctor."

THE SECOND SCREENING was the cherry on the cake of the pile of steaming turd that had been the last twenty-four hours, but it was a relief to know she was clean. She'd tried to tell them that the Devourers were trying to kill her, they weren't setting a ticking time bomb in her shredded brain, but at least now she was sure. A shower and a bowl of syntha-noodles later, and she was dressed and leading Mei Yin through the lower reaches of the Quitz district, following the faint pull of her psi-dart as it led their Lawmasters a winding path downtown.

"They're moving," Anderson shouted into her comm. "They must have hid out in a safe house last night, or maybe something spooked them."

"*Can you follow the trail?*" Mei Yin yelled back.

Anderson nodded an affirmative.

But the thread was actually getting stronger. The kid was being moved closer to them. But then it veered off and wound along the high wall that used to line the river that had fed the old city, now nothing more than a dried-up junk-strewn trickle.

Finally, they were looking at the dark, stinking, unwelcoming entrance to the sunken city. It was a maze of tunnels, originally used for commuter trains back when people lived in the country outside of the city limits, in land that had now either been swallowed by the city or turned into toxic desert. Either way the tunnels had long since fallen out of use. Cue the lowest dregs of society moving in and turning it into a hellish, subterranean town. It had been emptied out time and again by the Judges—there was no safe way to enforce the Law down there—but people always managed to creep back in and rebuild.

Judges generally thought of its inhabitants as scum, but Anderson couldn't help respecting their resourcefulness. Amongst the gang-bangers, drugheads and pure criminals, there were cits down here too. Poor people, families that would be forced into the cubes for vagrancy if they hadn't come here. She saw the sunken city as a symptom of a broken system. Not that she would say that too loudly around another Judge.

"Seriously?" Mei Yin asked, pulling off her helmet.

Anderson just nodded.

"I was part of the first clearance. Never thought I'd have to go back into this sewer again."

Anderson got off her bike. "Never say never."

The Lawmasters would have to stay behind. There were no clear roads down there, and besides, they didn't exactly want to announce their arrival.

"I'm gonna call this in, find out if a quad has detected any activity from here. And get some backup. If this is it, we're gonna need it."

"Don't you want to be sure first? This might not be their HQ; it could just be a safe house or something."

"Could be, but we've seen what they're capable of now. I didn't think it was possible, but they're stronger than they were the first time round. If they can take you down—"

"But they didn't. I'm still here."

"Barely." Mei Yin looked her in the eye. "It was close, Anderson. If they hadn't been interrupted, who knows what would have happened?"

"I'm stronger than you think."

"Are you? 'Cause I think you're pretty gruddamn strong. I don't know many Judges who could have survived what they did to you. And that's what's got me spooked. If a Judge of your power can't withstand them, what chance do the rest of us have?"

Anderson took some deep breaths and rolled her shoulders as Mei Yin spoke to Control. Despite saying she was ready, she really did feel as though she'd been torn apart and taped back together again.

"Okay, they're sending a psi-squad. We should wait for them before we go in."

"Agreed."

They settled in to wait, watching the foot traffic tramp in and out of the patchwork entrance. It was a large tunnel that had been crowded with stalls and the odd food cart, selling scavenged junk and broken tech. A few cits were eyeing them warily, but a couple of Judges hanging around outside couldn't have been unheard of. They were probably just wondering whose time was up, and hoping it wasn't anyone they knew.

After about fifteen minutes, a shabby-looking little man dressed in a suit about three times too big for him strode out purposefully, his feet taking him on a direct path to them.

"That's close enough," Mei Yin drawled, putting her hand to her daystick.

He stopped and held up his hands. "My name is Travis McMillan and I am the elected leader of the Sunken City market traders. I just wanted to come out and see if there was anything I could help you with."

"Help us?" Mei Yin repeated. "And what could you possibly do that would be of any use?"

He took the burn on the chin. "I just don't want there to be any violence. We've seen enough of that down here, and people are tired."

"Plus it can't be good for business," Anderson said.

"That's true." He smiled nervously. "Look, whoever it is you're looking for, wouldn't it be easier if we could help you find them? Rather than charging in and knocking in teeth until someone talks."

It wasn't this guy's first rodeo.

"Didn't think the Sunken City would be very friendly to snitches," Mei Yin countered.

"No, and you'd be right. But after the last clear-out, we decided that we needed to do things differently. If you bring the Law in, then on your own head be it. Don't drag the rest of us down with you."

"Well, in that case—" Mei Yin reached out and touched the top of his greasy head. Before he could protest, she dropped into his mind, projecting what she found to Anderson as she did so.

The people in the Sunken City were rattled. There was some sort of low-level anxiety making everyone jumpy. Well, maybe not everyone. Probably just those with some level of psychic ability.

"Anyone go missing lately?" she prompted him.

Worried parents at meetings. Those who had kids of screening age. A stallholder whose six-year-old grandson had gone missing.

Mei Yin met her eyes. Sounded about right.

The older Judge let him go, and he staggered back. "There was no need for that. I would have told you anything you wanted to know."

"Sorry." Mei Yin didn't sound sorry. "It was quicker this way."

"When is that backup getting here?" Anderson said, eyeing the entrance. "Tell them to stop a few blocks away and make the rest of their way on foot. We don't want them announcing their entrance."

Anderson turned to Travis, who was looking simultaneously pale and indignant, as Mei Yin called in the instructions. "Did anyone unusual come through here recently? We're looking for a girl—"

He was about to answer when his head exploded in a shower of bone and blood.

Anderson lost her connection to the kid.

As both Judges dived behind their Lawmasters and activated their defences, the fiery heavens opened and erupted upon them, lighting up the twin spheres of the shielding zone around them.

"Ha!" Mei Yin's voice was full of excitement. "Never had a chance to use this new shielding in the field—it's impressive!"

"Well, I'm glad you're having fun," Anderson replied, aiming her Lawgiver in the direction the firework show was coming from.

Mei Yin hopped onto her Lawmaster and trained her sight just above the flaring source.

"You'll bring the whole entrance down!"

"Exactly!"

"Wait!"

Anderson was relieved to see her actually pause.

"There are cits in there—the *kid* could be there..."

Mei Yin huffed like an impatient teenager. "Fine, you got a better idea?"

"Yeah." Anderson flicked her hair out of her eyes and locked in her cannons. "Follow my lead."

She hit the gas and drove straight into the fire, hoping that the shields could withstand this level of close-range heat. It was like driving down a corridor of lasers. An orange warning light started to flash.

But now she could see two men with mounted rapid-fire blasters set up just inside the tunnel entrance.

"Red warning! The shields won't take much more of this," Mei Yin yelled through the comm.

The moment she was close enough to see the spittle flying as the men cursed and shot, she set her bike cannon to concentrated burst and fried one of them, his chest obliterated in molten flesh before his corpse even hit the ground. Mei Yin took care of the second by blowing his head clear of his body.

Two shots flared on her shield in a feeble anticlimax as a third figure made his escape into the dark jumble of stalls, the cits quivering behind counters and barrels and whatever cover they could find.

Jumping off her bike, Anderson gave chase, hearing Mei Yin yelling into her comm that the backup needed to drive right into the entrance and fast. They were going in.

This was a nightmare of a place for a Judge to find herself chasing down a perp, let alone a group of psycho psychics. The air was thick with the smoke of cook fires and the stench of unwashed people living in the damp close confines of the underground labyrinth. Further in, makeshift shacks were tacked together to make tiny homes. Swathes of ragged fabric hung between them; strings of tiny coloured lights blinked over narrow corridors between the huts.

The perp swung a left and Anderson skidded to a halt, aiming around the bend before following, just in time to see him ducking behind one of the larger, sturdier-looking houses. She ducked as he shot at her before disappearing again.

"I'll go around," wheezed Mei Yin from behind her.

Anderson nodded and moved with her back close to the hut wall, fully aware that the sleazebag was probably just a decoy as the rest of them got away. She counted in her head. There had been five last night escaping with the girl, met by two more in the van. With two of them down and this guy leading them a merry chase, that still left four of them somewhere with the girl.

They hadn't tried a mental attack yet, which was a relief. Perhaps two Psi-Judges posed too much of a challenge.

She twisted sharply around with the corner cannon aimed for a killing shot, only to come face-to-face with Mei Yin.

"Drokk it!"

They both pivoted, trying to see where he could have disappeared to. They were in a small, darkened makeshift square, where a number of huts backed onto each other. Laundry was strung between them, forming a limp shadowy ceiling where the dim light didn't penetrate.

"Hello, Mei Yin."

Anderson trained her gun on the man who had just appeared, as if he had materialised from the thin, dusty air, at the edge of the darkness behind them.

Mei Yin, on the other hand, had frozen, her arm hanging loosely by her side.

It was the man from last night, the leader, dressed again in a clean, expensive-looking light grey suit, his shock of white hair striking against the grubbiness around him.

"Where is the girl?" Anderson demanded.

He ignored her.

"It's been a long time, Mei Yin. You're looking... old."

"Howl, how is this—you're—?" Mei Yin trailed off. She shook her head. "You're dead!"

His mouth curled in a half-smile.

"Not quite. Karlul saved me. He was not finished with me yet."

Anderson was appalled to see that Mei Yin was shaking.

"Okay, that's enough small talk." Anderson projected her laser sight at his forehead, purely for effect. She didn't need it at this close quarters. In fact, this was definitely a shoot-first-ask-questions-later situation.

As her finger tensed against the trigger, she was hit by a psychic force so strong she instantly fell to her knees. He turned his cold pale eyes on her, and smiled.

In that moment, Mei Yin seemed to come out of her trance. She whipped her hand down and gripped Anderson's shoulder tightly, and immediately the pressure eased as they linked, Mei Yin's extraordinary power feeding her strength.

She looked up as three figures, two women and the man she had just been chasing, emerged from the darkness. She recognised one of the women from last night, but the kid was nowhere to be seen. They must have knocked her out as soon as they realised she was linked—she was probably unconscious somewhere, guarded by the seventh disciple.

All thoughts of the girl were driven from her mind as the cult members breathed in in unison and hit them with a vicious psychic attack. Mei Yin's fingers dug into her shoulder as the two of them braced themselves against the onslaught with everything they had. It was as if the weight of the earth above them was bearing down on their defences. Gritting her teeth, she pushed herself to her feet to stand shoulder-to-shoulder with her partner, and braced herself.

Gather your strength, Mei Yin projected. *In 3, 2—*

Together they slammed into the driving forces with a focused, needle-sharp precision, finding the weakest point and tearing a hole. Anderson shot a dart through it, and was rewarded by the man that she'd been chasing collapsing to the ground.

The opening slammed shut as the leader—Howl—snarled with frustration.

"It's no use, Mei Yin. We've been here before, haven't we?"

Mei Yin let out a ragged cry, and Anderson sensed her focus waver, before her defences seemed to grow even stronger.

"That was a long time ago. You'll never—"

A pulse as she sent out an attack aimed at his core.

"—get the better of me—"

She was gathering her resources, pulling strength from Anderson as she readied herself.

"—again!"

Her attack exploded in a wave of anger and pain, pummeling their three assailants with pure psychic acid.

One of the women screeched as she fell to the ground in a heap. Anderson wouldn't have been surprised to see steam rising from her scorched brain.

But at that moment the final woman showed up.

Anderson felt her presence behind her as a thrumming static, and twisted just in time to see her raise her hands and slam her psychic power at them.

Caught in a pincer between the two forces, it was all Anderson could do to hold them back. Mei Yin had used up too much of their strength in her attack. Perhaps that had been his intention in goading her.

Mei Yin staggered and broke contact, severing their link.

Anderson grunted as the assault began to shake her barriers.

"Mei Yin!"

The older Judge was breathing hard, her eyes locked with Howl as he advanced on her. She began to shake her head, back and forth, as if mere denial would stop him.

"You're not worthy, are you, Mei Yin?"

She did nothing but continue to shake her head.

The pressure was too much. Howl's power seemed to buckle the air around him, blurring him into slow motion.

"Say it with me," his lips moved, his speech drawn out, insidious as it smacked into Mei Yin's defences.

"I."

Mei Yin opened her mouth, but did not form the word.

"Am."

She let out a ragged breath. "No!"

"—Unworthy."

"*NO!*" Mei Yin erupted in a mushroom cloud of force, driving him back two steps.

But her power then seemed to invert, curling back in on itself as it formed a shielding, suffocation cloud around her body. Tremors started at her hands, then overcame her, and she fell to the earth in a twitching pile of limbs.

"Mei Yin!"

Anderson leapt to stand over her, spread her hands and screamed her rage as her last vestiges of strength were hurled at the Devourers.

"You can't keep that up for long!" Howl shouted.

Then something came over them. The woman behind her ran around Anderson and grabbed hold of his arm.

"Master! They come!"

Howl looked Anderson deep in the eyes as she stood over a now limp Mei Yin, his ice-filled stare now burning with hatred.

"This isn't finished," he spat, before merging once more into the darkness.

They'd gone? What had forced them away? It certainly hadn't been her.

And then Judges poured into the space as backup finally arrived. Anderson fell to her knees and pulled Mei Yin into her lap.

"That way," she managed to gasp, pointing to where she thought Howl had gone.

She felt at Mei Yin's pulse points. She was still breathing faintly.

"I need a medic!"

It was all she could do to drag herself away as they got a resuscitation unit on her, and watch as they pulled Mei Yin onto a stretcher.

She wasn't surprised to hear, as they loaded her into a medwagon, that the Devourers had disappeared without a trace.

"We took two of them down, though," she whispered to Mei Yin's still form.

Nine

THE SEA

ANDERSON SHIFTED ON the hard metal seat next to Mei Yin's bed—
it was like they didn't want you to get too comfy or something—
and looked around the med bay. Clean, but battered white walls
and tiled floors, a sharp medical smell and the distant beeps and
whirs of medical machinery. It had been less than a day since
she'd been here laying in a med-bunk. She was starting to get
way too familiar with this place.

Had she looked so small, though? Mei Yin didn't need a
respirator, but a nutrient drip had been punched into her arm,
which was worrying. How long did they think she'd be like
this?

"Hey."

She jumped as Judge Chilton came in holding a luminous
green bottle.

"Thought you could do with some jump juice."

"Thanks." She twisted off the top and took a syrupy swig.
"What are you doing here?"

"I came in to report and heard about Mei Yin. Just wanted to
come by and see how bad it is."

"Yeah, that's what I'd like to know. No one is telling me anything."

"What happened out there?" Chilton leant on the door frame.

"I don't know. One minute we were linked and facing down four Devourers, and drokk is she *strong*. I wouldn't have made it if it hadn't been for her. But then—something their leader said spooked her. She overspent and then just sort of imploded. Shut down. I've never seen anything like it."

Chilton took a deep breath. "I have. What was it you think triggered this—episode?"

Anderson pushed her hair back from her forehead, trying to remember. "Something about having been here before. They seemed to know each other. She called him Howl."

Chilton hissed and straightened. "Howl. You gruddamn bastard."

"You know this guy?"

He looked up and shook himself. "Come outside, we need to talk."

THEY LEFT THE ward and headed to the high balcony on floor 102. Anderson was glad of the air and to get away from the chemical med-bay smell. Chilton went to lean on the balustrade and Anderson joined him, letting her eyes drift over the sea of lights below them.

"So who is this creep? And what the hell's going on with Mei Yin?"

Chilton took a deep breath. "Sorry, it's hard to talk about. For any of us that lived through it. Palmer brought it all back today."

"Drokk. With everything that's been going on—I didn't even ask you how he was doing."

Chilton shook his head. "The same as the rest of them.

Strapped to a bed while he raves about being unworthy. I don't think there's anything to be done."

She bit her lip. They had to stop this thing before anyone else got hurt. It had been a close call with Adjonyoh, and now Mei Yin was out of action. She waited for him to continue.

"Back then, no one was safe. We didn't have the screening process down—there was no way to know who had been turned and who hadn't. People were going missing, turning up dead. You couldn't even trust your own partner—"

"Look, if the high-ups had put two and two together a bit earlier, instead of twiddling their thumbs and keeping it to themselves, the Devourers never would've got to Palmer. Not with you around."

Chilton smiled. "I appreciate that. But I wasn't talking about him."

He paused, as if deciding whether to go on.

"You might have noticed, but Mei Yin, she keeps people at arm's length."

Anderson actually snorted before she could stop herself. "You're telling me."

He grinned, but it quickly fell from his weathered face.

"She doesn't do partners at all, actually. Not until you, anyway."

"It was grudgingly, believe me." Anderson turned her back to the city and leant back onto the barrier. "I'm hard to get rid of."

"Well." He turned towards her. "She has good reason not to trust a partner. Back then, she was young, and partnered with another young Judge. He was confident, talented—and pretty good-looking, too, if my memory serves. The rules were less strict back then about Judges being off-limits to each other, and rumour was at the time that they were involved. Drokk, I think everyone was a bit in love with him."

He let his gaze drift away as if looking into the past. "I was younger. All I wanted was to be like him one day." He shook his head. "I'm gruddamn lucky I turned out about as different from the worm as can be. At the height of the Devourer thing, our strongest two Psi-Judges disappeared. We all feared the worst, but we didn't know just how bad it was until months later, when we found Mei Yin.

"Her partner had revealed himself to her as the very leader of the Devourer Cult. But he *did* love her, in his own twisted way. He kept her locked up for months, torturing her day-in and day-out to try and turn her to the cause. But she was too strong for him.

"When the Cult was finally overcome, and they'd destroyed every member, they found her in their lair, catatonic. She'd managed a level of mental shielding beyond stopping others from getting at her from the outside. She sealed herself in."

"Her own partner did that to her?" Anderson broke in, horrified. The trust shared between partners was sacred. She couldn't even imagine what that would be like mixed up with a romantic attachment. Perhaps that was why they were so strict against it now.

Chilton nodded. "And that partner was Judge Howl."

ANDERSON FELT SICK, and it wasn't just the lack of sleep, her pounding head and the sugar surging through her from the jump juice. She'd left Chilton on the balcony and went to splash some water on her face in the washrooms.

No wonder Mei Yin had trust issues. She wouldn't want a partner either if something like that had happened to her. But they *were* partners. She felt as though a bond had formed over the past few days—a grudging respect growing.

Which meant she just couldn't afford to let her down.

She marched back to the med ward, determined to put things right.

"Hey," she said to the first medic that crossed her path. "I need to talk to Judge Mei Yin's doc. Now."

The medic put a data pen behind her ear and pushed her glasses up her nose. "We're pretty busy here, if you hadn't noticed. All the Psi-Docs have been worked off their feet. Now that Judge Mei Yin is stable, Doctor Marks is attending to one of his many other patients."

Anderson squared her shoulders and looked menacingly into the smaller woman's eyes.

"Did I not make myself clear? This is a judicial matter of the utmost importance. And"—she stepped in—"I'm gonna start making a fuss if you don't get him right away."

The woman took a step back. "How dare—"

"Calm down, please, the cavalry's here."

Anderson turned to see a short, somewhat rotund man with greying hair and a rumpled quality to him step out from an office. "It is I! Psi-Doc Marks. What's up?"

She was a little taken aback by his demeanour, but managed to blurt out, "What are you doing to break through Mei Yin's shielding?"

He rocked back on his heels. "Ah. Judge Anderson, I take it?"

She nodded, and followed him as he swept past her on his short legs towards Mei Yin's room.

Mei Yin was exactly as she'd left her: still, limp, and faintly breathing.

"She looks positively sweet like this, doesn't she?" he said, walking around the bed and turning to face Anderson.

"Look, this isn't the first time she's been like this, is it?" Anderson demanded. "So you must have it on file how to get her out, right?"

He touched his wrist and projected a file from his holo into the air above Mei Yin's body.

The vid was of a young Mei Yin, pretty, her hair long, dark and sleek like her niece's had been, sitting limply in a chair, staring into space.

"This was taken a month after she was rescued," Marks said.

"There were no Psi-Docs then, just norms doing their best. But with the help of a few specialists, it took them this long to merely get her to open her eyes."

He changed the file, this time showing an older woman holding either side of her forehead, her eyes boring into Mei Yin's in concentration.

"This is three months after rescue. They'd given up trying to break through her barrier by this point and were trying a new technique. It was a mind-to-mind melding; very tricky work, especially back then. It calls for the Psi-Doc to enter into a state of absolute calm, then bring down their own mental barriers. They must become both completely vulnerable and at the same time a haven of tranquility.

"They then had to send soft waves of clarity to her, inviting her to come to them. It is a slow, painstaking, highly skilled procedure, and one that we do not at this moment have the resources for."

"But it's different this time. She hasn't been tor—"

She cut herself off.

"No, she hasn't been tortured this time," Doc Marks finished for her.

Well, he obviously didn't care about privacy that much—she actually couldn't believe he had just shown her those files.

"But her body," he continued, "her mind, remembers. Her neural plasticity was forever changed by what was done to her. There must have been something that made her subconscious think that she was about to experience it again. I'd imagine it was an involuntary post-traumatic response."

Well, that did make a lot of sense.

"Not some*thing*," Anderson said, "some*one*. He was there. The man that did this to her before."

Doc Marks' eyes widened and he wrapped his arms around his body, nodding vigorously.

"Ah, yes. That would do it, all right."

"But don't you see?" Anderson leant across the bed and grabbed him by the shoulders. "That's why it is so important we get her out of this, and fast. Judge Howl is alive. And she's the one Judge left that knows everything about him."

Doc Marks cleared his throat, and she realised that she was almost nose-to-nose with him as they both leant precariously over Mei Yin's prone form.

She let him go, and he made a point of straightening his hopelessly creased white sleeves.

"Let us say that I agree with you. Let us say that I want to help you. What can we do? There is no one available right now, that has the psi-strength or the capacity for calm, who could attempt it."

"What about you?"

"Ha!" he said, his face creasing into a smile before quickly changing to something more serious. "Well, I'm flattered, but I know my limits. I'd need to ready my mind, meditate, take a week at the spa—"

"How about you cut the crud, give me the info and I'll get this done myself?"

He paused, clasping his arms behind his back and looking above him as if for inspiration. "Are you a particularly—*calm* person?"

She took a deep breath.

"I take your point. But if I have to learn how to gruddamn *fly* for this woman, I'll give it my best shot."

TWO HOURS AND a crash course in mind-to-mind healing later, and Anderson sat again on the hard metal chair beside Mei Yin's still form.

Doc Marks had shut the door, closed the blinds and dimmed the lights. He brought out a vaporiser that pumped some sort of mild relaxant into the air, and came to stand behind her, his hands resting lightly on her shoulders.

It would have helped if the whole thing didn't feel completely ridiculous—this was all in aid of calming *her* down, not Mei Yin. But that's what it was going to take. Mental transference of her calm, safe, welcoming reality onto Mei Yin's dark, dangerous, frightening one.

"Okay, Anderson. Breathe in, slow and deep. Make sure you get a real lungful."

She could really do without his quirky turn of phrase right now.

"Let go of your pain, let go of your fear, let go of the fighting, the psi-bombs and blood, the enemy attacks."

"You're not helping. The whole point is to *not* think of that stuff."

"Just breathe it all out, Anderson. Breathe it out."

She tried. She focused on the feeling of the heavy, vapour-filled air as it went into her lungs, letting it out slowly. Whatever was in it was actually working—she could feel her muscles uncoiling, the tension in her shoulders ebbing, the tight, anxious knot that she always carried in her chest ease.

"Now imagine your safe place," Doc Marks' voice broke in, jolting her out of the calm she'd found. "I'm going to leave you on your voyage sailing the tranquil waters of the river ease, may the oars of your mind not leave so much as a ripple on the crystal—"

"I'll show you where my oars go if you don't leave me alone, Doc."

"Calm, Anderson, calm and peace and ease," he responded to her threat. "Now. As soon as you feel that perfect moment of golden peace, begin the mental transference."

She kept her eyes closed and heard the door click quietly as he left.

"I know, I look ridiculous," she told Mei Yin. "But I'm doing this for you. Don't judge me." She grinned at her own joke.

Okay. Time to get serious.

She deepened her breathing again, felt herself drop into the place of calm she'd nearly felt before. Now to picture her safe place. That was the trickiest part. She'd really struggled to come up with somewhere she felt safe. Finally, she settled with riding her Lawmaster along a long, straight, empty road, returning from the Cursed Earth the year before. The hot wind was throwing her hair back, she'd just wrapped up a case and she wasn't driving anywhere in particular. Just the motion and the speed and the wind—it was almost like she was flying.

Then an image of that guy Travis's head exploding flashed into her mind from nowhere. Gruddamn it.

She started again with the breathing, building herself up to that beautiful empty highway—and then Palmer was filling her mind with his mental agony as he projected his psi-bomb over HQ. Start again.

Again. And again. The hours ticked away.

Finally, she was on that highway, and it *felt right*. She was safe, she was warm, she was happy.

Slowly, she reached a hand out to rest on Mei Yin's forehead, and begun the process of mental transference. Her own mind ebbed as she soaked slowly into Mei Yin's. She felt herself slide off impenetrable barriers.

A sheer, polished stone wall rose up beside her endless road. She tried not to react, just kept driving, feeding her peace out so that it washed over the wall.

They stayed like this for what felt like a long time. The driving, the wind, the freedom of the open road.

That was strange. There was a tree on the side of the escarpment; a pine, she realised as she drove past it. And there was another one, taller than the first. They began to rise up from the earth around her, and a sweet, clean, earthy smell rose from their deep green branches.

A forest. Guess inner foliage ran in the family.

She was now driving down a tunnel of trees. The wind still blew beautifully through her hair, and her calm was deepened by the fresh cool air of the wood.

The road narrowed, and began to wind down a steep incline. Anderson's breath was taken away at the next bend, when she was met by a vast, glistening, deep blue body of water. Was that—was that the sea?

The road ended on a grey pebbled beach. The trees stretched their long boughs over as if reaching for the water.

Getting off her Lawmaster, she walked towards the small figure sitting on a boulder under the protective boughs, staring out to sea.

She had her knees up hugged to her chest, rocking slightly. And she was young, maybe the same age as Anderson.

"Mei Yin," Anderson said softly.

The girl shook her head, keeping her eyes on the sea.

"It's okay. You're safe. No one's going to hurt you."

She continued to rock, holding herself tightly.

Anderson stepped closer to her and carefully laid her hand on her shoulder. The girl flinched and ducked her head, and Anderson let go.

"It's okay, it's me. Anderson. You remember me? I might be annoying, but I have your back. I'm your partner—"

"Partner?" Mei Yin whipped her head around and stared angrily into her eyes. "Partner?" She stood up, so that the boulder was between them. "I'll show you what a *partner* does."

The beach was gone. They were in a small, dark room, empty but for a mattress and a stinking bucket. Mei Yin was huddled at the back of the sorry excuse for a bed, eyes wide and pinned to the door as she heard it unlock. In stepped a young, pretty blond man. His cleanliness made Mei Yin feel ashamed of her filthiness, even though he was responsible for it.

"My love."

Her stomach clenched with anguish and hatred. Those words

used to fill her with something so pure, so hopeful. Now they made a mockery of everything she thought they shared. She'd been pathetic to have loved him.

She was pathetic to love him still.

He took a few steps in, and it was all she could do to meet his eyes.

"I have such wonderful news, Yinny," he said, kneeling on the edge of the mattress.

She flattened herself against the wall. *Yinny.* She'd always hated that gruddamn name.

"Karlul wants to meet you. I told Him all about the little misunderstanding we've had. But I've assured Him we're ready to put all that behind us."

She was shaking her head. "No. Please. I don't want to do that again."

His benign smile fell. "Do what again, Mei Yin? You only just arrived yesterday. We had an argument. Remember? We both said some things I know we didn't mean."

Every time the same. He would act as if this was the first time, the only time, he had subjected her to this. She'd come to understand that in his twisted mind it was a way of having a fresh start. She had to admit his level of denial was impressive.

She didn't struggle this time as the two Renfields—psychic slaves—dragged her down the grotty hall to the chamber, and strapped her into the cold, metal chair.

Inside she was building her defences, reinforcing her walls, drawing them up over her frailty.

"Ah, to commune with a god. Yinny, how did we ever get so lucky?"

He reached down and pulled the lever that let power flow into the chair.

Anderson, there but not there, watched as Mei Yin's body began to jerk. Was it some sort of psychic amplifier?

Howl pulled back the lever and as her body stilled, he snagged a metal disk suspended from the ceiling, flashing with lights, and pressed it to her forehead.

Then Mei Yin stiffened, and her eyes rolled back into her head.

No, it was worse than that. The disk was the psychic amplifier; the chair was some sort of electrical shock device. She'd read about the old-world treatment for mental ailments, but this was not a healing. This was to weaken her body and mind, to open her up like a cracked egg before the psychic amplifier blasted whatever evil influence it channeled into her. Minutes passed with Howl bent eagerly over her body.

"Submit to Him, my darling Yinny. Submit."

Her eyelids began to flutter, and he scowled, removed the amplifier and pulled the lever down. Mei Yin began to convulse again.

Anderson couldn't stand it.

"This isn't happening right now, Mei Yin. You survived this. You were stronger than him. This is over. It's done."

"It's never done." Mei Yin stood beside her, the now Mei Yin, her grey hair cropped short, her body broader.

Anderson bit her lip.

"You were stronger than him then, and you're stronger than him now."

They were back on the beach. Mei Yin sat on her boulder again, this time in her true form.

"I wasn't. He was there and he—it was like before. He always had such power over me."

"No, he didn't." Anderson knelt down beside her. "The only thing you could do last time was retreat. Build your blockades and resist. You had to be so strong to withstand that. I am amazed that you did."

Mei Yin shook her head. "I trusted him and he—he was *too strong*. I was a fool."

"No. *He* is the fool. *He* is the weak one. He has let some monster from another dimension possess him. Feed his pride with promises of power. You would never, ever be that weak." Anderson took a deep breath. "Now is the time to fight, Mei Yin. Now is the time to take your revenge for every moment of pain that he gave you."

"Revenge. There is no peace in revenge. I thought he was dead already. It didn't help me then and it won't help me now."

"Maybe not. But it would help me." Anderson stood up, taking a calming breath whilst staring into the glare off that rolling, beautiful sea.

"We need you, Mei Yin. *I* need you."

Mei Yin looked up at her. Shook her head.

"I will not face him again. And there is nothing you can do to change my mind."

Anderson gasped as she was flung back into her body, opening her eyes to the med ward. Mei Yin was gone. Her body was here, but her mind was no nearer to being healed than it was before she started this damn psychic transference business.

She pushed her stiff body up, cracked her neck and strode out of the room, nearly bumping into Doctor Marks as he walked past.

"How did it go? Is sleeping beauty awake?"

Anderson shook her head, horrified to feel her tired eyes burn with the threat of tears.

"So, what are you going to do now?"

"I'm going to kill that Gruddamn bastard."

Ten

BLOCK BOX

She parked her Lawmaster three blocks away from the Sunken City. The night was closing in. There was a looming presence hanging over the city—even more so than usual. She could feel something gathering, a building energy that tugged at her psi-consciousness.

Ducking into a likely-looking junk shop, she bought a raggedy, greying blanket from the bored server and wrapped it around her head and shoulders. She approached the Sunken City warily, keeping to the shadows. Someone would be keeping watch on the entrance. Her disguise wouldn't stand close scrutiny, but it might buy her some time.

Luckily, there was a buzz of people moving in and out of the entrance, workers returning home from their labours or leaving for their night shifts. She slipped into the darkness of the tunnel and wove her way through the stalls and milling people, keeping her head down.

She hadn't taken the place in, the first time she'd been here. The market was vast, the stalls stretching into the darkness. She kept to the main strip, the narrow thoroughfare clogged with customers and hawkers alike. It was a whole other world in here.

And despite the damp and claustrophobic closeness and the absence of any natural light, it didn't seem like the worst place to live.

But how was she going to find anything in this mess of humanity? She stepped into the shadow of a tatty stall, as if she were admiring the rag rugs laid out in front, and took a slow breath. She reached for the calm she had felt earlier, and opened her mind to the psionic frequencies. She could feel it, a menacing coagulation of psychic power, like a blood clot.

Anderson stepped back into the flow of foot traffic and veered off down a smaller tunnel, connecting the market to another great hall parallel to the first, although this one held shacks instead of market stalls. She kept walking, amazed at the level of organisation this place sustained. Another branch and she could feel the pull getting stronger. She reinforced her protective walls and pressed herself into the shadows as a group of robed, hooded figures passed by the end of the tunnel.

They looked weird—like something from an old-world religious group. Definitely culty.

She followed them through the maze of zigzagging tunnels, moving as quietly as she could, staying far enough back to remain unnoticed, but keeping them in sight. It was hardest whenever they turned a corner or took a new passage; she had to run to where they'd disappeared, then gingerly peer around to make sure they were still moving away.

Finally, they came to a large rusted metal door, where two more robed Devourers stood guard. She watched as the group entered and the door slammed behind them.

She eyed the guards as they settled back on their heels. She'd have to take them both out before they could raise a mental alarm. Setting her blaster to silent, she leapt from cover, her blanket falling away as she came up from her roll and knelt, braced her blaster against her thigh and shot a clean hit into each of their foreheads. They both slumped to the floor.

It was over in seconds. Had she been quick enough?

She ran to the door and listened for movement on the other side. She sensed a large mass of consciousness on the other side, much as she would if she listened outside of a large building with many rooms. They weren't all waiting on the other side of the door.

"Let's just hope they haven't planned a welcome party."

Reaching down to drag a large set of keys from one of the guards, she unlocked the door quickly, pausing to grab one of their robes. A little bloodstained, but the material was dark enough it should go unnoticed.

She was in a narrow, metal-walled hall, blessedly empty. It looked like an original structure: perhaps some sort of service station. Another corridor branched to the left, but she decided to stick to the route directly in front of her. Pulling her hood down, she walked past a succession of doors, some closed, some open. The open doors showed pallets and neatly folded blankets—sleeping chambers. But where were the people? She had to find the kid, make sure she was safe before she ripped Howl's head off. She was starting to wonder if she'd been too hasty coming here on her own. But this was a situation that called for stealth. One person was much less likely to be discovered than a squad of Judges bulldozing their way through the market.

A door at the end of the corridor led to some sort of ancient control room, with long-dead surveillance screens and panels of useless buttons, repurposed as a sort of cafeteria. She could smell the fug of greasy vats of stew and the acrid tang of petrol-fuelled heat-plates. But again, it was empty.

Two other doors led from it. Through the open door on the right she could see what looked like some kind of classroom, rows of benches facing a raised platform. This must be where they trained up new psychopaths.

The door on the left was open a mere crack, and through it she could hear the muffled monologue of a self-important orator.

Creeping to the door, she made out a small platform, with two sets of metal stairs leading down to an enormous, circular room, filled with over a hundred robed figures, all looking up adoringly at Howl's pristine figure, standing on a small podium at the far side. Crossing her fingers he wouldn't look up, she knelt down and peered in through the crack. It would be suicide to try and step inside.

"My warriors! My champions! My avengers!"

A roar went up from the gathered crowd.

"The time is close to put all our years of planning into action. Together, we have worked our fingers to the bone, our bodies to the extreme, and our minds to exhaustion, all in dedication to our Lord Karlul.

"The Law has made slaves of our minds, poisoning Karlul's gift and using it for its own dirty benefit. I feel His pain. I feel His anguish."

Howl paused, placing his hands over where his heart should be in his hollow, evil chest.

"In His infinite wisdom, He looked into our broken world, where people live in separate oblivion, with no connection, no collective consciousness, and found within Him the generosity to gift us with the power of awareness.

"And what did we do with it? Did we become aware? Did we see the truth He laid out for us?"

He stepped to the edge of his platform, looking into the eyes of the gathered crowd.

"No! We twisted it, darkened it by using it only to control those around us. And I was a part of it!"

He hung his head.

"To my shame, I was a part of it. I was one of them, the Judges. Lost in a sea of discipline and dry logic. But Karlul, He came to me. He felt my pain, and made it His own. He felt my suffering, and eased it with purpose.

"All I did was try to make this world understand. Understand the vast power of Him. And what did they do to reward me?"

He took a deep breath, his face contorting in anguish. "They killed me."

He didn't look very dead.

"Or so they thought. But a man who has the power of a god behind him is hard to kill." He raised his arms. "If you trust in me, in Karlul, you too shall become immortal. You too will receive His fathomless gifts."

The assembly raised their hands in turn, a waving carpet of idiocy.

"Karlul, we praise You!"

KARLUL, WE PRAISE YOU! the crowd parroted back.

"We give of our souls to Your keeping."

WE GIVE OF OUR SOULS TO YOUR KEEPING!

"Our divine Lord, we are Your willing vessels."

WE ARE YOUR WILLING VESSELS!

"We *are* worthy."

WE ARE WORTHY! WE ARE WORTHY! WE ARE WORTHY!

The chant was taken up with a sort of abandoned delirium. Sensing a climax to the pantomime, Anderson stepped back and straightened. She needed to find somewhere to lie low until she could work out how to get to Howl and end him.

Retracing her footsteps, she discarded the small rooms she had passed. There was nowhere to hide in there and she didn't fancy being in such a tiny space if she was discovered.

She went back to the main door and swung a right down the passage she'd passed earlier. This one led to one single locked door. Pulling out her stolen keys, she opened it and slipped inside.

She gasped, taking in what she had just stepped into. The

chamber was broad, but its real vastness was its height. The walls were lined with mesh cages, filled with prisoners. There must have been over a hundred of them altogether.

What the drokk are they using them for?

They avoided her eyes, assuming she was a Devourer. She walked to the nearest cage, where a teenage boy sat dejectedly beside an elderly woman.

"Hey," she whispered to the boy.

He shied away.

She pulled down her hood. "I'm not one of them. I'm a Judge. I've come to help. What are they doing with you?"

He came to the bars. "You gotta get us out of here."

"Do you know why they've captured you?"

He shook his head. "I've been here two weeks, some of the others have been here months. They just keep bringing in more. I don't know why."

She let her mind travel lightly over them, feeling their misery and their panic. They all had one thing in common. There were varying levels of psi-ability among them. For some it was only a trace, but she detected some with a lot of untrained strength—especially in the younger ones. Looking to where she sensed the brightest sparks, she was dismayed to see the small figures of children. This is where the kids had been disappearing to.

And kept here. But why?

"I'm going to get you out of here, okay?" She kept her voice low, she didn't want to start a mass hysteria. The boy nodded. She couldn't risk a psi-call to HQ or the Devourers would know she was there in an instant.

She bit her lip, scanning the room. "A little kid come in here yesterday? Brown skin, curly hair?"

He nodded. "I think she's somewhere up there." He pointed into the abyss above.

"Okay, sit tight."

She went to the narrow metal stair—more of a ladder—and climbed.

"*Kid*," she hissed as she peered into each cage. She climbed to the next level, and there she was, sitting at the back of an otherwise empty cage in a miserable heap.

"Kid!"

Her big brown eyes lit up and she ran to the front of the cage, gripping the mesh.

"You're here! I felt you coming after me. But then you were gone. I thought you'd given up!"

"No." Anderson grinned. "Never."

She fumbled through her set of keys and was annoyed that none of them fit the cage's lock. The lock looked pretty flimsy.

"Stand back."

She fired an Incendiary round at the lock, and it melted in an explosion of sparks. Kicking the door open, she knelt down to grab the little girl in a fierce hug.

"Sorry I took so long, kid."

"You know, my name's Maya."

Anderson smiled. "Okay, Maya, let's get you out of here."

All thoughts of a stealthy assassination had disappeared when she saw her. She'd have to act quickly once they were outside. She'd slip out with the kid—Maya—and call the full might of Psi-Div down upon these lunatics as they made their escape through the Sunken City. If she timed it right, they wouldn't discover the girl was missing until it was too late.

"Come on." She held out her hand and together, they walked along the shallow walkway and down the narrow stairs.

She paused outside of the boy's cage. "I'll come back for you."

"You're not taking us now?"

"It isn't safe, I need to call in reinforcements to make sure nobody gets killed getting you out."

"I don't care about any of that. You can't just leave me here."

Anderson's heart ached as she saw tears welling in his eyes.

"I promise you. I will come back for you."

"She will," added Maya. "She always comes back."

"DON'T LEAVE US HERE!" he yelled, as they slipped out of the door.

"Can't we take him now?" Maya said as they hurried along the corridor.

"I can't keep you safe if there are any more of us. I have to look after you right now."

She knew she wasn't being fair. Why this girl, over any of the others in there? But it was true that she couldn't take more than one on her own, and she felt a connection to this child.

She knelt down, the corner still shielding them, and took her little shoulders in her hands. "I'll come back for them all. I promise."

She stood and poked her head out to check the coast was clear. "Hello, Judge."

She saw a mouth full of rotten teeth form the words from the darkness of a hood before the lights went out.

SHE AWOKE WITH a thumping pain in her head. Blinking to clear her vision, she raised her fingers tentatively to her scalp; they came away sticky with blood. Great.

She pushed herself up. She was on a low bunk in an otherwise empty room, lit by a dim bulb recessed into the ceiling, probably so that it couldn't be pulled out and used as a weapon. She'd lost her daystick, her blaster and her data strip. They'd stripped off her jacket and left her in her vest and trousers, even taking her boots. Her skin crawled at the idea of them touching her when she was out of it.

"Fine mess you've got yourself into, Anderson."

She leant her forehead on her knees and gathered her wits, sending out a psi-alert that should bring down the whole of Psi-Div to her aid.

She felt it slide off the walls like water off oiled paper. Gruddamn it, some sort of psychic block box.

She looked up as Howl entered, flanked by the man with rotten teeth and a younger woman with red hair scraped back.

"How honoured we are, Judge Anderson."

She stared at him in silence.

"Whatever winding path led your feet here, I know that Karlul brought you to us for a reason."

She snorted in contempt. "The winding path that took me here is leading to your death, *Howl*."

He smiled and twitched his head to the side, regarding her thoughtfully.

"Stronger have tried and failed. As have you."

"I haven't even started yet."

"Enough!"

Rotten Teeth cracked a fist into her cheek and she reeled back, wiping a smear of blood from her cracked lip with the back of her hand.

She leant back on the wall and graced them with her brightest, widest smile, making sure to bare her bloody teeth.

"You get off on this, don't you? All these years and you still like keeping women locked up in little rooms."

Rotten Teeth moved in for another go, but Howl held up his hand.

"No," he said. "No, I do not enjoy this at all. This is all in the name of Karlul."

"It's because we're stronger than you, isn't it? You can't control us, and that scares you. Well, it didn't work with *Yinny*, and it's not going to work with me."

She felt bad for using the hated pet name, but she felt that Mei Yin would forgive her when she saw the response. His face drained of colour at the mention, throwing him off course.

"So, she's been feeding you lies, has she? Spreading her poison around once more."

"It's hard to lie when someone is inside your mind. I know what you did to her."

Did his mouth tremble slightly?

"She trusted you. She *loved* you. And you tortured her. For months."

"No."

"But she didn't break. She was stronger than you—"

"She was *WEAK*," he spat. "And she still is. The same closed cold little infantile girl she was forty years ago."

Well. A blast from the past seemed to have had some effect on him too.

"But that does not matter now," he said, collecting himself in front of his disciples. "It only saddens me that she did not choose the light of His love. When Karlul the Devourer comes, she will not be spared. She will not rise with me to rule this world as I'd once hoped. I was trying to *save* her, do you see? Everything I did to her was to try and make her understand."

"Oh, she understands. She understands you very well. None of this is for her, for your followers. This isn't even for Karlul. This is about you. You and only you—"

She faltered as his maniacal laughter drowned her out.

"Do you actually believe that I have need of your approval, little girl?" he said eventually, wiping his eyes. "No, I do not. It is too late for you to be turned to the cause. But such strength will not be wasted. Oh, no. Your presence is most welcome, Judge Anderson. Most welcome indeed."

Eleven

DOORWAY

ROTTEN TEETH CAME for her later. It might have been the next day or it might have been a few hours, she had no way of knowing.

She'd tried and tried again to break through the psychic blocking, but stopped when she realised she was just tiring herself out.

He was accompanied by the red-haired woman again. She hadn't taken much notice of her before, but focusing on her now, Anderson felt the psychic practically leaking from her.

"You're coming with us," said Rotten Teeth. "If Incra picks up on you so much as *thinking* of sending out a psychic SOS, I'll kill you, simple as that. Got it?"

Anderson stared him straight in the eye and he smirked, roughly taking her arm and dragging her out of the block box. They walked back through the control-room-cum-cafeteria, and down into the now-empty hall, their steps clanging hollowly on the metal stair: Rotten Teeth in front, with Incra's scrutiny boring into the back of her head. With her walls up, Incra couldn't know what she was thinking, but the instant she brought them down to send out a signal, the game would be up.

Halfway down the stairs, she grabbed hold of the metal handrails, rocking back to smack into Incra's nose with the back of her head as she kicked out and sent Rotten Teeth flying to crash down and into the dirt.

At the same moment she blasted a message to HQ, telling them she had found Howl, the heart of the cult, and that she needed backup yesterday.

Before she could broadcast her coordinates, she was slammed with a psi-blast from behind, sending her tumbling after Rotten Teeth. He grabbed her by the neck and slammed her into the earth.

"What did I say? *What did I say?*"

He straddled her chest, pinning her arms with his knees, and delivered a ringing punch to the side of her head.

"Enough!" Howl's clipped tone froze Rotten Teeth's arm mid-strike. "Take her to the Doorway as planned. By the time Psi-Div arrive, it will be too late."

Rotten Teeth dragged her to her feet and pushed her to the back of the room, where a panel rose to reveal a spiral staircase, descending into the gloom. It was cold on her bare feet, the smell of damp earth rich in her nostrils. This was not part of the original construction. It had been dug out recently.

The bottom of the stair led to a close, dingy passage that had been blasted out of the bedrock. Anderson was not prepared for what it opened out on.

A huge, circular void with dank, rot-black walls stretched out ahead. A huge metal disk rose from the floor; the enormous archway at the centre of the disk was big enough for a truck to drive through. An elevated walkway led from the passage, ending in some sort of a podium a few metres short of the archway. A helmet rested on the podium, cables trailing into the base of the arch.

But it wasn't the contraption itself that stunned her; it was the people strapped to the thrumming metal. The prisoners. Steel shackles pinned them down in a regular pattern across the base. Some were still struggling as they were strapped in.

"What is this thing?" Anderson whispered, without expecting an answer.

"You'll see," said Rotten Teeth as he shoved her from behind. She scanned the room for Maya, but couldn't make her out in the gloom.

She resisted as Rotten Teeth forced her down, and two other Devourers came to assist in dragging her arms and legs to the manacles, shutting her in tightly.

When she hit the metal, she finally understood. This was an enormous, energy-sucking psionic amplifier, and she and the other prisoners were the unwilling power supply.

As they secured the final captives, the Devourers went to lock themselves in. Howl walked the outer ring to secure the disciples' final manacles. Not even they could back out now, even if they wanted to.

He straightened his suit as he approached the podium, his smart shoes clanging on the gantry, and raised his arms to address those prone below.

Talk about a captive audience.

"Chosen ones! This moment marks the fruition of our long-held, divinely cherished dream. The Opener of Minds cometh!"

His language sure did get flowery when he got excited.

"Children of Karlul, we have been orphaned by a vile system, ostracised as mutants, controlled by the Judiciary, brainwashed and tricked into enforcing their laws.

"Soon, you will feel the love of your Father, come to raise up His children to lead this broken world to glory!"

He reached up and put the headpiece reverently on his head, and suddenly the amplifier came alive.

She felt a shift as the Devourers began to feed their power willingly, and slammed up her walls to stop her own psychic energy from leaving her body. It was like hanging from a cliff face by her fingernails as a strong wind sucked her legs into the abyss. It ripped her away to hurtle into the vortex at the disk's centre, spinning around the archway in an electrified mass. She could feel Howl focusing the energy, channeling it to pull apart the barrier between dimensions.

Head flung back, arms outreached, feet braced, he worked his mouth as the walls thinned.

It was agony, but at the same time, joined as she was to a hundred souls as their collective energy was bent to a purpose, she was filled with a sickening euphoria.

Within the eye of the storm, the air began to change. A shape began to form, massive and impossibly real. It was monstrous, hunched with powerful limbs, yet still too faint to see the detail of its being. Gruddamn it, she *couldn't* be a part of unleashing this monster on to the world.

She gritted her teeth, straining at her bonds. The daemon was getting clearer; two burning copper eyes began to pierce through the gate, a glowing animal energy pouring through the connection, its one, searing emotion pummeling her and all the poor souls strapped in.

It was *ravenous*.

"Howl!"

The daemon flickered as Howl's attention was broken.

Mei Yin! Anderson's heart flared with hope as she saw her partner standing, feet braced, at the entrance to the tunnel. She strode down the aisle, resolve suffusing every movement, and ripped the helm from Howl's head, throwing it to the side to dangle from the podium.

She swung an uppercut that connected solidly with his jaw, elbowing him sharply as he doubled over. He recovered immediately, shoulder-barging her, and the two fell back, grappling on the walkway.

Anderson tried in vain to pull free. She had to get out of this! She watched helplessly as Howl threw Mei Yin over the side to crash onto the metal floor below.

"You presume to put your hands on me?" he spat. "Now, in this most sacred of moments?" He jumped down to loom above her, and she leveled a double kick into his ribs.

Pushing herself up, Mei Yin struck him a blow to his windpipe, but the power was gone. She was tiring.

"Judge," came a small voice by her ear.

"Maya?"

The girl was crouched low beside her head.

"How are you free?"

She grinned. "Something I learned ages ago when the bad men would tie me up. I pulled my arms up away from the floor as they strapped me in, but without making a fuss, making them think I was going along with it. They weren't paying close enough attention and clipped me in too loose."

"Well done. Can you get me out of here too?"

The girl worked quickly, freeing her feet.

"Hey!" A Devourer had seen them, but they were all strapped in too.

Howl had grabbed hold of Mei Yin and was dragging her, kicking, to the edge of the amplifier. He dropped her and kicked her devastatingly hard in the ribs. Mei Yin curled in to protect herself from another blow.

Maya freed her right hand and Anderson turned to pull her other hand free.

Howl was kneeling now on Mei Yin's neck.

"Stay here," Anderson cautioned the girl, and ran at Howl with all the consuming hunger the daemon had poured into her. Grabbing him by the throat, she hurled him away from Mei Yin to crash against the base of the walkway. He jumped to his feet, turning on her with berserker eyes.

224

She stood between him and Mei Yin, ready for another round.

At that moment, an ear-splitting screech cracked through the air. All eyes turned to the gate as the head of the Devourer began to emerge.

"No!" Anderson cried. They were too late. The gate was opening.

Its vast reptilian head broke the hazed waterfall of the dimensional wall, the huge jaw open in triumph.

Howl rose on shaking legs, his face suffused with a sickening adoration.

"My Lord Karlul. It is I, Your servant in all things." He fell to his knees as the fiery eyes turned to him.

"Father, I give You this lowly world. I have dedicated my life to bringing You into it so that I—"

A dart of pure psionic energy blasted from the open maw of the Devourer and exploded into Howl's chest. The blast catapulted Anderson and Mei Yin into the air, crashing painfully into the wall of the cave.

Anderson struggled to Mei Yin, who was stunned by the impact.

"Mei Yin, you're here! I thought you'd still be on that beach of yours."

The woman smiled grimly. "Maybe you *can* teach this old woman a few things, cadet. You were right. I had to face him."

Her smile dropped as another terrible screech rent the air.

"We have to stop it," Anderson said. "What do we do? How do we send it back?"

"It's too late." She gritted her teeth and pushed herself up the wall. "Now that it's breached the barriers, we'd need twice the power to send it back."

"There has to be *something!*"

The Devourer roared, the walls vibrating with the terrifying sound. She saw it edge forward, the hint of a massive shoulder start to push its way through.

"This way!"

Anderson gaped as Judge Chilton, followed closely by Chief Smee, ran from the tunnel entrance, only to skid to a halt at the sight that waited for them. Behind them, more Psi-Judges began to crowd out of the tunnel.

"We have to add our power to close the breach," Mei Yin shouted.

Chief Smee, eyes fixed on the gruesome being forcing its way through the gate, shook herself out of her reverie, coming to kneel beside them.

"What the drokk is going on here?"

"This is a massive psychic amplifier," Anderson explained. "There are cits and cult members strapped into it. They've opened a gate into the daemon's dimension—"

"We have to get them out now!"

"No!"

Mei Yin grabbed Chief Smee's arm as she turned to give the command.

"We still need their strength. If we don't close it *now*, the Devourer is going to come through and suck the souls out of every person in Mega-City One."

Chief Smee blinked, sat back on her heels, and nodded.

"Right, everyone into the metal basin *right now*. Go, quickly!"

They dove onto the metal as the monster freed its shoulders.

It had to be the whole of Psi-Div, she thought, watching them pour into the room as Smee directed them to crowd onto the metal plate.

Judge Adjonyoh clocked them and ran over as she came out of the tunnel.

"What's going on?"

"We need to get onto the basin, now!" Anderson said, grabbing the Judge by the forearm.

Mei Yin clutched at her.

"Take me to the controller, Judge. I need to finish this."

Grabbing an arm each they helped her to her feet, half dragging the limping woman towards the podium where the helm still hung.

Passing Howl's smoking corpse, Mei Yin let out a little bark of laughter. "Reckon he's really dead this time?" she said as she aimed a kick at his trailing arm. But the movement made her cry out in pain.

"What's wrong with your leg?" Anderson demanded.

"Broken," she pushed out through gritted teeth.

"We can do this. Wait here and—"

"No, Anderson. Get me there. Adjonyoh, get onto that amplifier now! We'll need all the strength we can get."

Adjonyoh scrambled down and Anderson and Mei Yin staggered the last few feet together. The screeching of the horrible creature echoed around the chamber.

Mei Yin gripped the edges of the stand as Anderson positioned the helm onto her head, and looked her in the eye. "Get down there, kid."

Anderson nodded grimly before diving from the walkway. She knelt down and slammed her palm to the metal, willingly joining her power to it.

She could feel it now. With the focused power of the Judges, the base swelled with power.

She felt it channel to the controller, where Mei Yin had braced her good leg. She was staring into the eyes of the devil now, screaming as she aimed the collected force of Psi-Div full into its hideous face.

Anderson winced as the Devourer let loose another punishing blast of psi power, this time aimed straight at Mei Yin's diminutive form.

But Mei Yin was ready. She met that wave with the immense power building around her. The room shook as the two forces met, pressing against each other in a frothing blaze of power.

Mei Yin leant into it, forcing the inferno back, centimetre by centimetre, towards the monster.

Anderson was dripping with sweat, her muscles cramping as her mind asked more of it than it had to give. But still they needed more. She pushed herself, looking around to see others doing the same.

With an almighty yell, Mei Yin flung out with every ounce of power they had. The beam rocketed into the monster's power, reversing the flow, exploding into the gaping maw, driving it back.

As soon as it was out of the way, the barrier snapped shut, banishing the Devourer into its own realm once more.

Everyone collapsed as the connection was broken, utterly spent.

Anderson looked around. Maya was curled into a heap, her eyes screwed shut, her little body quivering. She gathered the little girl into her arms.

"Is it gone?" Maya said, her face pressed into Anderson's shoulder.

"Yes, it's gone. And you helped us do it."

With dismay Anderson looked up to where Mei Yin was laying crumpled on the walkway.

"Wait here, kiddo," she said, but Maya clung to her hand as Anderson walked—she didn't have the energy to run—over to her partner.

Collapsing beside her, she drew Mei Yin's head into her lap, and checked her pulse. It was there, but dangerously faint.

"I need a medic!"

Mei Yin's eyes fluttered open.

"It is done," she breathed, before falling back, a small smile on her lips.

Epilogue
MEMORIAL

THE EVENING SUN washed red over the rooftop of HQ, casting a hellish glow over the gathered Psi-Judges. They were lined up in smart rows, their uniforms crisp, their boots polished, their badges proudly gleaming.

To the right stood the grey-clad ranks of the cadets. Feeling a pair of eyes on her, Anderson winked at the small cadet with neatly braided hair, her skin glowing with health. It was amazing what a few weeks of regular meals and a safe place to sleep could do to a kid. Maya grinned back.

"Psi-Division," Chief Smee's voice rang out over them, drawing her attention away from the good that had come out of all this, and back to the cold reality of all they had lost.

She stood next to a huge shining metal sphere, with a flame projecting vertically into the air.

"We light this fire tonight to remember those that fell in this second war of the Devourer. It symbolises the burning strength, the courage of those we have lost, and in turn our fiery determination to remember them, and to never again allow such evil to poison our ranks."

Anderson bent her head, the sadness swelling inside. She saw Judge Chilton clenching his jaw with emotion. Palmer hadn't made it; none of them had. Apparently, the moment that Howl had died, they had lapsed into a coma, braindead.

"But they did not die in vain. Together, we have defeated an enemy more powerful than we could have imagined. Together, we can hold our heads high."

Chief Smee allowed one of her rare smiles that actually reached her eyes.

"Today, I am proud to be looking into the future with every one of you. Together, we are strong! Together, we *will* overcome!"

A cheer went up, and Anderson felt herself lifting her own head in hope, mirroring the movement of Judge Adjonyoh in front of her.

As the crowds dispersed, Anderson felt a tug at her jacket, and turned to see Maya. She knelt down, and allowed the girl a quick hug before holding her at arm's length.

"You polish up into quite the cadet," she said. "How are you liking your new home?"

Maya looked thoughtful. "It's better, safer than before. But it's strange. There are a *lot* of rules."

"You'll get used to those. Have you met your teachers yet?"

"Only the most important ones."

They both turned as Mei Yin wheeled her med-chair up to them, her leg supported and outstretched in a cast.

"Just wait till she gets out of that thing, Maya. You're not going to know what hit you."

Maya ducked her head shyly, but Mei Yin took her chin in her hand and lifted her face so she could look into her eyes.

"I won't go easy on you, cadet. But it's for your own good."

The girl straightened to attention, and saluted her superior.

"Yes, Judge!" she replied formally.

"Cut the girl some slack, Mei Yin," Anderson said. "You never know, she may turn out to be your partner some day."

Acknowledgements

With special thanks to Lucy Smee, my partner in crime, and to Maura Sills, a real-life Psi-Judge. And also to David Thomas Moore for asking me to write *Devourer* and to Kate Coe for being such a great editor, it's been a joy!

About the Author

Laurel Sills is a writer and editor who lives in South East London with her partner, daughter and two cats. She's had stories published in *Sharkpunk* and *Game Over*, both with Snowbooks. She was the co-founder and editor of the award-winning *Holdfast Magazine*.

FLYTRAP

ZINA HUTTON

To the niecelings and my friends from Twitter:
I wouldn't be here without you nerds.

MEGA-CITY ONE
2102 A.D.

Prologue

DESPITE LIVING IN Wormwood Block her entire life, Jax still finds herself turned around and twisted up every single time she leaves the cube of an apartment that she shares with her robo-goldfish—the apartment that she used to share with her sister before the clod went and got herself locked up for spitting on the street in front of an extra-sensitive Judge.

Especially when she's just coming back from running errands for folks that have business outside of the block and she's still running on adrenaline from dodging a Judge on the lookout for folks like her.

It's always just so... disorienting, coming back to the building and trying to find her way through the maze-like hallways back to her cube.

Jax has lived in Wormwood Block since she was born—she was actually almost born in the hallway in front of the elevators on their floor, and there are signs and screens everywhere to point residents to the nearest exit or anything else they can possibly need—and yet, here she is—

Lost.

Again.

She knows that she's on the right floor, because she can at least manage an elevator when she needs to. She realises that she's on the wrong side of the block when she squints down at the far end of the hallway, catching a glimpse of weak sunlight at the very end. Only floors above the three-hundred mark of this block get anything close to 'natural' sunlight thanks to the bigger blocks that surround it... but it's coming from the wrong direction.

"Grud," Jax says, her voice edging into a whine that'd make her wince to hear it come from anyone else. "Now I'm gonna have to walk all the way back to the other side of the block."

Jax mutters to herself the whole time that she tries to retrace her steps, stomping her feet as if that childlike expression of annoyance helps make up for the injustice of it all.

It doesn't.

Right as she reaches the elevator, Jax swears that she can feel someone standing right behind her, practically breathing down her neck. A tense prickle rolls down her spine and her mind goes immediately to the knife that she keeps tucked into a deep pocket of her puffy rad-green jacket. She's not supposed to have a weapon, no one in the block is, but with all the work she's done outside of the building and all the trouble she's gotten into inside of it—

Having a way to defend herself is worth the risk of getting hauled off by a Judge if she ever has to use it. After all, better to be stuck in an Iso-Cube for a year or two for assault than permanently laid out on a slab.

With her hand on the hilt of her knife, Jax whirls around only to see the empty hallway stretching behind her.

"Imagination on overdrive," she says to the air, uncurling her fingers from the knife and smoothing down the front of her jacket. She keeps walking, trying to ignore the anxiety making her teeth itch.

The elevator doors slide open with a muted hiss of hydraulics. Considering how many people live in Wormwood Block, Jax is surprised that it hasn't opened sooner to spew out a couple dozen residents all over the place.

Instead of a seething crush of busy humanity, however, the elevator's only occupant is a little kid with skin the same shade of synthcaff brown as Jax's own. Barely knee-high to Jax—who isn't all that tall herself—and with a mop of curly blue-black hair that leaves their face obscured, the kid doesn't look like much. Most kids don't.

Mind already on her mattress and a night watching vids with her fish, Jax starts to head off. She doesn't get far.

"Excuse me," the kid in the elevator says in a high-pitched, almost squeaky voice. "Can you help me get home? Please?"

Jax's first instinct is to say no. Kids aren't her thing. She didn't even like them when she *was* one. She even opens her mouth to tell the kid to "go find a map."

But her mouth doesn't cooperate with her mind.

Neither does the rest of her body.

Instead of... all of that, Jax hears herself tell the kid, "Yeah, sure thing, kid," as she steps into the elevator and takes the kid's small left hand in a loose grip. With her free hand, she hits the buttons for one of the lower floors, her mind not even registering the numbers even though she's looking right at them.

When the kid looks up at her, Jax realises that there's something... strange about the kid's eyes. They're bright brown, almost glowing in the flickering light from overhead. And they're the only part of the kid's features that Jax can register in her mind. The rest is replaced with a fuzzy brown blur that makes her own eyes water.

"Wh-what?" Jax's tongue feels thick in her mouth, her head heavy. When she tries to look down at the child again, her head doesn't move. She's a passenger in her own damn body. "Wh-what's going on?"

The little kid laughs as if Jax is being *funny* and then tightens their grip on Jax's hand, tiny fingers squeezing hard enough that ragged-edged nails bite into Jax's skin.

It *hurts*, and Jax hears a weak whimper slip free from her mouth as her fingers flex in an involuntary response.

"Be *quiet*," the kid says in a whisper too harsh for their little body. "And stop moving."

And, despite her best efforts to resist the force controlling her, Jax feels her mouth snap shut and her body freeze. By the time the elevator reaches whatever floor Jax's fingers had pressed, it's like she's not even *in* her body any more.

When the elevator doors open, Jax's vision goes black as a pulse of white hot *pain* stabs into her mind.

Her last conscious thought is that *A little kid has no business being this strong.*

One

Several days later

ON ONE OF the highest floors of Wormwood Block, the park that takes up most of the space is one of the few rec areas in the tower with an actual view of something other than another building. The park is usually quiet; peaceful, despite being a high traffic area.

Until it isn't.

In the early evening, a sudden burst of screaming overwhelms the piped-in sounds of nature circa 1987. The sound, a primal noise that echoes *fear-loss-confusion* coming from a vaguely person-shaped lump on a bench, jolts the residents who'd come up to socialise in the holopark, and several people leave without a backwards glance.

Sticking around when a futsie goes off is *so* not how most people plan to spend the evening.

Leaving, as always, remains the smartest decision.

WHEN THE PERSON on the bench gets off it, Mahren S., 255th floor, is the first person to approach. Fueled partly by bravery

243

and partly by a desire to live out her unfulfilled dreams of being a Med Division Judge, Mahren leaves her wife and daughter behind—along with her common sense—because she just wants to help.

"You're okay," Mahren croons, creeping close enough that she can peer into wild blue eyes that stare at her out of a face that's practically more bruise than unblemished skin. "You're going to be fine."

I'm a mother, Mahren thinks to herself. *I can handle this.*

Boldly, bravely, she reaches out and rests one slight hand on the shoulder closest to her in an attempt to comfort the shaking, still-screaming person in front of her.

And promptly gets punched in the face for her troubles.

Despite how much crime goes on in the city, Wormwood Block has always been relatively non-violent. Aside from the occasional spat between neighbours who've practically grown up in each other's armpits, Mahren swears that this building has rarely seen actual violence.

At first, the pain of being hit in the face is so overwhelming that Mahren simply doesn't register it. She can't. She hears the faint crunch as cartilage crumples and then tastes a salty rush of blood—her blood—as it spills down her face and stains the new sweater she'd bought just the other day.

And it still feels as though it's happening to someone else.

The pain hits moments after she lands on the ground; a double dose from the blow to the face as well as from the futsie riding her body to the ground, using her as a cushion from the synth-grass that isn't half as soft as it looks.

Screaming—from her wife and daughter, from the bystanders around them—echoes through the air a few seconds later.

Mahren tries to talk, but the words come out in a wheezing warble that's thick from the pain radiating from her face and the blood trickling back into her throat.

"St-stop," she whispers, eyes wide with pain as she tries to focus on the skinny girl currently trying to stand on shaky legs mere feet away. "I—I just want to help."

Her words are in vain, however.

The next person that the frightened futsie launches herself at lays her out flat with a right hook.

Mahren drags herself up into a seated position, waving away her wife's assistance when the older woman rushes to her side with their sweet daughter not far behind, and takes in the unconscious girl laying in a crumpled heap on the scratchy synth-grass.

"We—we need—" Mahren clears her throat and then, not-so-discreetly, spits out a stream of blood that spatters across the too-bright green of the fake grass underneath her. "We need a Judge. Now."

THE MOMENT THAT Anderson sets foot in the indoor part at one of the highest floors of Wormwood Block, her head starts to hurt.

It's not that surprising.

From the moment that she and Judge Lee—a street Judge with only slightly more experience than Anderson has—exit the elevator onto the floor that leads to the scene of the disturbance, they come face-to-face with what seems like half of the block's population.

Their minds push at Anderson's shields, concentrated eagerness lashing against her mind so hard that the mere *effort* of holding the thoughts at bay makes her wince and want to backpedal into the relative safety of the elevator.

As they approach the park, the crowd of nosy residents intensifies, thickening around them. If not for the fact that they're clearly marked Judges—both in their uniforms, with the shining black of Lee's helmet standing out against her brown skin—Anderson knows that they'd be at risk of a swarm.

By the time that Anderson actually sets one booted foot down on the bright green grass, her head pulses with a spike of sharp pain. She gets flashes, nothing that seems serious at first—

A hallway.

Uncomfortable chairs.

Bruises on brown skin.

And then, a bright flash of deep red that can only be blood, makes Anderson stagger, coming close to falling flat on her face.

A strong hand at her elbow just barely keeps that from happening.

"Lee—"

The other Judge's gloved fingers flex against the sleek black of her suit, the pressure steady and sure. Grounding.

"Do you require assistance?" Lee's voice is low but intense as she dips her helmeted head so that she's no longer towering over Anderson's shorter body. "I can clear the floor out for you in minutes, Anderson."

It's a kind offer, but not a smart one.

Anderson bites back the first, second, and *third* responses that come to mind, settling instead on telling Lee that, "If you clear the entire floor, then we'll have to hunt down potential witnesses instead of having them come to *us*. Just because I *can* do the extra work, that doesn't mean I want to."

Despite choosing the gentlest way she could think of to point out the flaws in Lee's attempt to 'help,' Anderson realises that even *that* isn't gentle enough by the blotchy flush stealing across what Anderson can see of the other woman's face.

Grife.

"You can go in first, though," Anderson offers a little belatedly, hesitation tripping up the words on her tongue. "Read the room, clear a path... That sort of thing."

Lee's mouth thins with a tense frown. "I know how to do my job, Anderson."

Ooh.

Chilly.

Anderson resists the urge to shiver. They're far too public for that kind of thing and she's probably pushed Lee's buttons enough. Besides, street Judges never seem to get Anderson's brand of humour.

It'd just be a waste.

Instead, she inclines her head in a sharp nod that sets her hair to swinging.

"Go ahead, then," she says, gesturing for Lee to precede her through the mass of people who don't seem to have the sense to get out of the way.

It doesn't hurt to let Lee go first. The other Judge is taller, and broader. When she moves across the fake grass, the residents nearly trip over themselves to get out of her way.

Which means that they're not in Anderson's way either.

Lee stops without warning, without *thinking*, and Anderson walks right into her. Without the protection of her helmet, Anderson's nose bounces off of Lee's armour so hard that tears well up in her eyes.

Before Lee can turn around or, actually, say *anything*, Anderson rushes to cut her off.

"I'm fine. Just a little bump."

She inches over to stand at Lee's right elbow, shooting a glare at a gawker who waits until the last possible moment to get out of her way.

Between the headache and the annoyance at the crowd around them, Anderson is so busy trying to bolster her flagging shields that her gaze almost skips right over the scene in front of her.

She sees the blood first. Most of it tacky and drying on the face of a woman with panic-blown eyes and a white-knuckled grip on the hand of the woman beside her. A few feet away from the two women, a prone body is lying so still that, if not for the faint rise and fall of their chest and the lingering psionic energy that Anderson can sense crackling around them like a halo, she'd assume that they were dead.

"Tell us what happened," Lee says, her tone cool and imperious as it cuts through the chatter around them.

The woman with the bloody nose speaks first.

"M-my name is M-Mahren," she stutters, voice thick and hard to understand thanks to her busted nose. "I-I tried to help, but—but—"

The woman besides her leans forward, dark gaze intense. "She hit my *wife*," she says, just shy of a snarl. "All Mahren was trying to do was help her when she was *obviously* in distress. It's not *her* fault that that *futsie* lashed out at her for no reason."

Both women are telling the truth. Or the truth as they know it.

But then, no one ever does anything without a reason.

Anderson jerks her head in the direction of the unconscious young woman, addressing Mahren's wife without breaking eye contact with her. "So, what happened after she attacked your wife?"

ANDERSON HAS SOME medical training.

She knows the basics of putting broken bodies back together and she's even decent at it—though not as good as she is at manoeuvring through a mental minefield. When she kneels beside the unconscious young woman, she flashes back to her training, gaze skimming over too-cool flesh as she takes stock of the woman lying in front of her.

When she rolls the other woman over, onto her back, the first thing that she notices is her head wound. The half-scabbed-over cut stretches up from just above her left eyebrow, across her forehead, disappearing into her thick hair. The bruise surrounding the injury is dark, too new to have made it very far on the healing process. When Anderson touches the bruise, the young woman tenses, but otherwise doesn't move.

"She had this injury when she came here," Anderson says, looking over her shoulder to address Lee who had insisted on standing guard over her. "It's not new enough to be caused by whatever happened here." Anderson's gloved fingers brush over the farthest edge of the cut, barely skimming over it. "See how it's scabbing over?"

Lee leans close enough over Anderson's shoulder to make her feel faintly claustrophobic.

"She didn't get any of these injuries from fighting with that woman," Lee points out, her voice cool.

"No, she didn't."

After a moment of tense silence, Anderson resumes her careful study of the unconscious woman's body. She plans on trying to reach out to her mind: after all, that's why Anderson is here. But first, she has to have some idea what she's working with.

"Make sure no one gets too close," Anderson says, glancing up at Lee with her mind already skipping to the task ahead of her. "I'm going to check her for other injuries and then try a mind probe."

The girl is *covered* with bruises and injuries—many of which are shiny patches of brown skin that look inflicted by a laser cutter and quickly healed. All of them seem older than a day or two and many of them are half-healed.

As far as Anderson can tell, none of the wounds are defensive ones. The closest things—bloody bruising on the knuckles of one hand—seem fresh enough that Anderson can probably attribute them to Mahren's busted nose and the tussle just before.

She'll check that against the girl's memories, of course, but it seems likely.

Aside from the lack of defensive wounds, there's another anomaly—

"I don't see any marks from restraints," Anderson tells Lee.

"With how many injuries she has and how bad some of them look, I'd be expecting some kind of restraint marks on her skin. I won't know until I do the probe or until the Med-Judges get a look at her, but it almost looks as though she just... sat there and let this happen to her."

"So, do the probe then," Lee says. "The sooner you check her, the sooner we can find out who did this and move on." The impatience is a little novel. Usually, the Judges that Anderson gets saddled that *aren't* from her division are a little more close-mouthed about their impatience. They may fondle their Lawgivers and step a little close to her as if that'll speed her along, but they rarely ever come right out and say anything.

Novel doesn't mean it's not annoying.

Anderson grits her teeth hard enough that she swears she can hear them *creak* in response, but holds her tongue.

Instead, she steps closer to the young woman still lying unconscious in front of her and presses one gloved hand to the girl's forehead before she slowly and carefully releases a trickle of power.

THE MENTAL IMAGES come in a wave almost too fast for Anderson to make sense of.

Not that there's much that she can recognise at first, aside from the girl's hazy, half-frantic memories of lashing out at Mahren and the fear of being somewhere unfamiliar before being knocked into unconsciousness from a blow to her already-aching head.

Half of the images in her mind seem almost... scrambled, and Anderson largely can't see anything that she can recognise. She presses forward with her power, mentally brushing past memories that she can't see until she sees her first truly clear ones.

An elevator.

A small, blurry face.
High-pitched laughter.
A gloved hand with a laser cutter.
Pain pain pain.

Anderson starts to see another memory; of a curious sensation, one that she can only identify as 'being led.' She gets a fraction of a second to contemplate that feeling as she drifts through other memories but, before she can do anything about it, another psionic presence *shoves* her right out of the girl's head.

The force leaves Anderson reeling, so confused that she almost doesn't remember where she is. It takes Lee's strong hand on her shoulder, firmly tugging her back and sending her head wobbling back and forth, before she snaps out of it, staring blearily at her surroundings. Despite Lee's presence and the standard fear of Judges that the residents of Wormwood Block should have, the crowd of people around them is closer than it should be. The residents encircle them tightly enough that they block out even the faintest glimpses of the path and the flickering holographic trees lining it, all but obstructing Anderson's view of the door. There's a moment when all Anderson's bleary gaze can register is the almost claustrophobic feeling of being surrounded by people more interested in news they can take back to their fellow residents than in their own safety.

And, going by the way Lee *growls* as she jerks as if to rise to her feet and glares at the crowd, the residents *should* be concerned with their own safety.

"Wh-what happened?"

"You zoned out the second you touched her. The futsie stopped breathing for a moment."

The helmet—and Lee's attempt at maintaining her calm—does nothing to mask the unease in her voice.

"What?" Anderson barks, at the same time that she reaches out with her senses to feel—*nothing*.

Where there once was a fast-moving torrent of memories, there's now an empty blankness, as if everything that the young girl ever *was* has been locked away behind a door that Anderson has no hope of unlocking. Locked away—or erased.

The girl is breathing now. Slow and unsteadily.

But Anderson can't *feel her*.

"Did you find anything?" Lee asks.

"Her name," Anderson says, her own voice hushed. "Her name is Jax. And, Lee, I believe a psi is responsible for this."

Interlude

KILLING SOMEONE ISN'T very difficult.

People are fragile enough.

Even with the many life-extending modifications residents can get done from the comfort of their own small apartments and the widespread access to healthcare, it doesn't take much to take a life. All it takes is a little mental nudge, a little shock to the system; a pinch of pressure or a sharp jab to one of the many major arteries in the human body.

But silencing them, mentally wiping out everything that makes a person a person?

Now that's harder than it should be.

He sends the order through the communicator that goes up to the apartment, the text on the screen telling them to "Take out the trash."

Simple enough.

If they don't think about the fact that the words refer to a person instead of actual garbage due for the incinerator, that is.

Alone, Ness doesn't have the strength to snuff out a life several dozen floors up. Her younger sister Helen, whose power grows at a pace too wild for Ness to document even in her own mind, has the strength, but still can't figure out how to focus it.

So, this kind of mental murder takes a team effort.

It would be easier, if they had already been upstairs with *him* in the first place and therefore closer to their prey. But then, *he* doesn't want them being seen together in public. Not in a way that might link them together as potential accomplices, or worse—a family.

"Ness," Helen says, her voice quiet but intense as she glances between the screen and her sister. "We should hurry."

It's not that Helen *wants* to hurt people, Ness thinks. But when *he* isn't happy with them, they suffer. Either *he* 'forgets' to bring back food for them to eat, or *he* keeps them apart, sometimes for *days*.

Sometimes, if *he's* really angry, *he* does both.

The first touch of Helen's soft little hand isn't quite enough to open the connection that has existed since the moment that Ness first held her younger sister in her arms. At this point, the full connection isn't automatic; they have to *work* to access each other's power and enhance it. It's like... unlocking a door with a palmprint. It should work the same way every single time, but there's always that fear that somehow, this time, their palmprint won't match. Or, in the case of Helen and Ness, that their powers won't work, or that their connection will be too shaky, because they're hungry or because they haven't done it in a while.

This time, Ness's fear is unfounded; their link comes online. The sensation of being in each other's heads is uncomfortable at first, the way it always is, and Ness blinks rapidly to try and get used to seeing through her younger sister's eyes as well as her own.

"Come *on*," Helen whines into the silence, jolting Ness back into focus.

Once linked, it's easy enough to retrace their psionic energy back to the mind several floors away. With the mind comes the memory of their name—*Jax*—and Ness shudders at the thoughts of what *he* did to leave them in such a sad state.

Ness feels Helen reach for Jax, her powers pressing forward along the thread of energy that stretches between them and their prey. There's another presence upstairs, another persistent press of psionic energy nudging against their combined strength and keeping them from getting a good grip on Jax's already overworked body. The mind that brushes up against theirs, that tries to *probe* theirs, is new. New, but experienced in a way that makes the sisters balk at tangling with it. It's the sort of presence that can only belong to someone with power.

A Judge.

When Helen falters in her attempt to snuff Jax out like a light past its expiration date, the other presence pushes against their combined powers, nudging them back and back until—

"I can't keep doing this," Helen says through her clenched teeth. "I can't—I can't get a good hold on Jax's brain." The hold, Ness thinks to herself, is necessary, if they're going to snuff it out.

But if they can't...

"Do you trust me?" Ness asks aloud.

Helen's small head bobs.

"Send out all of your power in a blast," Ness says. "Wipe Jax out."

Ness hates the way her voice sounds, all cold steel as she orders her little sister to do something just as bad as killing. But she's the only one who *can* give the order.

When Jax's frantic mind blinks out like a dying lightbulb a moment later, Ness tells herself that the sacrifice was necessary.

It always comes down to sacrifice.

Either *his* victims or them.

And Ness will *always* make the choice that keeps her little sister safe.

Two

ANDERSON ISN'T A fan of surprises.

Especially when said surprise ends in mental backlash so bad she's smacked back into her skull and immediately gets a headache. The pain lingers several minutes after she's forced out of Jax's mind, long after someone comes for Jax's deathly-still, slender body to take her back to headquarters for further inspection. The blowback felt almost physical, and Anderson catches herself blinking back the tears that threaten to stream from her eyes.

"Grud," she says, breathing out, one gloved hand flying up to rub at the corners of her left eye. The pain is... persistent, battering against her brain like someone with a particularly large grudge. Her shields, as ineffective as they are most of the time, are battered and breaking down. It's going to take time to strengthen them on her own.

Time that she doesn't have, because she has to figure out if Jax is still *Jax* or if her consciousness has been wiped away entirely. She has to find answers. Not just because that's her job and she intends to be good at it, but because she *knows* she wasn't imagining another presence forcing her back on the mental plane.

She knows she shouldn't let her shields stay in shreds, but they'll have to wait.

Moments after *that* realisation, Anderson senses Lee's approach. The other Judge comes around on Anderson's left side, walking slowly as if she doesn't want to surprise Anderson and wind up brain-blasted for her troubles. Even if Anderson hadn't been on alert with her senses cranked up *high*, she'd still be able to sense the worry that cloaks Lee.

It's both unwarranted and unexpected. Lee shouldn't be feeling worry.

Worry is one of those pesky emotions that good Judges just don't feel. Especially not for a Psi-Judge, someone that's just one difficult day away from being just another case.

That sense of worry increases as Lee comes closer, and Anderson's mouth twists with an expression she knows won't make anyone around her feel better.

"You need to get your head checked," Lee says. The words are firm, almost an order. "Who knows what happened when you tried to read that futsie—?"

Anderson feels her lips tighten in a frown and she makes a point of not turning to track Lee's approach. "I'm *fine*."

"You and the futsie checked out at the same time," Lee fires back, an unsubtle sharpness in her tone. "'Scuse me for not wanting to work with a partner that might self-des at any moment. Get your head checked or I'm filing a complaint."

There's smugness in Lee's voice and in the thoughts running through her head. Even if Anderson *does* allow the techs to check her out, Lee is thinking, she's still going to let someone know about this—

About how Anderson is "a thick-skulled Psi that could be compromised."

Anderson bites back the mean smile.

Lee's complaint, if she even remembers to make it after they're done for the day, will be just one of a handful that she gets every time that she's partnered up with a new street Judge.

It's not like any of the higher-ups will be *surprised*.

"Once we're finished interviewing residents, we have to stop by Psi-Division HQ so I can get a second opinion about Jax," Anderson says, still not looking up at Lee. "I'll get a scan while we're there." She pauses, feeling that sharp smile settle on her face. "Since you're so worried that I'll break."

NORMALLY, ANDERSON DOESN'T sleep unless she has to.

But by the time that she and Lee finish tracking down and interviewing every single person that'd been in the holopark when Jax had gone off script, she feels as though she could even fall asleep on the unnervingly crisp fake grass under her boots.

And her headache is still there.

Mostly, because her shields are *not*.

And there's still work to be done.

FINDING WHERE JAX is laid out in a scanner bed is easier than expected.

Headquarters is, as always, packed to the brim with busy, distracted Psi-Judges focused on the next crime, the next poor decision made by a (supposedly lesser) mind. Some of the Judges she recognises, and they clearly recognise her, judging by the way that they either dip their helmeted heads in greeting or sniff disdainfully at her appearance. Most of the Judges they pass, however, barely gift Anderson and Lee with a glance as they make their way to one of the wards that they use for particularly interesting suspects… or victims.

* * *

LYING COMATOSE IN a scanner bed, Jax looks so much smaller than she had previously. So much younger. The sight of her, dressed in a robe and all hooked up to more devices than Anderson can name, makes Anderson feel like she's looking at a child—even though she knows, from the resident files she'd gotten from one of the block's supervisors, that Jax is only a few years younger than she is.

The tech at the foot of the scanner bed looks up when Anderson and Lee walk in. Pale, with blond hair buzzed short, pale green eyes, and thin features that almost put Anderson in mind of a straw. Anderson recognises him immediately; he's one of her cohort at the Academy, a Psi with a knack for healing and an interest in tech. He's patched her up a couple of times, mostly back when they were both in training.

His name escapes her mind even as she wracks her memory for it.

Of course, the slip isn't missed.

"It's Miles, Anderson," he says with a faint smile, voice almost fond. Aside from letting him patch her up whenever she'd gotten hurt, Anderson can't understand what she's done to earn it. "You never could bring yourself to remember my name."

Anderson shrugs. "It's been a while."

"Long enough," Miles says, simply. "I've been expecting you."

Anderson nods once, barely acknowledging his words. "I'm supposed to check her out again. Have there been any changes?"

"I've been monitoring her since she arrived, and nothing has changed," Miles says without glancing down at the tablet in his hands. "She's alive, thanks to the machines, but far from aware."

Anderson stares down at Jax, biting her bottom lip as she thinks.

And thinks.

"Get me a chair," Anderson says to Lee. The order is delivered without thinking and with an accidental, but not insignificant, mental coercion. Because Anderson's shields are *shot*.

When Lee returns with a chair—a hard-backed monstrosity that is not going to be comfortable in the slightest—she slams it down hard enough to make Anderson wince.

"Do *not*," Lee says, biting the words out through her clenched jaw, "do that to me again."

Anderson opens her mouth, fully intending to apologise and offer an explanation, and then... stalls. She can't admit to being so fried and frazzled that she uses her power without thinking. Not in front of Miles *and* Lee. Especially not after Lee's thoughts from before. That's a fast track to a deep brain scan and some time spent being poked and prodded and *thought at*. Anderson doesn't have *time* for that.

Her apology, when she manages to make it a moment later, is weak. "It won't happen again," she says.

The jut of Lee's jaw and the way her gloved right hand curls into a fist says volumes about her patience. And her anger.

"It better not."

REACHING INTO JAX'S mind is different than it was the first time. Instead of the images she'd seen before, flickering flashes that still barely make any sense at all, all Anderson registers now is a steady dark space that feels like an empty room.

Empty, aside from the remnants of the strange psionic energy from the backlash, and several thin threads that blink in and out alarmingly when Anderson tries to touch them.

"What *are* those?" Anderson can hear her own voice aloud, fear and frustration tripping on her tongue. She's never seen a mind like this before. It's somewhere in between a mind-wipe and... *something else*.

Jax's *self*, what little of it Anderson had been able to read back in the holopark, isn't really present; but it's not entirely gone either. Instead of a full mind-wipe—it always makes Anderson's skin *crawl* when she has to brush up against an erased mind— the thread-filled blankness makes Anderson feel as though her own mind has been set... adrift. Like a wipe-job left half done.

Anderson dives deeper, trying to trace the threads back to their source and what she suspects are the remnants of Jax's *Jaxness*. It feels as though she's extending her own mind on a thread, and as she searches for those blinking threads and where they must lead, she feels her own thread thinning.

Stretching.

And—

Unceremoniously, Anderson finds herself dumped back in her own body.

It *hurts*.

Her previous headache, the one that she'd been hoping in vain would go away on its own since she couldn't find any time to rebuild her fleeting protections, is twice as bad, twice as painful.

Forcing her aching head up, she pins Miles with a sharp look.

"Sorry about that." The other Psi holds up his hands in an attempt at a don't-bite-my-head-off gesture. To her eyes—and Lee's, undoubtedly—he looks contrite, but Lee can't see the surety and smugness in his aura.

"You were in too deep," Miles says. "Your heartbeat slowed, and I could sense you drifting away. If I hadn't intervened, you would be right next to Jax on one of these beds."

Anderson frowns. "I almost had her," she insists.

Miles' head tilts. "Really?"

Well...

"Well, I think I have a lead," Anderson admits, speaking slowly. "I don't yet know who's responsible for her physical injuries, but I do know one thing. The psi that did this? Isn't a professional." Anderson pauses to rub at her temples. "This isn't a proper wipe. Some part of Jax is still in there, somewhere."

"But if you try to reach her," Miles says, in that pleasant tone that doesn't match the steel in his gaze, "we could lose you too. I'll make a request for an amplifier and a more experienced telepath. One that isn't half-fried and exhausted."

"But—"

Anderson wants to whine. Wants to remind Miles that this is her—*their*—case and victim. Honestly, she wants to kick something. She does none of those things.

"While we're here," she says, "I need your help with something."

HONESTLY, ANDERSON IS used to having other people in her head. Has to be; privacy is a fantasy that Psi-Judges aren't allowed to have.

But having Miles in her head as he tries to divide his attention between scanning her mind and memories and helping her start the long task of rebuilding her shields is... frustrating. Technically, Anderson can do both of those things on her own.

One at a time.

On a day when she isn't worn thin in all the wrong ways.

So his help is... necessary. But frustrating.

"Would you mind thinking a little quieter?" Miles says aloud, mostly for Lee's benefit. The other Judge is a silent shadow on the far side of the room, still standing over Jax's prone body. She'd chosen to stand there instead of at Anderson's side, and that's fine by Anderson. "I'm trying to focus."

Anderson bites back an instinctive (and insincere) apology and tries to concentrate. Which is... harder than it should be.

"Can we patch my shields first?" Anderson asks, hating the words as they slip out of her mouth. They're weaker shields than she should have with her experience, and she's never quite managed the hang of blocking other people out of her head unless they're an active threat, but... they're *her* shields. And they *do* help.

Most of the time.

Miles utters a quiet huff and flares his nostrils. "Shields first," he agrees. "Then scanning."

IT FEELS LIKE hours pass.

Endless, boring hours.

But finally, Miles steps away and nods, looking satisfied with his work if not with hers.

"Your shields are back to some level of usefulness," he says. "And I've done a preliminary scan."

"But..." Anderson trails off expectantly.

"You should try not to extend yourself any further," Miles points out. "Your shields are flexible enough, but I can sense your exhaustion. If I thought you'd listen to me, I'd suggest taking an hour or two to rest."

Anderson has *never* been that good at listening to other people.

Or taking care of herself...

She brushes off Miles' words as if he'd never said them, turning to her next concern. "Did you sense anything with the scan?"

Hesitation thickens the air.

"The backlash you felt earlier, the presence that tried to wipe your victim's mind? *That* caused your headache. And if you'd decided to ignore it the way I know you'd've preferred to, I have a feeling that it would've only gotten worse. Much worse."

Great.

Just drokking great.

"Can I leave now?" Anderson asks. "I want to go back to the block."

263

Miles doesn't frown.

Much.

"I think you need rest," he says again, "but since you insist on working until you drop..."

Anderson is out of her chair and halfway across the room before Miles has the chance to finish talking.

Interlude

NESS DOESN'T HAVE time for guilt.

She'll make time later, when she doesn't have Helen holding her hand and all of her attention focused on scanning minds for someone that meets *his* specifications in the dozens of people that chose that exact moment to rush around to various parts of the block.

As she scans, she counts fifteen people eager for a look at the holopark from earlier today and a chance at another potential 'futsie sighting,' twenty people thinking about sleep in such deep detail that it makes *her* yawn, and at least sixty people who will probably get arrested by a Judge before the night is out.

But at least they'll (probably) be alive.

You're thinking too much, Helen projects, her voice made stronger by the physical contact and their own unique bond. *The quicker we're done here, the quicker I can go back to sleep.*

The mild scolding makes Ness's cheeks warm and she sighs and squeezes her little sister's hand.

"Fine," she says with her mouth instead of her mind, eyes narrowing as she surveys the crowd. "I don't want to be out here any more than you do, so..." She trails off as she feels someone approaching their hiding spot on the west side fiftieth floor. No cruel thoughts or even unfriendly ones leap out at Ness as she and Helen scan as a unit.

Their unfortunate future victim is... nice.

Nice enough that when he sees Ness and Helen huddled together in the hallway, the first emotion he feels is worry.

For *them*.

"Are you girls lost?"

The concern is touching.

Most of the time, when they have to grab someone for *him*, they go for the folks that don't like kids or that would actually harm them if given a chance. That way, Ness doesn't have to feel as guilty about what she has to do, or what *he* makes them do.

The man is tall enough that when he comes closer, Ness has to tilt her head back to see more of his face than the inside of his nose and the wiry red of his bushy, busy beard. He looks like he could've been a Judge in another life, on another world.

"Can you help us?" Ness answers his question with a question of her own, trying her best not to convey any of the anxiety speeding up her heart. She manages a smile for the man in front of her and then holds out the hand that isn't holding Helen's. "We're trying to get downstairs."

Ness doesn't have time for guilt right now, but as the deep-voiced and *nice* man curls careful fingers around her own, she knows that she'll feel guilty about whatever happens to this one.

Three

IF ANDERSON THOUGHT the emotional resonance around the holopark was tough to wade through earlier, it's nothing compared to how it feels on their return to the building.

The brightly-lit hall leading from the elevators is devoid of residents aside from one of the block's supervisors—a man named Rowan, who'd met them on their way into the massive building—but Anderson still feels like she's walking a gauntlet. She's surrounded by the lingering thoughts from the rush of residents, a great mass of people who have managed to make a sort of path to the holopark and through the hall—an almost physical pressure from thoughts and sensation and commentary, none of it very helpful.

After all, everyone thinks that they know something.

By now, news of the previous disturbance has made its way across the entire block, twisting in the telling.

For some people, the story is that a mutant got loose and attacked a family. For others, the story they heard was about a futsie that *ate someone*. Somehow. At no point in the multitude of minds that Anderson brushes against as the elevator shoots up does she come across a single person that knows *exactly* what went on in the holopark earlier in the day.

Even though she *knows* that Rowan, an earnest man that'd given her Jax's information without needing to be asked, had sent out a bulletin to every single resident.

Rowan, a slim man that looks around the same age as Lee—not that *that* gives a clue to his actual age with all the work that people get done on their bodies out of boredom—starts to drag his feet as they get closer to the entrance to the holopark. He's even fidgety enough to stall them.

"Stop that," Lee snaps, reaching back and urging Rowan forward with a not so gentle tug. "You're the one that volunteered to come up here and override the security lock. Quit lagging. You're slowing us down."

AFTER A QUICK but fruitless scan of the holopark, Rowan insists on taking them down to Jax's cube of a room. Despite Lee's gruffness, Rowan is helpful. Strangely helpful. As they walk through the hallways, Anderson frowns at his narrow back. No one in Mega-City One is ever helpful, even if their lives literally depend on it.

"Did you know Jax?" Anderson ask the back of Rowan's head.

The man's shoulders rise and fall in a shrug that says absolutely nothing.

Anderson bristles, feeling downright spiky. "Well?"

"She did some... er... *errands* for anyone that could afford to pay her," he says after a hesitation that makes Anderson and Lee share a silent look. That was not information that Rowan had volunteered before. There are tens of thousands of people living in Wormwood Block. Even a supervisor—and Anderson highly doubts his position in any way has actual power—shouldn't be able to single out any one person that lives here and isn't related to them.

But before Anderson or Lee can ask a follow-up question, Rowan rushes to fill the silence, spitting out a rapid-fire rush of words that makes Anderson consider stunning him.

"I didn't use her that often," Rowan says, sounding defensive to Anderson's ears as he babbles. "She dealt with things I didn't care for, and I never really trusted her not to turn on me." He continues speaking into the tight tension of the silence that stretches around them. "She was always running around the place on her deliveries. Probably making enemies. You know?"

What she can read of his thoughts—a similarly hectic stream-of-consciousness—isn't much better than the words spilling out of his mouth. Or much slower.

With how fast Rowan's mouth and mind are moving, Anderson can honestly only pick out a small percent of what he is actually saying and thinking. All she can gather is that Rowan is hiding something—probably that he had used Jax to do something unsavory at one point or another.

This stream of too-quick talking and thinking continues right up to the beaten-up door for Jax's apartment cube. Rowan unlocks the door for them and then stands back almost expectantly.

Before Rowan can invite himself deeper into their investigation, however, Lee stops him. Forcibly. One hand pressed flat to his sternum hard enough to make the man grunt and wince, pain tightening the corners of his eyes.

"You can go."

NOT ONLY IS Jax's apartment so small that Anderson and Lee barely have room to move around one another, but the filthy room doesn't even have a window. In its place, she has a battered vid screen that doesn't even take up the whole of the wall it's mounted on. When they walk into the apartment, the monitor cycles through a series of images clearly tailored to Jax's... sad little life. Including a message thanking Jax for dropping off an order from two days ago.

There's nothing that stands out about Jax's life. Everything in her small apartment is mundane. Lee finds some drugs and a few small knives, but... she's normal. Boring, aside from the errands that she runs in order to afford her habit. As hard as they search, Anderson and Lee can't find anything that would explain someone hurting her and trying to wipe her mind.

"Jax is small-time," Lee says as she scrolls through the young woman's messages on her tablet. "Everything she's delivered in the past few weeks is junk or just illegal enough to be someone else's problem." Lee sets down Jax's tablet and casts a disdainful look around the messy, minuscule room. "This is a waste of time."

Stomm, what's crawled into her helmet?

Sure, aside from the strange circumstances of her appearance in the holopark, everything about Jax's life seems too normal, right down to the robo-goldfish taking up a prime position on a large table, but this can't be a waste of time. If only for the fact that it's one of the few places in the building where Anderson can actually hear herself think.

And that gives her an idea...

"I know you're annoyed, but could you do me a favour and keep quiet while I do a scan?" Anderson asks, aiming for a polite tone instead of an order that she knows Lee will bristle at. "When I scanned Jax earlier back at HQ, I noticed some things that I want to check out. This apartment might be the best place to try and find answers about Jax and whoever attacked her."

"As long as I don't have to go back out there with Mr. Helpful, you can do whatever you want," Lee grumbles, just loud enough for Anderson to hear. She stands back, holding up the nearest wall with her broad shoulders, watching with a weighty silence as Anderson clears trash off the least disgusting chair in the room and then sits down, preparing to drop onto the psychic plane.

Four

In her mind's eye, Anderson's view of the apartment shifts. On the psychic plane, Jax's apartment isn't as filthy. It is coloured by the young woman's presence in the tiny space, the imprints giving Anderson the same impression as the threads she had noted in her scan of Jax's nearly wiped mind—but for the most part, that's it.

And then Anderson shifts east and notices the same presence that she'd gotten from her scan of Jax's mind and from the psychic backlash in the holopark. She realises, then, that *normal* isn't quite the word for the space she inhabits on the physical plane. Jax's impressions are all muddled and murky, as if the same presence that tried to wipe her from existence at the holopark had tried to do the same in here.

At first, it seems like it will be easy to locate the source of that strange psychic presence, because Anderson is literally surrounded by it. But the moment she tries to engage the presence, she gets a rude awakening. The presence—which should *not* be able to move—is difficult for her to get a grasp on. What had initially seemed stationary jerks away, slipping through her psychic fingers through the apartment wall—or where the wall would be in the waking world.

This is harder than Anderson expected it to be.

She realises *why* when she hits a psychic hotspot, a trap set by the source, and plunges headfirst into a memory that is definitely not hers.

SHE'S SEEING THROUGH someone's eyes as they look down at a floor stained with rust-brown splotches of what is very likely blood, and pitted from some sort of chemical (acid?). The hands are small, gloves covering the skin well past Anderson's limited field of vision. In the right hand is a bottle of some kind of solution. In the left, a cloth that's clearly already been put to use scrubbing the floor.

"Do a good job," Anderson hears a muffled voice snarl from overhead. "We're going to be having another guest soon and I don't want any cross contamination."

Anderson watches as those small, gloved hands shake, spilling the cleaning solution across the floor. Despite her hopes to hear the voice of the person cleaning up or even feel their thoughts, the person's head simply bobs up and down in a nod.

Silent, even in the safety of their mind, the only thing that Anderson can even sense from the person trying to clean is a sense of bone-deep weariness and fear.

When she tries to interact with the memory, to get a better look at her surroundings, the scene... *shifts*.

I DON'T WANT to do this.

I want to go back to sleep.

Another memory.

This time, with a running thread of thoughts unlike the emotion-filled mental silence from before. Anderson is in another mind. Another body. This one feels... different from the first, and when light floods the room, Anderson realises why. Where the memory from before had nearly no identifiable details about the person whose memory she was riding, several details stand out in this one:

Small brown hands and chunky wrists.

Dark hair brushing the side of Anderson's borrowed face.

Rounded cheeks brushing against rough cloth.

I want my bed, the mind thinks. *I don't want to be useful.*

Slowly, Anderson realises one important detail about the memory she's currently inhabiting.

It belongs to a child.

A child so young that they're still being carried around and their entire internal monologue revolves around how tired they are. How much they want to be back in bed.

The thought about being useful, though; now, *that* throws Anderson.

As with the previous memory, Anderson tries to interact with the setting. She tries to flex those little fingers she can see curled in the collar of a shirt or turn the head that keeps focusing on how much they'd rather be asleep.

A sudden jolt makes her flinch across the psychic plane and she 'hears' a new thought:

You're not supposed to be here.

The thought comes along with a challenge, a child's curiosity and annoyance spiking into Anderson's mind before that memory dissolves too, depositing her straight into—

Where she started, Jax's apartment. Only now the psychic energy from before, the strange presence she'd been tracking, is nowhere to be found.

"What—?"

Anderson grits her teeth, feeling the pressure even in this plane, and tries to reach out again in another scan. Wormwood Block is as massive as any of the other blocks that Anderson has had to scan in her time working as a Jay, but there's no way that a presence that strong could vanish as if it had never even been there.

What she finds in her scan isn't what she wants, but it might be another clue: a stray, panicked thought from someone on a lower floor on the other side of the block. *I just know that Baker wouldn't stay out without telling me. Why isn't he answering his drokking comm?*

The thought comes from a worried sibling. Anderson can pick that much up from the flurry of frustrated and fearful thoughts that bleed through across the plane.

The other thing that she picks up?

A thought about this missing sibling stumbling across a child in one of the hallways.

Anderson drops out of the psychic plane and back into reality with an exultant cry that visibly startles Lee. Even though the other Jay tries to hide it, Anderson has to smother a laugh at the way the tall woman struggles to collect herself.

It takes a moment or two, but finally Lee asks, "Any luck with the scan?" in a gruff tone.

Anderson feels a sharp grin settle on her face. "We're going to need to head downstairs. I think I was in the mind of the person responsible for trying to wipe Jax." She pauses to rub at her temples in an attempt to ward away the headache that threatens. "It's a child, Lee. And there might be another victim."

Interlude

THE MOMENT THAT the sisters feel the Judge's psychic scan, two things happen.

First, Helen responds to the brush of the Judge's focused energy with her own. Only, her press of psionic energy is much more like a slap to Ness's senses. Or rather, it would be if not for the fact that Ness isn't Helen's target.

As for the second—

Ness panics the moment that she feels that unfamiliar *searching* presence pass through the block, insinuating itself into all of the nooks and crannies as the Psi-Judge tries to track their energy from... Jax's room. *Oh, no.* Ness reaches for her sister on instinct, strengthening her attempt at the sort of psychic misdirect that she's used several times in the past. It's protected them from the notice of other Psi-Judges and sensitives before, and it *should* protect them this time.

If only Helen would stop trying to reach out—

"Stop *struggling*," Ness hisses, digging her fingers into Helen's skin as her sister tries to throw her off and reach out, her desire to get at the Judge going against everything that they'd learned together.

Helen shakes her head, uttering an angry, wordless cry as she shoves against Ness's grasp and the wavering misdirection field.

Ness refuses to let go.

"Do you *want* her to find us?" the older girl whispers, terror shaking the words as they leave her mouth. She has one hand curved around her younger sister's upper arm and the other pressed to the right side of her forehead as she tries to focus—

It's just so hard to focus with a squirming kid flailing at her and trying to pick a fight that she's much too small to win.

The only comfort is that *he* isn't here to see this. That she doesn't have to shield themselves *and him*, because *that* requires some form of physical contact. That if she fails, there's nothing *he* can do to punish her for it because the Judge will already be involved.

"I need you to listen to me, Hel," Ness says against the shell of her little sister's right ear. "I know you think that this is a game, a challenge, but we can't fight this Judge. We can't even let her know that we can sense her." She shakes her sister, just a little. "So please, stop moving. Stop reaching out. Just... *stop* and let me do this."

Helen *growls*. "But she shouldn't *be* here—"

"Hel, *please*," Ness breathes. "I need you to be good and listen to me."

It takes a moment too long for Ness's liking for Helen to stop struggling against her body, but eventually, Helen blows out her breath in a huffy sigh and slumps. Without her resistance, Ness is able to shore up the misdirection field.

As they sit in a tense silence, they feel the Judge's probe pass over them.

So much trouble in such a short time...

At least, Ness thinks to herself, *we're safe for now.*

Five

SKINNY AND PALE with a shock of bright red hair clipped back from her wide forehead, panicked thoughts full of her missing sibling, the woman doesn't seem to register Anderson as a Judge at first. When she answers the door, hope blazes on her face, quickly melting away into annoyance.

"You're not Baker," she says in an accusatory tone. "What do you want?"

Gesturing at Lee, who couldn't look more like a typical Judge if she was in the middle of punching a criminal in the face, Anderson offers the woman a smile. "This is Judge Lee, and I'm Anderson. We're here to help you."

Wary disbelief shines in the woman's eyes and is reflected in the emotions Anderson can feel without even looking too closely at her. "*Help* me? How?"

Anderson points at her head. "I'm a Psi-Judge and *you* have been thinking very loudly about your missing brother. Are you going to invite us in?"

* * *

THE WOMAN, WHO introduces herself as "Kay" after closing the apartment door behind them, offers Anderson and Lee seats in a room that is significantly larger (and *cleaner*) than the one that they'd just come from upstairs, but refuses to take one herself. Instead, she paces round and round the room, her thoughts on a constant loop of *WhereismybrotherWhereismybrotherWhereismybrother.*

Sometimes—all right, all the time—Anderson wishes that people could just think a little quieter.

"Baker never stays out without letting me know," Kay tells Anderson, her voice earnest, head wobbling on her tattooed neck. "If he's going home with someone, he sends me a message and shows up in the morning to spill the deets. This is *not* like him."

Anderson has to hold back a thoughtful frown.

Normally, a single missing person in a block populated by tens of thousands isn't something that'd be *her* problem. But a missing person vanishing shortly after a futsie attack linked to a possible rogue psi? After she's just caught a glimpse of a too-clever child with more power than she'd expected?

That makes it her problem.

Anderson puts her hands on her hips. "And what did you two talk about, the last time you spoke?"

It'd be easy to pluck the answer out of Kay's mind if she needed to, but she really doesn't *want* to.

Kay frowns.

"You know," she says, one side of her wide mouth twisting, "it was a couple hours after that futsie went wild." Kay pauses to touch the tip of one claw-tipped finger to her bottom lip before pressing on: "He'd messaged me from downstairs, said something about coming home early since the clubs were already boring him—"

"And then?" Anderson interrupts, carefully keeping the impatience out of her own voice.

"He told me he'd be right back after he helped some lost little kid find their way back home."

There it is.

"A kid?" Anderson asks, leaning forward into Kay's space before she catches herself. "Where? What'd they look like?"

Kay shrugs, the gesture uncomfortably casual despite her missing brother. "He really didn't say," she says, "I mean—I don't *remember* him saying, anyway."

"I can help you with that," Anderson says. "But you're going to need to sit down next to me and focus as you walk me through the last time you spoke with him."

When Kay is close enough to touch, Anderson grabs her right hand in a tight grip and tells her to, "think back to your last conversation..."

WHEN HER COMM alerts her to an incoming live message from Baker, Kay *almost* considers muting it. She loves her brother a whole bunch, but it's too damn *early* for him to be calling her to let her know whether he is or isn't coming home for the night.

Kay glares at her comm, willing it to go silent so that she can go back to playing games on the net with some kids too young to know that they're *literally* getting played. She plans to take them for everything they've got, and she can't do that with her big brother bothering her.

Her comm goes silent.

For about five minutes.

Then it comes back on with an even louder tone, Baker's *answer-or-else* tone that he programmed into the device back when they'd first hooked it up.

"Let's pick this up in a bit," Kay says to her prey, pausing it in the next moment so that she can shut off the game and pick up her comm, shifting her VR headset with her free hand so that she can see her comm display as well as the game's paused screen. Baker's face is on the screen, his bushy beard, the shining metal rings through his eyebrows and nose, and his usual big smile so warm even in an image that Kay immediately feels some of her annoyance melt away into familiar fondness. Tapping on his name, she answers.

"What do you want, Baker?"

Baker's voice rumbles through the tinny speakers. "Is that any way to greet your favourite brother?"

Kay rolls her eyes. "You mean my *only* brother?"

Huffing, Baker says, "You're so mean to me."

"Whatevs," Kay drawls, settling back in her gaming chair and wriggling around until she gets comfortable again. "So, who're you going home with this time?"

Baker laughs. "No one, if you can believe it," he says. "Everyone's so busy talking about that futsie that no one's actually dancing or doing anything *fun* in the clubs." He heaves a sigh so *clearly* overblown that Kay has to muffle her own laughter in the palm of her free hand. "Here I am, dressed in my second-best pants, and I can't find anyone interested... I'll be back upstairs in a tick. Take a break from bothering the kidlets on the net and watch something with me."

It's Kay's turn to sigh.

"Oh, I suppose," she huffs. "I *was* about to clean them out, but for you I guess I can take it easy on them." She taps the side of her VR headset, sending out an automatic forfeit. Sure, it stings to tap out, admitting defeat to a bunch of babies with good stuff for grabs, but—

Kay *does* like spending time with Baker.

They don't do it enough any more.

"Done," she says into the mic on her comm, "Now, when will you be home?"

Silence, for a heartbeat or two.

"Hold on a bit, Kay," Baker says, sounding distracted.

"There's a *kid* wandering around out here. Grife, *two* of them. They look lost—"

There's the sound of Baker's big hands fumbling with his comm, then the video on his comm turns on, showing Kay a view of the hallway and a fuzzy view of two dark-haired kids that leaves Kay with more questions than anything else. For some reason, even though Baker has the camera pointed right at them, neither one is in focus. Aside from the hair and their height—one is taller and stylus-skinny, while the other is knee-high and round—Kay can't tell anything about them.

Baker continues speaking as the video moves closer to the kids. "Lemme see if I can help them out."

That's her brother, always trying to help people out.

If she didn't love him, she'd feel obligated to take advantage of him.

"Well," Kay says, "Don't take too long. Just stick 'em on the nearest elevator and head back. I don't want to be up all night while you play around with some embryos."

Instead of an answer from her brother, even a snappy comeback, Kay glances down at her comm and sees... nothing. The call has ended without so much as a 'goodbye' from her brother.

When she tries to call him back, the comm goes straight to the message service.

As Kay's memory of her last call with her brother fades and she slumps against the arm of the couch in a numb haze, Anderson sits back, her mind racing.

This can't be a coincidence.

She looks over at Lee, with a frown. "It's the kid I saw when I was doing my scan," she says. "Only, there are two of them."

Two suspicious kids with enough power to throw up shields and hide their appearance over *video*? When Anderson thinks about how these kids have *also* gotten themselves entangled with the attempted murder of one person and the disappearance of another—

She shudders.

This *can't* end well.

"We're going to need to return to Control," she tells Lee. "We need to file a report and a request for more Judges to help us get through the block. On our own, this will take too long."

Lee bounds to her feet in one fluid movement and makes for the door, not checking to see if Anderson is behind her or not.

Anderson hesitates, glancing at where Kay still sits frozen.

Sympathy is a weakness.

Anderson knows that.

And yet—

"We'll do everything we can to find your brother," she tells Kay. "Starting by letting security know he's missing and in danger. They'll put out a bulletin in the block."

Kay sniffles, the sound wet and thick. "D-do you think Baker'll be okay?"

It would be so easy to lie, to tell Kay that her brother will be fine. That he'll show up again in one piece.

Instead, Anderson doesn't say anything at all, turning on her heel and heading for the door where Lee waits, bristling with her own impatience.

First thing in the morning, they'll be back, and Anderson *will* get to the bottom of things.

Interlude

He COMES BACK to their rooms in the dead of night, waking them with the sound of *his* heavy footsteps. Not that this is any different from usual. *He* never makes much of an effort to be anything *close* to kind and polite as far as they're concerned, and that extends to not waking them up in the middle of the night.

He knocks once on the door that Ness and Helen share when he allows them to stay together. A sharp rap of his heavy knuckles that sends Ness's pulse leaping up into her throat as Helen stirs in her arms.

"I know you two are up," *he* says as though it isn't the middle of the night. "Come out. I have something for you."

Ness feels her mouth twist with a grimace.

No matter what *he* has—a reward or a punishment for something that *he* only *thinks* they did—Ness wants no part of it.

His rewards are never really for them.

They're for *him,* and the pleasure *he* gets out of disappointing them. She's known *him* for five years, ever since their mother died and *he* took them in "out of the kindness of his heart" and not once has *he* ever given them a 'reward' that wasn't painful or embarrassing.

Food they can't eat.

Clothing they can't wear.

Souvenirs from victims they have no business remembering.

And *his* punishments aren't much different.

LEGALLY, *HE* IS their guardian.

Not their father.

Not by any meaning of the word.

When Ness thinks of 'father,' she thinks of the man that made her mother smile. She thinks of strong, brown arms lifting her to touch the ceiling of their apartment and of being read to in the shelter of those same arms as Helen dozed in her lap.

Whatever *he* thinks he is to them—owner, guardian, *master*— it isn't *that*. And something about having to hide herself and Helen behind the misdirection field reminds her of what it meant to have a father.

He's sitting in one of the chairs scattered across the main room, long legs loosely crossed at the ankle. *He* looks comfortable. As usual. As they approach, Ness cradling Helen's sleepy little body in her arms, *he* smiles.

It isn't a nice smile.

It is *never* a nice smile.

"I see my girls survived *two* run-ins with a Jay," he says. "I'm proud."

It's hard for Ness to miss the possessiveness in *his* voice, and she has to hide her disgust in the cloud of Helen's soft, dark hair.

"She almost caught us," Ness says, her own voice hushed. "I tried—"

He cuts her off.

"Yes, I know you two failed at following my orders," *he*

says, sneering as *he* speaks. "The girl is still alive, and I only know *that* because another Judge is trying to be *helpful* and keep me informed about the status of this 'case.'" *His* sneer strengthens, making his face appear even uglier to Ness's eyes. "I should be downstairs, playing with the toy you two found for me, but instead, I have to keep an eye on that Judge. I'm disappointed."

Disappointment is never good.

Ness wobbles on her heel, trying to keep from backing away and making *him* angry.

"Th-the Judge won't get anything," she insists, trying to insert more confidence than she actually feels into the words. "We did our best—"

"And your best wasn't good enough," *he* says, voice raising loud enough to actually wake Helen up. When Helen starts to stir, mouth moving with sleepy little murmurs, *he* settles back against the chair, looking too pleased with himself.

"Now," he says, the smile on *his* face showing too many of his straight, white teeth for Ness's comfort, "I *did* say that I had something for you."

Despite herself—and knowing better—Ness is hoping for dinner.

Real food, and maybe something to drink.

Anything that'll keep her and Helen from simply keeling over after using so much energy doing *his* work for him.

Instead, *he* tosses two wrapped bars at them.

Tosses them.

Ness is so shocked that she forgets her promise to herself to stay silent and not cause any trouble for them.

"What is this?" she blurts out, eyes widening. "Th-this isn't enough food for—" One of them, she thinks. Much less two.

His smile is still one of the worst things that Ness has ever seen.

"It's what you deserve."

Fly Trap

* * *

IT TAKES HOURS for *him* to leave, but the moment he does, Ness turns to a now wide-awake Helen. "I'm hungry," she says, in a sullen murmur.

"Don't worry, Helen," Ness says, not bothering to speak quietly now that *he* has already left the apartment to go back to *his* playroom. "I'll go downstairs and get you something to eat."

Her stomach growls, a faint sour rumble underlying her words.

It's been a while since she had more than synthcaff and water in her stomach. With all of the energy they've used since waking up in the early hours of the morning, it's a wonder that they are not dizzy, or stumbling all over the place. Aside from a few of those all-in-one meal bars before they could even see the sun from their shared room, they haven't eaten anything in a number of days.

Too many days.

"I'll get you something good to eat," Ness promises, sighing a bit as she tries to remember what times the restaurants and cafeterias scattered across their side of the city block shut down and send food to be recycled or repurposed. "Just—just be patient. Drink some water."

"Water doesn't help," Helen insists, staring up at Ness with a stern look on her face.

Ruffling her hair as she stands, Ness manages a soft smile for her little sister. "Water will help, for now."

Six

THERE'S ALWAYS SOMETHING wrong with the incinerator on the west side of Wormwood Block.

Always.

No matter how many times maintenance comes by to fix the drokking thing, within a week or two, it always goes back to its normal, mostly broken original state. Cutting out, uneven temperatures, sometimes burning so hot it sets unintended things on fire. That's why, with a rotating crew of thirty-two residents on top of the robots that aren't as helpful as they should be, it has the most people working in that incinerator block out of the entire building.

Thirty-two people working round the clock to catch what the incinerators miss in their first pass.

Maz and the early morning crew—made up of fellow sixtieth-floor residents Deke, Xoe, and her own sister, Yannel—are the ones responsible for emptying the ash pans and sorting through what's left to find: things that the intermittently-broken incinerators simply couldn't handle.

They've found strange things before. Of course. It's

Wormwood Block; and the residents of this block aren't any less likely to toss weird crap down the incinerator chute than any other.

Toys, food, clothes, the occasional robot housekeeper. You name it; they've probably hauled it out of the ash pan...

Of course, this *is* the first time that anyone on the morning crew has dug up human *bones* from the ash pan during their shift.

AT FIRST, MAZ isn't quite sure what she's looking at when Xoe scurries up to her, the familiar stiff sway of her prosthetic hips hurried in the dim light from the flickering light strips overhead.

At first glance, the thing in Xoe's gloved hands looks like a pipe. A half-burnt, burnt-grey *mess* of a pipe, but... that's all it looks like. At first. Until Maz realises that Xoe's hands are shaking and that the other end of the potential pipe looks an awful lot like a—

"Is that a bone?" Maz is proud of the way that she doesn't let her voice shake as she takes in the length of not-pipe in Xoe's long-fingered hands. "A *bone?*"

Xoe nods, her dyed blue hair swinging back and forth. "Deke and I found a ton in the ash pan all the way on the end."

Maz blinks, nonplussed. "A... ton?"

Shrugging, Xoe attempts to correct herself for accuracy's sake. "At least a whole body's worth."

Not that either of the two of them actually know how many bones are in a human body.

Maz resists the urge to fling the bone away and pretend that she's never seen it. It'd be the easy thing to do, but if Maz wanted *easy*, she'd've never begged for this shift in the incinerator, where she has to wade through other people's junk *after* all the usefulness has already been burnt out of it.

"Let me see them," she says, shoving the bone back into Xoe's hands and striding away in the next moment. "Maybe we'll get lucky an' they'll just be what's left of someone's dinner."

Needless to say, Maz and her crew are *not* lucky.

As she walks up to Deke with Xoe right on her heels and holding that—that *bone* in her hands as if she's not sure what to do with it, she realizes that he's holding something as well. Something smaller and rounder...

"Tell me that's not what I think it is," Maz says, her voice edging into a whine as she catches her first glimpses of empty eye sockets and sooty teeth. When both of her subordinates give her a familiar (and frustrating) blank look, Maz sighs. "Tell me you found that skull somewhere else. Anywhere else."

Deke shakes his big head. Two feet taller than her and built like a wall, strong enough to match, Deke is the biggest member of her crew and—unfortunately—the one least likely to understand sarcasm or anything like it.

He's honest to a fault and doesn't seem to get the dry but almost desperate tone in Maz's voice.

"It was with the other ones," Deke says, anxiously. "Only, this one isn't burnt that badly," he adds, tilting the skull so that Maz can see the star-shaped hole at the very top of it. "It's broken. Just broken."

Grud.

This is not how Maz wants to spend her morning.

Or any part of her life.

She sighs, reaching up to rub at her forehead with sooty, gloved fingers before she remembers the state her hands are in. All she's managed to do is smear filth across her eyebrows, across inked and pierced skin that *really* didn't need any of it.

Yanking her hands away from her skin and trying hard not to blister her team's ears with what she *wants* to say, Maz settles instead for giving orders.

"Deke," she says, snapping her fingers to get his attention. "I need you to sift through the ash and put every single bit of bone that you can find in a bin. If it looks like it belongs with that skull, put it in." Then, she turns to Xoe. "We all got that announcement from the Jay that stopped that futsie from eating that woman. Think you can get security to send a message to her?"

Xoe is, unlike the rest of them, in *good* with security in Wormwood Block. Mostly because she's been living with one of the women in charge for a few years now. If they need a message sent out to one of the Jays, she's the best one to try and get it out.

Xoe nods, and heads to the quiet(est) corner to ping her lover on her comms.

That leaves Yannel.

Sun-starved, with skin so pale she looks almost translucent, Yannel drifts up to Maz's side as if she's the spooktacular star of one of those old films she keeps meaning to pirate. Big, bruise-ringed eyes blink at Maz.

"And what am I doing?"

Maz sighs, gaze shifting across the garbage and ash pans that they still have to go through before their shift is done.

"We're going to do our jobs," she says, "and hope the Jays don't keep us from finishing before it's time to head home."

Seven

THE CALL TO return to Wormwood Block comes mere hours after Anderson and Lee return to Control. The sun—or what little of it that Anderson can see when she races her Lawmaster through the foggy streets right on Lee's rear tire—is barely up.

It is, in a word, too drokking early.

But crime waits for no Judge.

Backup, their backup, meets them at the front of the block. While Anderson doesn't know every single Judge on the street, she does recognise one of the two standing in front of her.

Cato, a Psi-Judge a decade older than her but with more experience, is a tall woman with heavily freckled brown skin, dark eyes that can't be seen behind the visor of her helmet, and a scar that traces down the left side of her face, causing her mouth to twist in a permanent grimace. Anderson has no idea how Cato had gotten that scar, but she doesn't plan to ask.

Her partner is drawn from the usual Street Judge stock: big, broad, and already completely done with the very idea of Psi-Judges interfering in what should be, to his mind, an easy case. He's also, like Lee, wearing his uniform properly. Including the helmet. What skin Anderson can see is light and scarred as well, the product of a life spent protecting the city and fighting scum.

While Cato greets Anderson with a sharp smile and a brief incline of her helmeted head, her partner sniffs.

Loudly.

Anderson doesn't need her powers to see he doesn't have much use for them.

"Why are we even here?" The first words from Cato's partner drip with derision, as if he needs to let them know that he's thinking that this is all a waste of time, that this is a case a Street Judge could have wrapped up in two hours instead of two days. His thin-lipped mouth curls in a sneer and Anderson feels the fingers of her gloved right hand curl into a fist looking for a home on that strong-jawed face. "This should be an easy case."

Anderson bites the inside of her bottom lip. The pain, slight as it is, keeps her from saying something that will get her reported.

Not, she notes absently, something that she'll *regret*.

"We need help finding suspects. That's where you two come in," Anderson says instead, trying not to sound as smug as she feels at getting to delegate caseload duties to Judges with more experience on the street. "We're looking for two children: one is small and round, the other is a tall, thin teenager. Any relevant details are filed in the report we turned in last night. We'll handle things at the incinerator."

Before Cato's partner, whose name Anderson still doesn't know, can get green with her, Anderson jerks her head in the direction of the incinerator bank and heads off, with Lee following near enough on her heels to annoy her.

Payback for the close bike ride, Anderson figures.

ANOTHER MORNING, ANOTHER gauntlet of gawking residents lining a hallway that they have no business being in. The residents' interest batters at Anderson as she and Lee shove through the closely packed hallway on the way to the incinerator, the source of the call from earlier that has them out before basically anyone else.

Thoughts on thoughts on thoughts.

Ugh.

Another futsie?

Cannibals?

I wonder if they found the whole body?

Why won't they fix the incinerator?

I wish these freaks would move so I could see.

Anderson grits her teeth as the residents come closer. "Lee?"

In front of her, Lee's shoulders tense up. "Yes?"

"Make some room."

Honestly, Anderson suspects that Lee must get some amount of pleasure out of muscling her way through the crowd that tightens up around them. There's a distinct sense of glee colouring her aura as she shoves, kicks and—in two cases—headbutts residents that dare to get in their way as they walk towards the entrance to the incinerator on this side of the block.

Anderson knows that she should probably be a little... worried that her current partner is this bloodthirsty, but anything that gets her through a crowd of this size without having to get her own hands dirty is fine.

Acceptable, even.

THE ROOM WHERE the incinerator banks are kept smells like burnt meat.

Burnt meat, garbage, and—this is probably Anderson reaching a bit—*fear*. Like the hall outside, the incinerator banks are packed with gossipers trying their best to get a good look at the carnage and chaos that Anderson and her partner are about to discover.

It takes more of Lee's punchy approach to crowd control and

the frantic wave of one hand by someone Anderson assumes must be the crew on duty when the bones were found, but finally they make their way to the back of the incinerator banks, to the one oven that isn't on.

"Are you the ones that found the body?" Anderson asks, glancing at the four people in front of her.

Nods all around.

The person that waved at them before steps forward, drawing immediate attention thanks to the tattoos that mark her light skin from her hairline down.

"We don't usually find things like this in the incinerators," she says earnestly. "Most of the people in the block don't even eat meat. *Can't* even eat meat. And this… wasn't meat."

Anderson and Lee lean in to look at the pieces of bone and ash that rest in a bin. Anderson's nose wrinkles at the smell.

"What made you think this had something to do with that bulletin?"

The woman, with one gloved hand that trembles as it moves, sifts through some of the burnt debris and then holds up a soot-covered ring that shines silver in the dim light.

Oh.

That looks like one of Baker's facial piercings, one of the steel rings that Anderson remembers from the image she'd plucked from his sister's memory. If his piercings are here—

"Let Cato and her partner know that I need them to deliver the news," Anderson says, her voice quiet. It's cowardly, and Anderson knows that, but—

Frustrated, she doesn't wait for Lee to get in touch with their backup or to shove through the crowd of people now even more interested in the remains they've found. As Anderson pushes back the flood of people trying to get into the incinerator room, a skinny slip of a teenager—dark skin, a shock of curly black hair, knobby knees and elbows—brushes past her. Anderson manages to get a glancing look at the girl's face, from that brief encounter, but what she gets from that brush of skin on skin is worth even more.

Energy crackles between them like a jolt from a stunner. The contact briefly disrupts whatever shields Anderson and the girl have, sending backlash between them.

There is a rush of rapid-fire flickering impressions and emotions.

Fear. Anger. Disgust. Hatred.

Copper-stinking blood.

Swollen fingers clutching at a softer, smaller hand.

Anderson senses power, but not much skill. She recognises the energy as belonging to the presence that had been in Jax's apartment the day before, and which had appeared to be responsible for the woman's condition. Sticky, cloying, as though the energy is reaching out to Anderson.

The girl bolts before Anderson can do anything about her.

Anderson manages to shout "Stop right there," her voice rising up against the noise from the gawking crowd around them, but then the crowd surges again and she loses sight of the girl in a matter of moments.

Lee arrives at her side moments later, frowning.

"They're on their way to Kay," she says. Glancing around, she asks, "What were you shouting about? Who were you shouting at?"

"The girl was here," Anderson says, snarling. "Now we're going to have to find her."

Interlude

NESS TAKES THE long way back to the apartment that she and Helen share with *him*. Alternating between the maintenance stairs that are so rarely used these days and the service elevators in different sections takes time—time that Ness doesn't think she actually has, what with the memory of that Psi-Judge's energy still clinging to her like dust.

Of course, in a block populated by hundreds of thousands of people, Ness has run into other people with psionic power before. For the most part, though, the people that she brushes up against in the hallways or elevators barely have enough power to give her a bit of a buzz. They can't read her mind on the fly or make her do anything that she doesn't want to do. They can't see her aura or anything *interesting* like that.

The most that anyone has been able to do—where *anyone* is the man that pretends he's their father when it suits *him*—is throw up a hasty and hard-to-batter-down shield.

But this Psi-Judge is different from those others.

She reminds her of Helen.

Or, rather, she makes Ness think of what Helen could be if

she wasn't stuck here, subject to the casual cruelty of their very own private monster.

Helen could be a Psi-Judge. She could be a power in her own right. She could be *somebody*.

If she'd only been allowed to grow and learn without *him* stepping on her throat and keeping her from actually using her power for anything *other* than helping *him* hurt and kill people.

If Ness was stronger—

If she could be braver—

They wouldn't be in this position.

BY THE TIME Ness makes her way back to the apartment the three of them share, she's out of breath. Out of breath and so sweaty that her palm slides right off of the palm-reader at the front door the first time she tries to unlock it.

When the door opens to a setting right out of a homey vid— Helen sitting on *his* lap as *he* lectures her in an almost kind, almost... *fatherly* way—she knows she has to say something.

Ness knows better than to interrupt when *he's* busy, or talking, or *anything*, but she can still feel the sensation of the Judge's power sliding across her skin and trying to reach into her mind. She doesn't know if the Judge got a good look at her face, but what she did get—that flash of uncontrolled power— is good enough.

If she's right, then this will only end badly.

And soon.

"I think she saw my face," Ness says, speaking to *him* without looking up. With her chin pressed pointy into her collar, her words come out in a mumble that even she has trouble understanding. "You know—the Jay who tried to read th-the one you let go."

Even though she knows Jax's name, Ness can't say it aloud. Guilt and shame trip up her tongue and she feels tears prick hotly at the corners of her eyes. But she doesn't cry. She doesn't let herself.

Crying, she's realised over the years, is just a way to show *him* that *he's* won and that *he's* that much closer to turning them into mouldable monsters for *his* evil.

Ness sniffles once, deeply enough that she nearly chokes on the snot in her throat, and then pushes on.

"She'll be looking for me," she says.

He smiles and then rises to *his* feet, directing *his* full attention at Ness. Before, when *he'd* been sitting down with a newsvid up on the nearest screen for Helen to go over with *him,* and cradling a cup of synthcaff in *his* hands, it's almost possible to pretend that they're part of a normal family. That when *he* calls them 'his girls' that *he's* coming from a place of love, not ownership.

It takes every single ounce of Ness's self-control to stop herself from flinching backwards or flat out running from the room and away from *his* searching, intrusive stare.

"Where is she?" *he* asks in a voice that'd seem gentle to an outsider. To someone that didn't know *him* and couldn't see— or otherwise sense—the cruelty hiding behind the mask.

Ness shakes her head twice before she can bring herself to answer with words.

"She-she's at the incinerator," Ness eventually manages to whisper, forcing the words out through a throat so tight it feels like she's choking on everything she says. "Th-they found b-bones—"

His eyes almost seem to flash in the light of the room and *he* launches himself forward, crossing the room in a matter of ground-eating steps so that *he* can grab at Ness's forearms. "*Bones?*"

Ness squeaks and tries to jerk backwards, out of *his* reach.

"Th-the incinerator wasn't working," she spits out, "I don't know why—but they got some kind of alert and called the Judges first thing. I—*oof!*" Ness doesn't get to finish the sentence that she'd only just begun. No sooner than that first syllable leaves her mouth does *he* shove her out of the way, stepping over her on *his* way to the door.

"What are you going to do?" Ness finds herself asking, breaking one of the rules that she'd set in place for herself since the moment that their mother died and *he* became a part of their lives.

It's only fair, though; by touching her, *he's* broken one of *his* own.

He doesn't look back or bother with one of *his* usual insincere apologies.

"I'm going to handle this," *he* snarls. "Don't leave the room until I come for you two."

He rushes to the door and then through it, leaving them to stare at the door in a sort of stunned silence.

"Ness," Helen whispers. "What is *he* going to do?"

Ness shakes her head and then gestures for her sister to come closer. Once they're in each other's arms on the floor, she sighs.

"I don't know," she admits, "but whatever it is, we're going to suffer for it."

Eight

THE MOMENT THAT they walk into the security station, Lee's body starts to vibrate with a tension that would be hard to miss even if Anderson wasn't able to read her mind.

"What's wrong?" Anderson asks, hand slipping down to her Lawgiver on instinct. For Lee to be so immediately and visibly upset, something has to be wrong. But what could it be?"

Lee's shoulders stiffen. "Mister Helpful is here. Again."

Anderson starts repeating Lee's words to herself, and then makes the connection.

"Rowan?"

He's the man from before, the one who'd let them into Jax's rooms and into the holopark. While his helpfulness isn't the worst thing that has ever happened while Anderson was working, he was somewhat... obnoxious in the help that he did give. Anderson tilts her head back to get a better look at the way that Lee's entire body seems ready to fight. Just because Rowan was helpful—

Interesting.

"What is it about him that has you this frustrated?" Anderson murmurs, glancing over at where Rowan seems to be all but holding court in a corner a few feet away from the main database for this section of the block. Rowan may be annoyingly helpful, but he seems harmless enough.

Lee shrugs. "There's something about the way he's been offering to help. I don't trust him."

Anderson doesn't blame her. Trustworthy and downright *helpful* citizens are hard to come by, and there's no reason for *this* one to be as helpful as he's been. It's not a crime, of course, but... maybe it's worth checking out.

"I'll handle him," Anderson says over her shoulder after she pushes past Lee and marches towards Rowan with purpose in her stride.

IN THE FEW seconds it takes for Anderson to reach Rowan, the crowd around him disperses, leaving him alone for her approach. He greets Anderson with a slow smile that even manages to reach his eyes, but doesn't last.

"How can I help you?" Rowan asks.

"You can help by giving me access to the block's resident files and inputting some data for me," Anderson says. "I have a potential suspect for the incident yesterday, as well as for the body discovered in the incinerator. We also have reason to suspect that there are other disappearances."

Rowan's flinch is so slight that if Anderson hadn't been looking for some reaction to her words, she'd've missed it. But when she tries to read his mind, she finds a whole lot of... nothing.

Rowan's thoughts slip right through her metaphorical fingers and, no matter how hard she tries to get a grip on them to see what he's thinking and *why* mentioning other disappearances made him flinch, she can't manage it.

Quickly, Rowan's smile returns, and he gestures to the station behind him. "I can do that," he says, "Just... bear with me. It's been a while since I've done any data input."

Inwardly, Anderson resigns herself to Rowan dragging his heels on this as well, but outwardly, she merely offers him a tight-lipped smile.

"Don't take too long," she says, a warning in her tone. "I'd like to wrap this up before the end of the day."

Anderson crosses her arms over her chest and then waits for Rowan to settle in, with his hands poised over input points. "Are you ready?"

At Rowan's nod, Anderson proceeds to rattle off every single detail that she can remember about the young girl that she'd bumped into earlier. And there are plenty of them.

By the time that she's done, Anderson feels as though there should be enough information to find her in a matter of moments.

Rowan, however, feels otherwise.

"This will take a while," he says, offering Anderson and Lee a hesitant smile. "Is there anything else I can do in the meanwhile?"

Anderson grits her teeth, biting back what she *wants* to say and instead telling Rowan that, "I need to know if there have been any notable disappearances in this block recently."

Rowan's eyebrows draw together as he thinks. Why he pauses to wrack his mind instead of looking at a computer screen is beyond her. Eventually, he shakes his head.

"This is a big building, Judge," he says, dipping his head in a nod that Anderson realises is supposed to be apologetic. "With tens of thousands of people living in it, sometimes people just... fall into the cracks. I couldn't tell you the names of anyone that lives outside of my specific section if I tried."

Considering what Anderson suspects about Rowan and Jax... she finds that hard to believe.

"Speaking of your section," Anderson says, drawing out the

words, "does anyone else live with you that might move around the building more?"

Rowan makes eye contact with Anderson at last and she gets a flash of thought that reminds her of the little child whose memory she'd slipped into earlier. Anderson jumps at that, but manages to control her face and not grin.

"Someone like... a daughter?"

The smile on Rowan's face vanishes entirely. He eyes Anderson warily, almost like a trapped animal, and Anderson thinks that if not for the fact that she *and* Lee are standing in front of him, that he'd bolt.

"I—I do have a daughter," Rowan confesses after the silence between them stretches tight for several minutess.

Anderson allows herself a smile. "And how old is she?"

Rowan shakes his head. "Not old enough to hurt anyone, that's for sure."

"I'll be the judge of that," Anderson says, speaking mildly enough that when Rowan's face turns a blotchy brown-red with poorly hidden anger, she's surprised by it. Instead of addressing that, she turns to Lee. "Send Cato a message letting them know that we'll be taking a trip upstairs to follow a lead. I want them to come and look through what data the computer spits out."

With that done, Anderson turns back to Rowan. "Lead the way," she says.

"Wh-why do you want to question my *daughter?*" Rowan blurts out.

Anderson shakes her head. "She might know something you don't."

Interlude

THE SECOND *HE* gets out of the elevator on their floor, they know.

Despite the fact that *his* own psi abilities are so small as to be nearly nonexistent, *his* arrival on the floor hits them immediately. So does the arrival of two other minds following closely behind him.

One, a normie Judge who can't stop thinking about how annoyed she is with how long this is taking, is inconsequential. Even though the woman's a Judge, she can't do anything to them that *he* already hasn't done. She isn't a threat.

It's the other mind that gives them pause.

The Judge from downstairs, and from the day before.

Unlike the other Judges that Ness has seen, the female Judge trailing behind *him* doesn't wear her name on her badge. That much Ness remembers from the basement incinerator. She also doesn't wear her helmet. It should make her seem kinder, more approachable.

That's probably why she does it, Ness thinks to herself.

However, with all of that psionic power that seems barely

contained in a body only a bit bigger than Ness's, there's no way that Judge can be anything *but* frightening.

Ness's fingers curl into a tight fist, ragged nails cutting into her palms until the pain blooms almost like a laser burst in her mind.

"*He's* going to want us to hurt those Judges, Ness," Helen says, her voice trembling with what Ness suspects is either taut fear or nervous excitement. After everything they've been through together and how hard *he* has been trying to make Helen like *him*, Ness *can't* know. "So they don't hurt us."

"They *won't* hurt us," Ness says.

Helen is too kind (and, Ness suspects, too *young*) to call her on the lie—or how badly Ness wants it to be true.

Ness reaches for Helen without looking, trusting that her little sister will come to her. In her arms, with Helen's baby-fine black hair tickling her chin and the weight of her power—too massive for such a small body—practically blanketing the two of them, Ness can almost forget what's going to happen next.

Once the door opens.

"Stop worrying," Helen says, resting the palm of her soft right hand flat on the curve of Ness's left cheek. Despite the gentleness of that touch, the look in Helen's eyes and the feel of her own psionic energy makes Ness flinch. "Worrying won't help."

Ness opens her mouth to reply, but before a single syllable can leave her mouth, she registers the presence at the front door to the apartment.

"They're here," she whispers, unnecessarily, her mouth hardly moving as she watches the door slide open with a muted hiss.

Nine

NORMALLY, ANDERSON WOULDN'T let someone like Rowan take the lead on the way to a secondary location that she hasn't been able to look at before. But while she may fling herself into danger all the time in the name of the Law, she wasn't born yesterday. She's not a rookie any more.

Anderson isn't letting *anyone* she doesn't trust walk behind her.

Not when she's on high alert and there's something suspicious about the way his mind feels when she dares to brush against it with an unsubtle use of psionic energy. The sensation of his mind is almost... *oily*, definitely unpleasant.

And, even more worrying, Anderson can't read more than a handful of surface thoughts.

Rowan's mood, his memories of earlier in the day, and even further memories about the girl that she'd seen in his head when she'd first peeked—

None of them are available.

Not without forcing her hand a lot earlier than Anderson wants.

"How long have you been a supervisor here?" Anderson asks as they walk through the maze-like hallways of the upper floors where Rowan and his family live.

"Five years," Rowan responds, without looking over his shoulder. "Give or take a few months." There's a story there, one that Anderson can sense and one that she *wants* to know.

So, she pries.

"And your wife," she asks, knowing full well that Rowan is listed as 'single' in the resident registry.

At that, Rowan's sloping shoulders stiffen with tension before spitting out, "She's dead," in a clipped tone.

The way he says those two words is clue enough.

However, Rowan's anger—at the death of his wife or, more likely, Anderson's intrusiveness—gives Anderson something else: a crack in his mental armour. Rowan's nothing like *her*, not in any way that matters, but he has enough psionic energy to block her, tangle up her attempts at reading him.

Until now.

Still walking behind Rowan with Lee behind her and silently watching *everything*, Anderson reaches out one more time, splitting her focus between making mental notes of their surroundings—Rowan's pace has slowed, and Anderson suspects that they're close—and trying to stealth her way into his mind.

It works...

...sort of.

Instead of the more-or-less-coherent stream of thoughts or memories that she usually gets when she tries, Anderson is hit with another wave of disjointed images and thought fragments. This time, reminding her of her brush against the gangly teenaged girl that'd bumped into her right outside the incinerator.

Only—

Worse.

Blood in sticky pools.

A bruise ringing a dark brown eye.

A large hand—Rowan's hand—helping a small hand clutch a scalpel.

A woman lying on a slab, unmoving.

Anderson comes to a sudden, jerky stop.

Unfortunately, so does Rowan; right in front of a door that slides open at their arrival. The opening almost seems to free a claustrophobic wave of psionic energy that grabs at Anderson and *pulls*.

"I—I—" Anderson feels her mouth open and close as she tries to figure out what the hell she's just seen, but nothing comes out. Certainly, nothing that would give Lee any clue that they're in the company of not just any killer, but one that's been killing for a long time—with the help of two tiny apprentices.

When she meets Rowan's eyes, she's not surprised to see the wide smile on his face.

He has them where he wants them, after all.

Anderson walks into the small apartment, not entirely of her own volition. Lee, following close by, nearly trips over her when the psionic force from before stops Anderson cold, right in the middle of the room.

"Watch it, Anderson! I could've been—"

But Anderson doesn't get to hear what Lee could've been because the next sound that she hears is a solid *thud* as Rowan ambushes Lee and the door slides shut behind them.

"You *do* understand that attacking a Judge will just make things worse for you," Anderson says, still frozen in place by that force. "You, your 'daughter'"—and here, Anderson allows the doubt she feels to slip into that one word—"and whoever else you have working with you; you're all going down for a long time. If my backup doesn't take you out first."

Anderson tries to lash out with her mind, to send out a psi-blast that'd alert, oh, just about every single Psi-Judge in her range (and her range is *wide*). But... nothing happens.

Nothing except for the same eye-watering backlash that all but *ruined* her day yesterday.

H-how—

The force holding Anderson in place loosens enough to let her turn her head and take in the rest of the room. And its other inhabitants.

Anderson recognises *both* girls.

The older of the two is the teenager that Anderson ran into earlier. The other, sitting on her hip despite looking a little too old for that, is the girl that Anderson had seen in Rowan's mind. They're obviously sisters, with their matching brown skin and the blue-black hue of their curly hair, but they don't look like Rowan. They do, however, look like the image of the dead woman that she'd plucked out of Rowan's head.

"So, you have *two* daughters," Anderson says, trying to sound flippant as she turns to look at where Rowan has Lee laid out on the ground, as if she's not a Street Judge with several years' more experience than Anderson. "Nice misdirection."

Rowan laughs, sending chills down her spine. "They're my girls," he says. "*Not* my daughters." He hesitates, the look on his narrow face almost thoughtful, before speaking again. To the girls. "Put her out."

Anderson jerks her head to stare at the two girls steadily closing on her.

Put her out?

Despite the headache pounding in her brain, Anderson tries to blast them. To stop them. To do *anything* to keep them from getting her in the same position as Lee is.

But her attempts fall flat, as a tiny, baby-soft hand touches her face, and her world plunges into darkness.

ANDERSON IS GETTING tired of headaches.

But when her choices are waking up with her brain doing its

level best to make her regret it, and not waking up at all... she'll take the headache.

When she first wakes up, swimming up from the depths of the darkness she'd plunged into when that small child had touched her, she can barely think past the headache pulsing in time with her heartbeat. She can barely manage to open her eyes wider than a sliver.

Anderson's tongue feels thick and fuzzy against the roof of her mouth, and when she tries to talk, her jaw doesn't cooperate at first.

Finally, she manages to stutter out a quiet, "Wh-what—" that leaves her throat feeling scratchy.

She's lying flat and—as she realises when she tries to move her arms and can't—being pressed down to a flat surface, she feels panic slice through her.

"Don't bother struggling," Rowan says, his voice coming from just outside of Anderson's currently limited range of vision. "You're not going to get loose anytime soon." He sounds smug; Anderson can almost picture the smarmy smile on his face. "After all this time, I can't believe a Judge like you just walked into my block. What luck!"

Ignoring him, Anderson keeps trying to yank free from whatever it is holding her fast. If she can just get an arm free, maybe reach down to the knife she keeps in her boot—the boot that Anderson realises that she's no longer wearing when she flexes her feet and feels air on her toes.

Anderson isn't wearing her boots.

Or her gloves.

Or, she suspects, any of the more useful parts of her uniform.

"If you're looking for your knife," Rowan says, speaking up again, "I have it now. It's a sharp little thing, isn't it?" There's the sound of metal on metal and then a low moan of pain that isn't Anderson's. "It works so well, doesn't it, Helen?"

Absently, Anderson registers a squeaky-toned noise of

agreement. One of the girls, then: the younger one, most likely.

What on earth does he have her doing?

Anderson flexes her foot again and bends her knee upwards, trying to pull away from her restraints. Despite her best attempts, her leg doesn't budge.

However, she does feel the pressure of a small hand closing tight around her ankle to keep her still.

The other girl.

Anderson bites back a frustrated snarl and drops her head back onto the surface with a dull thud. She wants to struggle more, but considering that she can't even manage as much movement as she did a second ago, it would be a waste of time. There's something about this girl and the effortless way she's able to hold Anderson down with just a touch of one slender hand—

It takes a moment for the realisation to hit, but when it does, Anderson feels as if she now understands everything.

Grife. She's using telekinesis.

Craning her neck up as far as she can, Anderson takes her time taking in the young girl's features, captive gaze lingering on the too-thin frame, fearful wide brown eyes, the massive bruise covering one side of her face. Anderson almost can't believe the girl in front of her is the same one that'd crashed into her. She almost can't connect this cowering girl that looks likely to tip over in a strong wind with those bones lying amidst the ash in the incinerator.

When Anderson tries to reach out with her own powers, at first it's more of the same. It feels as if she's crashing face first into a wall and no amount of effort seems capable of breaching whatever barrier is keeping her from using her powers. The headache she's had since reawakening pulses in time with her heartbeat, the pain returning with such ferocity that Anderson feels like curling in on herself and moaning.

Of course, she can't move.

But when she meets the girl's eyes, Anderson feels a jolt. The girl is looking at her in return instead of staring at what her guardian is doing to Anderson's partner. It's a wary look, one that dares to hope. A look that gives Anderson a little hope of her own.

The next time that Anderson tries to use her own powers, she holds eye contact with the girl and reaches out—

Can you hear me?

The first few times that Anderson tries to connect with the girl, nothing happens. Sure, her headache doesn't get any worse and she swears that the pressure, and the wall blocking her, both lessen somewhat, but the girl doesn't so much as flinch. It would be so easy to give up, Anderson realises. If she doesn't have a way out of here and her only hope is a little girl who probably doesn't even know how to use her powers to communicate—

No.

Do not give up.

She tries to focus past the pain in her head and readies herself for one final push.

Can you hear me?

At first, there's more of the same mental silence, but then—

What do you want?

Ten

THE CONNECTION ANDERSON makes with the mind of the girl sitting down by her feet, staring at her with a wide-eyed, suspicious gaze, is fragile. It keeps cutting in and out as they try to communicate with one another. After a few false starts, the girl reaches out to Anderson, using the physical connection to bolster their flagging mental one.

What do you want?

Anderson doesn't hesitate. *I want to help you*, she fires back at the young girl. *My name is Anderson, and if you'll help me, I know I can get you two out of here.*

The girl's expression shifts, nose wrinkling as she takes in Anderson's prone body with suspicion and no little disdain. Even without thinking it, the lack of faith she has in Anderson's ability to save herself, much less anyone else, is very visible.

How can you *help us?*

Anderson wants to be offended by the doubtful tone in the girl's mental voice, but then... she's the one stuck to a table while her partner gets tortured mere feet away.

A little doubt, in this case, is the least of what the girl is probably going through.

Anderson tries to imbue her mental voice with confidence she doesn't necessarily feel. *Tell me who you are and what's going on and I will help. I promise.*

The girl's eyes narrow and she glances between where she has Anderson restrained and over at where Rowan has Anderson's partner strapped to a similar table. What she sees there—because Anderson still can't turn her head to look— must be terrible, because in the space of two heartbeats she seems to give in.

I'm Ness, and six years ago, Rowan was our mother's partner, the girl says. *He might be Helen's father, but he's not mine. He was distant, not really interested in us, until right before she died five years ago. That's when he found out that we were hiding our powers. And two weeks later—*

Ness's mental voice takes on a jagged note that almost feels as if it's stabbing into Anderson's brain, and she winces in response. The girl realises what she's doing and reigns herself in somewhat.

—two weeks later our mother died, and he started looping us into his hobby.

Anderson feels a chill roll down her spine. *You've been doing this for five years?*

Ness's shoulders rise and fall in a quick shrug. *He only made us hunt for him at first, but he makes us part of what he does now. We're strong together, but—* The girl's face drops, her expression hopeless. *I don't know what he'll do to us if we fight back. There's no point—*

The anger that tears through Anderson in response to that sad, lost look on the girl's face is surprising in its intensity and immediacy.

I know—I know it's hard to get away from a dreg like that, Anderson sends, her grasp on her own telepathy still kind of shaky. *But I can help you. You're both already in trouble for helping this creepshow do what he's doing, but at least now you've got a chance of seeing life outside a cell. Either one of us dies, and that's it for you. Is that what you want for your sister?*

The girl shakes her head. *No!*

Another one of those too-loud bursts of mental noise ricochets through Anderson's brain. Anderson squeezes her eyes shut even harder and tries to focus on breathing through her nose instead of releasing a thoroughly embarrassing whine from the pain.

Slowly, Anderson feels the girl pulls back, physically and mentally.

Within moments, Anderson can move again, a little, and she turns her head to the left—only to see what appears to be Rowan vivisecting Lee while Helen clings to him, half hiding her small face underneath her dark hair.

The sight chills Anderson, but also solidifies what she has to do.

Then I need you to go get your sister and get her out of the way. I'll handle him.

It takes a while—too long—for Ness to find her confidence. She gets to her feet slowly, moving as if she aches, and then starts to walk over to Rowan's side with a just-barely-noticeable tremor in her lanky limbs. By the time she reaches where Rowan has her sister observing his... *work*, the tremor is all but gone.

"What do you want?" Rowan says, speaking almost absently at first before he registers that Ness is next to *him* and not, as she'd been before, Anderson. The man jolts, the blade in his hand falling with a clatter next to Lee's side. "I *told* you not to leave the Judge alone."

The words, spat out, put Anderson on alert—not because she thinks Rowan will do anything to *her*, but because Ness is nearby and very vulnerable. Tensing in preparation to attack,

Anderson holds her breath, trying to remain still and silent even as adrenaline floods her body.

However, Ness is quick with a retort.

"I don't know why you're so worried," she says with a careless shrug of her skinny shoulders. "We put her under again. It's safe to walk away."

Anderson can almost *feel* the suspicious look from Rowan, but she doesn't move.

Eventually, he turns back to his task. "Fine," he says, "I know my Helen wouldn't let me down."

It's a dismissal, yes, but not an effective one.

Ness stands her ground, squaring her shoulders and looking up at Rowan with just enough defiance on her narrow face to make Anderson feel a little itch of worry. "Helen needs to go upstairs. It's time for her to eat and take a nap."

From what Anderson can see of the little girl, her head tucked into Rowan's shoulder, it isn't necessarily a lie. If Helen is the one who put Anderson out and who is dampening Anderson's powers, her little body must be using up more energy than it can store.

But Rowan doesn't take the bait.

His eyes narrow and his hands curl into fists. "You're up to something, aren't you?"

Ness shakes her head.

"I want my sister," she says, tone sharp.

One of Rowan's hands grips the back of Helen's small head, holding her fast as she tries to look up at her sister.

"I will take care of her if she needs anything." The words are delivered in a calm manner, but something about the expression on his face—which Anderson can't see—makes Ness step backwards.

Shaking her head, she keeps at it.

"Please," she says, her voice trembling. "I just want my sister."

Rowan laughs. It's not a nice laugh at all.

"So, this is when you choose to fight back," Rowan says, sounding curious. "When I have two Judges at my mercy and another two combing the building looking for them?" His voice turns contemptuous. "You never were very smart. But then, that's what I have Helen for."

Ness utters a wordless *snarl* of pure rage and she *moves*—

Anderson barely registers the movement, but she feels the swell of Ness's power and sees the aftermath. Suddenly, Ness has grabbed Helen away from Rowan with one hand, and with the other shoved the man back hard enough to slam into the wall on their side of the room.

It's too much to hope he'll stay down.

Soon, too soon, he's back on his feet and staring between Anderson and Ness with betrayal and rage naked on his face.

"Y-you—"

Anderson forces herself to sit up and swing her legs off of the slab. Her vision swims in an alarming blur of colours after the swift movement, but thankfully she doesn't tumble off of the table as she turns in Rowan's direction.

"You should surrender," Anderson says.

Before Rowan can answer, Ness interrupts. "Should I—should I put Helen to sleep now?"

Anderson answers without looking at her. "That *would* be a great idea!"

The little girl utters an annoyed whine, but the sound cuts up abruptly.

Immediately, Anderson feels the shackles on her powers come undone and she starts to feel a bit more... balanced. She takes a time to do a quick mental check, barely a second or two, and then does a little multitasking of her own as she watches Rowan lurch towards them.

First, she shoots off a psychic message in Cato's direction that *should* serve as a beacon directing her down here. Then she knocks Lee out, sinking her under so fast that the other woman goes from moaning in pain to a sudden stillness in the blink of the eye. Finally, she slides off the slab and turns to face Rowan.

"You don't want to do this," she warns, watching Rowan's approach.

Rowan launches himself at Anderson, tackling her down to the ground hard enough that her shoulders smack against the hard floor. Pain pulses through her back and she jerks up, back arching as the air punches free from her lungs in a pained grunt.

Rowan has just enough hair to grab and Anderson makes use of it, tangling her fingers into his hair and *yanking* until Rowan's neck is tilted back, the tendons in his throat standing out against his skin. When he reaches up to try and pull her fingers free, Anderson tries to damage his; slippery with (*Lee's*) blood, it's hard for her to get a grip on his fingers at first, but she keeps scrabbling until she hears a staccato of sick-sounding pops and a hoarse cry of pain.

Anderson allows herself a fierce grin.

Her satisfaction doesn't last.

At some point during their tussle, Rowan has managed to pull free of Anderson's hold and get his mangled fingers around her throat. As he squeezes down on her throat despite what must be excruciating pain in his ruined fingers, Anderson tries to focus more on hurting him *back* than on her esophagus slowly crumpling under the pressure. She claws at every bit of Rowan's exposed skin that she can reach, even managing to get in a decent eye-jab or two as her vision starts to get blurry around the edges.

Surprisingly, Ness is who saves Anderson. She flings a shoe at Rowan, hitting him hard enough to distract him from his single-minded focus on strangling Anderson to death.

"Leave her alone," Ness cries out, voice hoarse.

Rowan... does. Somewhat. He loosens his grip on Anderson's

throat, letting her head drop back to the ground with a heavy thud that sends stars up in her eyes as he looks over at Ness.

"After I kill this Jay," Rowan says, tone almost conversational, "I'm going to kill you. And then I'm going to raise your sister just the way I wanted to."

That... doesn't sound good. Not to Anderson and certainly not to Ness, who sucks in a stunned gasp.

"You wouldn't—" Ness cuts herself off.

Just outside of Anderson's limited field of vision, she hears movement as Ness gets to her own feet and starts across the room.

"You would, wouldn't you?" Her voice is soft at first, but strengthens as she comes closer. "But I won't let you."

Rowan barks out a harsh burst of laughter.

"*Let me?* You're nothing more than a scared little girl. What can *you* do to stop me, aside from surrender?"

Lying on her back and staring up at the underside of Rowan's chin, Anderson can't get over what she's hearing. Ness may be a child, but she's strong enough to hold Anderson down and even push Rowan back with sheer mental force. She's dangerous, and Rowan seems intent on underestimating her.

Ness's voice comes closer now, from almost right on top of them. "Surrender?"

"If you promise to behave, nothing bad will happen to you."

Anderson sees Rowan's smile, feels the smugness practically *drench* him, and watches as he holds out a hand for Ness to take.

Bad idea...

When Ness's fingers touch Rowan's, there's a psychic pulse that lances through him, freezing him in place.

Rowan can't move, not even to blink or draw in air. This binding is stronger than the one Anderson had woken up to, and she's glad not to be on the receiving end. She wriggles out from under Rowan's frozen body, scooting backwards just far enough that she can get onto wobbly knees.

"If you do this, you'll be a murderer," Anderson says, her voice quiet. "I won't be able to help you."

When Ness turns to look at Anderson, the expression on her face is bleak. "I think—I think you've helped as much as you can."

And then, she uses her powers to crush Rowan's throat.

As THEY WAIT for backup to reach them downstairs, Anderson watches as Ness and Helen hold hands. She shouldn't let them: they're criminals, and at the very least should be cuffed and separated. But Anderson can't make herself do anything to part them.

They look so *small*, huddled together on a slab just feet away from Rowan's crumpled body. Anderson feels the guilt yank at her.

Children can be dangerous, and Anderson *knows* that these two are. Grife. She's just watched Ness kill a man with a single touch and was almost subject to similar treatment from Helen.

But—

Tired, with flushed cheeks smeared with tears and snot, they look like... kids.

"I can't let you go," Anderson says into a silence that is mostly unbroken except for Lee's laboured breathing and intermittent sobs from the sisters. At Ness's miserable nod, she forces herself to keep talking. "But, I'll—I'll do what I can to make sure that whatever happens isn't *too* terrible."

"Will they separate us?" Ness asks, her rough voice muffled, her mouth pressed into the cloud of Helen's dark hair.

Anderson opens her mouth to answer her question and then closes it without speaking. At least, for a few tense moments.

"I have no idea," she admits. "They might. Helen is too young for any of this."

In Ness's arms, Helen twists about, struggling until she can direct a surprisingly sharp stare at Anderson. "I'm not leaving Ness," she says, her voice rising into a shout. "You can't make me!" The temperature in the already frigid underground room seems to plummet in response to the little girl's words, and Anderson swears that she can see her breath misting in front of her.

Ness squeezes her sister tightly and, thankfully, the embrace seems to calm the tiny terror.

"We'll be fine, Hel," Ness insists. "We'll be *fine*."

Epilogue

PRISON IS NO place for a child, Anderson thinks as she walks through the brightly lit hallways that lead to the two sisters' cells. It may be safer for them than on the streets or back with someone like Rowan—if he were still alive—but to a one, every single person that Anderson passes in their cells or at the few manned security stations in the building is an adult. Someone either uninterested in or unsafe for two young girls who've already been through so much.

But this was their *choice*, Anderson reminds herself as she takes the final turn to the bank of cells where the two girls are. All Anderson can do is visit them to make sure that they're—

Okay?

Somewhat sane?

Happy with their decisions?

Scoffing at herself, Anderson shakes her head to try and clear it of the distracting thought just in time to reach the girls' cubes.

* * *

DESPITE THE FACT that they're in prison and haven't seen each other—or anyone, aside from the few humans monitoring them, the relative isolation of the Iso-Cubes seems to be good for Ness and Helen.

The sisters greet Anderson with matching smiles, running up to the transparent front walls of their respective cubes in order to greet her and press their hands up against the thick glass separating them from everyone else. Someone—and while Anderson has her suspicions, she also knows she'll never find out for certain—has provided the sisters with clothing that doesn't look like prison uniforms. Their brown skin is healthy and flushed, their dark fuzz of their shorn hair gleaming under the glare of the overhead lights and, unlike many of the other prisoners, they look as if they've *gained* weight.

They also, Anderson realises, have tablets for their personal use.

Mustering a smile for the girls, Anderson asks, "Are you both... happy?"

From where Anderson stands, she can see the confused and absolutely *lost* look that settles on the sisters' nearly identical faces. She finds herself torn between laughing at their shared expression and hating that they're in this position at all.

"Happy?" Ness repeats the word, crossing her arms across her chest. "Well, it's better than being with *him*." That last word she snarls, filling it with every bit of disgust that she can muster for the memory of Rowan's abuse and what they underwent at his hands. "We eat every day, now, and your people come by every other day to check on us."

Your people.

Other Psi-Judges.

Anderson starts. She'd honestly forgotten one of the conditions for the two girls' adjoining Iso-Cubes and retaining their powers had been mandatory training to be Judges at the end of a shortened sentence. With Helen's power and Ness's focus, they have the potential to be useful to Mega-City One.

"Are you sure that this is what you want?" Anderson gestures at herself, making a face.

Helen smiles widely, showing off a missing tooth that Anderson hadn't seen at first. "We want to be like you," she says simply. "Someone that saves people."

Yeah.

Except... she hadn't managed to save Baker, and Lee is *still* walking funny from what Rowan'd done to her leg.

With those bitter thoughts in her head, Anderson sighs and crouches down, touching her hands to the glass just above each sister's hands.

"I'll try and visit you both in another few weeks," Anderson says, hating herself for the fact that her words feel like a lie. "Maybe next time, you can tell me what they're teaching you both."

Later

"ANDERSON, CONTROL."

The call comes just as Anderson's flinging a leg over her Lawmaster, ready to head back out on the beat. "This is Anderson. What can I do for you?"

"You still at the Isolation Block?"

"Just leaving," she says, firing up the engine. "Why?"

"Great, then you're closest. Can you head to the morgue? Joe Dredd's asked for a Psi-Judge."

Anderson kills the engine, leans back in the seat and frowns. "Say again, Control? He wants a *Psi-Judge* at the *morgue?* What does he expect me to *do*, give a pep-talk?"

"Beats me. Request is flagged to a new case. All I've got is the case name, 'Judge Death.' Mean anything to you?"

"Not a damn thing. Alright, best go ask him myself. Tell him I'm on my way. Anderson out."

She kicks the engine back into life, keys in the route and pulls away.

About the Author

Back when she was a child, **Zina Hutton** once jumped out of a window to escape dance class in the Virgin Islands. Now she's a speculative fiction writer who tends to leap headfirst into new stories and worlds the second that inspiration strikes. Zina lives in hot and humid South Florida where she's never far away from a notebook and her precious Kindles. Zina currently works as a marketing minion, but she's also a writer with non-fiction publication credits in *Fireside Fiction*, *Anathema Magazine*, *The Mary Sue*, *Strange Horizons*, *ComicsAlliance* and *Women Write About Comics* as well as several short stories in different publications. You can find her at stitchmediamix.com and on twitter as @stichomancery.

CHAPTER ONE

I WAS NEVER a believer in predestination. Hell, if pushed I'd struggle to spell it. It seemed an unlikely state of affairs, your life attached to these rails that lead to one inevitable conclusion. It's a comforting school of thought, I have to admit, to consider that every shitty choice you ever made was fated to happen, that every bum deal you were handed you were never going to escape. Kinda takes the sting out of the guilt. *Que sera sera*, and all that—whatever will be will be, so fuck it, there's nothing I could've done to change it.

But I can't avoid accepting the responsibility, however attractive that sounds at the time. The trains I take are mine alone to board, and where they take me is a journey of my own making. I am the master of my own destiny, even if that destiny is to be a washed-up asshole with no prospects. I got myself to here through every bad decision and crummy situation I found myself in, and no matter how much I'd like to drink that knowledge into oblivion, the fact is that it's no less true. Nothing is fated; the future is yours to mould and shape as you see fit. Your life is in your hands, not the mysterious whim of the cosmos. Sure, I could blame a lot on the arbitrary roll of the dice, and the fact that Lady Luck's been mainly smacking me in the face lately rather than softly nibbling the nape of my neck, but I feel it's better to own your screw-ups rather than rant about outside forces you've got no control over. No one likes a whiner, after all.

So, yeah, I'm well aware of who's at fault for putting me in my current predicament, and I'm cool with it—in the sense that I'm not bitter as opposed to unwilling to change it, because I would be quite happy for the chance to climb out of this pit. But that would require commitment, sobriety and drive—attributes that I don't necessarily possess in abundance; and money too, and it's the lack of folding that's possibly the root of everything. Does my pursuit of the green get me into these scrapes? Probably. Does it plunge me further into debt, in an ever-tightening downward spiral of self-loathing, thereby necessitating me to take jobs that I would otherwise baulk at? Oh, most definitely.

Anyway—predestination. Not a believer. Or I wasn't. But sometimes I guess a moment comes along where you feel it's a turning point; it's setting your life on a path that you're not going to be getting off. It's got nothing to do with choice; the event's been handed to you as a *fait accompli*. Or what's that other Frenchie phrase? *Force majeure*. This is the universe taking that big old junction lever with both hands and giving it a wrench, tugging you onto a whole other set of tracks entirely, and you get no say in the matter: you just have to respond accordingly, which is mostly by barrelling along headfirst towards the new end-point. Now, you may disagree—you might reckon I could've done things differently at any time; taken a way out, a side exit, picked another route. But I suppose we'll have to not see eye to eye on that, 'cause as far as I'm concerned I'm sure—sure as eggs are cluckers—that my future was mapped out that night. Fate took a guiding hand, and swept me along a road I couldn't turn back on.

Fact is, the bottom crapped out of the world the evening I beat up the wrong guy. I mean on a global scale, not just in some localised woe-is-me way: the whole actual planet went down the shitter. I'm not naïve enough to think that what I did was the catalyst—I'm sure this stuff had been building for a while, and I only became aware of it in the slow, dim, dawning realisation of a man who's just been alerted to the fact that he's on fire—but it felt like a through-the-looking-glass episode. Everything was changed, both within and without.

Now, I don't make a habit of beating up guys, wrong or not. Or at least I don't do it for pleasure. But unfortunately it's something my somewhat sorry state of affairs has dragged me to, and efficient acts of moderate violence are one of the few skills I can legitimately lay claim to. Thirty years ago I was a boxer of reasonable standing—welterweight, semi-pro—and had the potential to make a name for myself in the ring. I was fit—frighteningly fit—and had ambition to burn; I used to spar with Thad Dewberry, if you remember him? This was before he became four times national champion, naturally. Knocked him on his ass on more than one occasion too. Freddy, my trainer, said I had raw, natural talent, and at the risk of blowing my own trumpet I *knew* I was good: I was fast, nimble, with enough aggression to power a decent right hook, and an obstinate streak that meant I never knew when to quit. So, of course, I took all that aptitude and ability and threw it all out the window in exchange for a serious gambling addiction. Cards, dice, roulette: I was a sucker for everything, and the more it took hold, the bigger my debts grew, and the faster that physical discipline drained right out of me. All I could think about was the next game, and where I could secure the funds to enable it, and with that my concentration was shot.

Organised crime circles the sport like sharks round a stricken dinghy, and outliers on the fringes of the Mob were more than willing to lend me the cash with an interest rate scarier than some head injuries I've received. I took a dive a few times, I'm ashamed to admit, and ploughed the payoffs I got from those straight into my next poker session. I did some bare-knuckle fights—cracked my eye socket, was hospitalised for a spell with bleeding on the brain (which may or may not have had more of a permanent effect than the quacks let on). I backed out of those pretty quick. By this point I was in my mid thirties and starting to feel gravity's sag. I wasn't the dancer on the canvas anymore; I was lumbering, and threatening to do myself wheelchair-worthy damage.

I retired from the ring while I could still see and speak without a slur, and got a job at an automobile plant. Picked up a nice little alcohol problem too, which made sure the ship sailed on the last of my fitness: pants got that much tighter, breath got a shade shorter, heart palpitated more times than I cared for. But I... Listen, I don't know why I'm telling you this, or why I think you would want to have all this personal info frontloaded onto my tale. Like, you didn't ask my life story, right? I guess the point I was making was that I wasn't always a bum, and that current fiscal circumstances are the reason I agreed to rough up a complete stranger. Once I abandoned the boxing, my income plummeted but unfortunately my love affair with the cards didn't lose any of its ardour. Next thing I know, I'm being informed that my debts that I'd spread around town had been consolidated into one big chunk of change that I owed a guy who called himself the Bushman.

I'd never met this dude, and still haven't; the reasons for his moniker are as shrouded in mystery as his facial features. I didn't know anything about him, but he sure as shit knew plenty about me. His intermediaries informed me of his preferred repayment plan, but made sure to point out that if I was willing to do him what they called 'favours', then he would see about shaving off a few kay. This sounded voluntary, but I never considered refusal was ever an option, and frankly a couple thousand off my tab looked better on the balance sheet than the inevitable broken limbs that were heading my way if I didn't start returning my loans. The Bushman was well aware of my former sporting prowess, and figured to exploit it, even though it had been a good half decade since the last time the old Jackson McGill piledriver had been called into use. It was still there, that jab, even if time had not been kind to the body that it was an extension of.

So I became de facto Mob-boss muscle, directed as required. I threw up after the first time I beat someone to a pulp, disgusted with what I'd become, and haunted by the look of fear on their faces just before I slammed my fist into them. They were squirrelly little saps for the most part—losers like me who thought they could take the money and run—and nothing like my opponents in the ring, who had come out of their corners snarling with the intention of delivering equal amounts of hurt. These submissive pricks, on the other hand, snivelled and blew snot-bubbles and apologised profusely, and sometimes I hit them more than was necessary just to get them to shut up. I didn't need to hear it—my own head was filled with doubts and regrets and broken glass, and I didn't want it to get too crowded in there. Block it all out, I told myself. Give the bozo some bruises to remember the Bushman by, and skedaddle. The drinking came into its own there, I have to admit; it was great for blurring memories. I embraced the bottle even more.

I know how all this sounds, and I'm not expecting you to like me. As I say, how I got here is through my own choices, and no one else's. If I was smart, if I truly wanted to get out of this life, then I'd knock the gambling on the head, stop racking up the debts. But I'm well aware that's not going to happen any time soon—and most pertinently, so does the Bushman. He's got no desire to lose me, I'm too much of an asset. Thus, here I find myself, trapped in a role of my own making.

I got the call just after five on my way home from work. I live a little outside of town in a two-storey shitpile on the edge of a derelict street just before the suburbs gives way to scrubland

and the woods, and it's a good half-hour drive past the factory stacks and abandoned car lots. I saw my cell chirrup on the passenger seat of my Pontiac as I edged it through the rush-hour traffic, rain splodging the windscreen. I knew who it'd be—they always texted from the same number and at the same time. I found a public callbox and pulled over, hitching my jacket collar up and ducking through the fat, warm drops to the kiosk.

I don't know if this is the benefit of hindsight colouring my recollection, but something felt off even then: more people seemed to be out in the weather than you'd expect, and they appeared agitated, restless. Sirens blared several blocks over. The radio said something about tailbacks across the river. There was an edgy vibe, as if tensions were going to spill over any second, but I didn't know for what reason. A guy slammed his palm against the callbox window and shouted something indecipherable, then tried to yank open the door; I told him to fuck off and he took the hint, but his eyes told me he was barely aware of what was going on. A few more just like him stomped past, and I remember pausing to watch them, this herd of crazies surging down the street, demented in their terror. That should've been the first sign, I guess, but I must've passed it off as random loons—the city wasn't short of them. Even the Judges weren't exactly stable, at the best of times.

I punched in the number and got the message: gimp staying at the RestEazy motel on Rothman, near the airport. He'd booked himself onto the 7.30 flight to Hugersfield, way up north. I was to stop him getting on that plane and gently remind him that he owed fifty kay in unpaid debts, a commitment he was freely welching on. Don't cripple him, they said, just make him piss blood for a week. They gave me a brief description, and I could picture him instantly, since he was virtually identical to every other sadsack that I'd put the frightners on—tubby middle-management drone drowning in a wretched coke habit, and not even embezzlement to the tune of a quarter of a mil could keep him supplied in snow and ensure his girlfriend was happy and sufficiently far enough away from his wife. Dabney Krinkle was his name, like it mattered—I whale on one of them, I've whaled on them all.

I had to book if I was to make to the RestEazy before he checked out, so I ran and slid back into the car, burning rubber towards the freeway. The news broadcasts weren't kidding about the traffic; the filter lanes were rammed nose to tail, and several of the drivers had given up entirely, abandoning their vehicles and fleeing along the hard shoulder. I still didn't have clear idea what had put a bug up so many people's asses, and the pundits on the radio weren't clarifying anything—I heard the word 'coup' several times, and listening between the lines it sounded like some kind of military takeover at the heart of Justice Department. A damn quiet one if it was, since there hadn't been any suggestion of small arms' fire from what I'd seen... but who knew what was going on in the Grand Hall? Something was certainly scaring the locals, unless it was mass hysteria: I'd seen pack mentality in action before. If I'd had the time, I could've stopped someone and asked if they knew what the hell they were running from, but I suspected I would've got little sense in reply.

Madness, I thought. I assumed it'd blow itself out by morning.

I got off the freeway first chance I could and tore down the back roads instead. The newsreader was now listing areas of the city that were either off-limits or impassable, and it seemed like they were radiating out from the centre, sectors being shut down systematically. No wonder so many cits were bolting; they were being forced out towards the edges. Static crackled from the speakers, and before I could retune the radio it went dead. Nothing was audible on any station other than a low hiss. That was disconcerting. Even the twenty-four-hour evangelist guy had been silenced, and not even the revelations about him and the fifteen-year-old had managed that. The car felt uncomfortably quiet and empty, and darkness was falling fast beyond the glass.

I was driving parallel to the airport, I realised, but on the other side of the chainlink fence nothing was stirring. No planes taking off or landing, no lights, no signs of life. It occurred to me that maybe all flights had been cancelled—grounding the aircraft sounded like the first sort of thing the military would do in the event of a governmental overthrow—and that I wouldn't have to worry about catching the mark before he departed. The counter-argument in my head reasoned that Dabney possibly wouldn't know that, and could still try to scurry away. I spotted the RestEazy and swung in to the kerb opposite the entrance, turned off the engine and leaned forward in my seat, arms on the wheel, confident I had a decent enough view.

A family were throwing their suitcases in the back of a taxi while the dad was shouting at the harassed-looking driver. They eventually drove off in a cloud of exhaust fumes, destination who-knew-where. Beyond the doors, I could see further consternation in the lobby as arm-waving dweebs berated the receptionist, luggage piled around them. It seemed like everyone was getting the shit out of Dodge; or at least they wanted to and were being frustrated by the lack of transport options. I looked up at the motel façade and saw a few lights on in the windows, indicating some residents at least were staying put, then thumbed the number for the place into my cell, gleaned from the buzzing neon sign hanging off the corner. It took several unanswered calls and a couple of redials before a female voice finally responded with a barked expletive.

I asked to be connected to Dabney's room and the line hummed, then rang. I remained optimistic: she hadn't said he'd checked out. The receiver was picked up after the sixth ring, though no one offered a greeting other than short, quiet breathing. I listened for a moment, waiting.

"Dabney Krinkle?" I asked.

No confirmation or denial, other than the breaths hitching up a notch. Then the line went dead. I scanned the front of the building again, watching the few illuminated squares that were the occupied rooms, and sure enough one blinked out seconds later. The spooked Mr Krinkle was on the move. I pocketed the cell and resumed my study of the main entrance, running his distinguishing characteristics through my head as I awaited his appearance.

People were threading out now into the street, bags gripped tightly in fists, glancing around, wondering where the hell they were going to go. A trickle became a crowd and I sat up, worried I was going to miss him. My eyes roved over the sweaty, concerned faces, trying to zero in on my target. Seconds later I spotted him—tubby, white balding dweeb, glasses perched on his conk, *snap!*—and I wrenched open the car door, tracking him as he stumble-tripped along the sidewalk, away from the bulk of the others, briefcase clutched to chest, head turning left and right as if hoping to catch sight of another cab. I followed discreetly, the others paying me no heed, more important things evidently playing on their minds.

I picked my moment just as he was well separated from the throng and crossing the shadowy junction with the RestEazy's underground car park. I closed the distance in a matter of seconds, wrapped my arm around his neck, and pulled him further into the gloom; he was surprisingly light, and shock meant he offered little resistance. I pushed him up against a wall, satisfied we were alone, and hit him hard on the bridge of the nose, just enough to make the stars dance before his eyes. I always lead with a good pop to the face, gets them disorientated. He gasped, glasses went flying, and his legs buckled. I caught him and propped him back up. He didn't let go of his briefcase though, I noticed. I gave him a couple of quick slaps to get him to focus.

Now I had his attention, I could go to work.

FIND US ONLINE!

www.rebellionpublishing.com

/rebellionpub   /rebellionpublishing   /rebellionpub

SIGN UP TO OUR NEWSLETTER!

rebellionpublishing.com/sign-up

YOUR REVIEWS MATTER!

Enjoy this book? Got something to say?

Leave a review on Amazon, GoodReads or with your
favourite bookseller and let the world know!

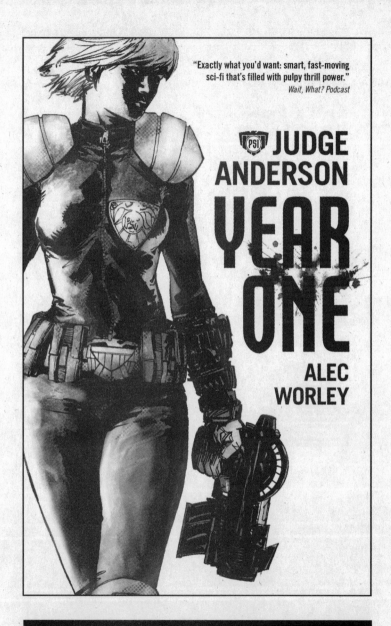